SPY TRAP

JOHN FULLERTON

LUME BOOKS

LUME BOOKS

Published in 2022 by Lume Books

Copyright © John Fullerton 2022

ISBN 978-1-83901-484-0

Typeset using Atomik ePublisher from Easypress Technologies

www.lumebooks.co.uk

Spy Trap

The colour of the cat doesn't matter, so long as it catches mice. –
Attributed to Deng Xiaoping

The Brodick spy trilogy is dedicated to all those who have worked as 'contract labourers' for the Secret Intelligence Service, whoever and wherever they might be.

List of Characters

Brodick, Richard, Secret Intelligence Service (SIS) officer in charge of UK Station which runs agents in 'denied territories' or 'hard target' countries, such as China, North Korea and Russia. Cover names David Webster and Dexter Fisher. Name in Mandarin (Pinyin) Bo Deli, in Cantonese Bo Deli. Chinese Intelligence Service code: 2904. Recruited by Fang, Chinese intelligence officer, in Beirut during the Lebanese civil war.

Du Fu, head of Shanghai Public Security Bureau, Du Lan's brother and Yao Tie's brother-in-law.

Du Lan, ambitious Shanghai socialite, wealthy business-woman and property owner married to multi-millionaire Yao Tie. Sister of local security chief, Du Fu. Known as GLUTTON's occasional lover and apparent assassin.

Fang, work name of Chen Meilin, deputy chief of Chinese foreign intelligence service *Guoanbu*, and head of *Guoanbu* 5th Bureau, responsible for counter-intelligence. Also known as Zhang Pusheng. She holds the rank of colonel in Chinese military intelligence, at this time known as PLA2. SIS codename DRAGON. Recruited by Brodick in Beirut during the Lebanon civil war.

Green, Jeff. Cover name of a CIA officer with an interest in DRAGON.

Ho Ping, Susan. Cuckolded wife of Roger Peacock, physics lecturer, owner-occupier of a flat on The Peak in Hong Kong.

MacGregor, Angus. Director-general of SIS, traditionally known as 'C' and based at Century House in the south London borough of Lambeth.

Marsh, Polly. SIS employee in London and Brodick's office assistant.

Peacock, Roger. Successful UK businessman who works as an SIS agent in the People's Republic of China and as financial adviser to Yao Tie, wealthy Chinese Communist Party Secretary in Shanghai. Married to Susan Ho-Ping, academic from Hong Kong. Peacock's SIS codename is GLUTTON. Brodick is his case officer.

Xie Rong, head of Chinese foreign intelligence service, the *Guoanbu*. Fang's immediate superior and a Party man rather than an intelligence professional. Opposed to political and economic reform and an associate of Yao Tie.

Yang Bai, head of *Guoanbu* field support group in Thailand.

Yao Tie, Chinese Communist Party Secretary for Shanghai, multi-millionaire, hardliner strongly opposed to economic and political reforms. Married to ambitious socialite, Du Lan. Employs Roger Peacock's services as financial and investment adviser.

1

Shadows come alive, murmuring at her approach, breaking up and moving aside in the corridor, shuffling out of her way.

Cops, technicians, chambermaids, cleaners, curious guests.

Lishi. Left this world.

Siwang. Died.

Zou le. Gone.

Dao Tiantang. Gone to heaven.

Qu jian Ma-ke-si. Gone to meet Marx.

The comedian who mumbles this last, anti-communist remark sniggers at his own wit and falls silent.

She smells fear and sweat, the musty, unwashed bodies of winter, halitosis, cheap hotel soap, apple-scented shampoo and coal dust.

A police detective guarding the door nods, steps aside, uses one arm to push it open.

The Englishman is motionless.

Fang sees him stretched out on his back on the hotel bed, his head resting on the pillows as if taking a nap. A big man, dressed in a white vest and striped pyjama bottoms, barefoot, no sign of a struggle, no blood.

Ready for the undertaker. Even his sparse hair looks combed.

Zou! zou! Move! Get out!

It's impolite, but effective.

The uniformed police officer, the detective in his padded coat, two hotel security men and the duty manager retreat down the corridor like scared children, along with the idlers. No-one objects. No-one questions the order. Only the last, the detective bringing up the rear who had secured the room and ensured that no-one else entered, hesitates, glancing back at her and opening his mouth as if he wants to say something, only to think better of it.

There is nothing for him to see; the intelligence officer's face yields nothing, her expression impassive, a blank mask of authority she wears for such occasions – and there have been plenty of those. Her iron mask.

They know what she is, not who she is. No-one identifies the 'what' by name, only as the 'relevant department', *youguan bumen*.

Fang moves fast. She slams the room's door in the faces of the forensics team waiting outside and hurries around the bed to the far side, near the window. She takes from her jacket pocket a tin box the size of a spectacle case, which she places on the bedside table. Opening it, she removes a syringe, attaches its needle, leans over the foreigner and inserts it into the man's right arm, above the elbow, drawing out a 5 ml sample of blood. From her pocket she takes a pair of scissors and snips a few strands of the man's greying hair. She holds his right hand – big and fleshy – in her left and with her right, using the same scissors, cuts off a slice of thumbnail, then adds them to the tin, which she snaps shut and returns to her pocket.

She makes two local calls from the bedside phone that together last less than 2 minutes and 20 seconds, during which she gives orders for the body to be removed to the mortuary. Cremation must proceed

2

at once. There is to be no autopsy. She needs the services of neither police forensics nor the pathologist. There is to be no police investigation, no photographs and no witnesses. All existing paperwork will be destroyed and nothing more is to be recorded in any form.

The woman has seen bodies beyond number. As a child during the Great Leap Forward, she saw people throw themselves into a river to drown, death being preferable to what awaited them in life, a slow death by starvation. She'd seen that the dead women lay face up in the water, the men face down.

The hotel audio and video tapes have already been confiscated, along with the visitor's passport and briefcase, and placed in Fang's custody. They are in the back seat of her official car, a boxy, black Red Flag limo with brown curtains over the windows, watched over by her People's Liberation Army (PLA) driver. Distinctions of gender seem to vanish on Beijing streets in winter because everyone looks similar; most wear long, padded coats and many women either cut their hair short or tuck it out of sight. Today it's 20 below zero.

The tapes and videos are not limited to the room itself but include the corridor, the lifts, the lobby, the bar, the coffee shop, the restaurant and the car park, the drive out front all the way to the gates and the street beyond. Everything from midnight until now: 10 hours and 43 minutes' worth of state surveillance.

At the front desk, all record of the *waibin*'s stay has been destroyed or deleted, along with the foreign guest's credit card details that were taken on registration and invoices.

Scrubbed clean, all of it.

Mr Peacock was never there, warm or cold, alive or dead.

It's a matter of national security. It takes precedence over everything and anyone.

The staff of the Friendship Hotel in Haidian district, Beijing municipality, have never seen him. They will remember nothing and they will not talk, not so much as another whisper or murmur, on pain of unemployment and a compulsory vacation at the state's expense in the *laogai* or camps.

By the time the colonel of the PLA's intelligence service, known as PLA2, who is also (more importantly) the director of the *Guoanbu*'s 5th Bureau, responsible for counter-intelligence, reaches her own office, a copy of the foreign ministry statement she dictated over the telephone lies on her desk.

A foreign businessman, Roger Atwood Herbert Peacock, aged 54, was found dead in his Beijing hotel room this morning by one of the cleaning staff. A UK national from Essex in England, Mr Peacock died of heart failure, believed to have been triggered by excessive drinking. No foul play is suspected. The British embassy in Beijing has been informed.

2

Poor old Peacock.

Who would believe that line about 'heart failure'?

I had read the Chinese foreign ministry statement, forwarded by Beijing Station overnight, followed within hours by an encrypted signal from DRAGON's 'One Time Pad' or OTP. It sought an urgent meet, using the pre-arranged code BLUE PETER. But I'm worried about something else far more pressing: saving my skin.

Our people were coming for me, and I was pretty certain why.

I had the dizzying sense of being flung back in time; a collision with a past, a falling backwards. A motorcyclist and his pillion passenger arrived at the park gates and triggered the unease. Dressed in black, they wore identical black helmets, visors down. Faceless death on wheels was a silly phrase that went through my mind.

This wasn't supposed to happen.

My instinct was to break cover, take off, but I told myself to get a grip, to stay where I was, to remain still, to look away.

You're innocent. You've done nothing, you know nothing.

That wasn't true, of course, but I'd faked it before and I'd do so again. Blood drummed in my chest and throat, pulsed in my eyes and ears, so that what I was seeing flickered like an old newsreel.

So sorry, Fang. I've made a mess of things. Or possibly – she had. Whichever of us caused this cluster-fuck, she was on her own. We'd never see each other again and I saw, for the first time, how much I was going to miss my partner in betrayal.

We'd done well so far, she and I, propelling each other to the top of the spying game. For a time we had our hands on the best kind of worldly power there is; the secret kind.

I didn't mean the 54 people – intelligence officers, assistants and secretaries – who worked for me at UK Station. Nor was I referring to the fact that Fang employed around four times that number in *Guoanbu*'s 5th Bureau, which was responsible for Chinese counter-intelligence on a global scale.

I meant that, by working in secret and in tandem for years, she and I had built up between us a fortress of lies and deceit and, with it, the ability to tip the world into mayhem – in pretty much any location we chose.

After all, the CIA and KGB had instigated murder and chaos for decades under the convenient label of Cold War. We Brits had done so for Empire and now, in the name of peasants and workers, the new superpower on the block – the People's Republic of China – was intent on something similar.

Dismounting, the pillion rider swaggered into the entrance and stood there in the stone arch, looking around, her manner nonchalant.

Me, a traitor?

As I argued with myself she looked at me, sizing me up, comparing me with whatever images they had been given in order to make a positive identification. Her male companion – I assumed he was male because he was bigger, bulkier – waited on the bike, head turned my way, revving the silver grey Triumph Triple in menacing growls.

They must have known I had a treff with the boss because he must have sent them instead. Some minion from General Service Branch would have briefed this pair on the who, what, when, where. I was shaking now as if I was running a fever.

Braced for the bullet.

Flight or fight?

The Firm had discarded my services, orphaned me, left me to my fate. It felt lonely. No-one was going to speak on my behalf or intervene, call out 'hang on, wait a moment, there's been a mistake'. It was no mistake. There were no mitigating factors, no excuses. I was a traitor and was as good as dead.

Admit it, Brodick. You've built a fine career on the back of treachery. This has included a decent wage at the taxpayers' expense. Not only that, your lies have allowed you to accumulate influence over others – who will never know it.

But by the time a second black-clad pair appeared, riding yet another bike, and they too lurched to a halt – this time at the park entry off Fentiman Road – I was up on my feet. I was ready to run; a middle-aged, two-legged animal with a paunch and an urge to throw myself against the bars of the cage I had built myself with such care.

Think, fool.

Run – where?

I wasn't carrying and it would not have helped much if I had been. Spies don't carry weapons, despite Hollywood's fantasies. This was London, after all. Home to me and my kind. South London in winter, south London in the lunch hour, in the polluted murk that passed for daylight.

A dark Transit van completed this macabre gathering. Black or brown, I couldn't tell, it drew up at the kerb on the third side of the park, on the far side of a threadbare hedge. It wasn't more than 30 metres from where I stood, braced for whatever was about to happen, *had* to happen, was something I'd been waiting for. The Richard Brodick of yore had gone – because I'd killed off that youngster with his passion for adventure, that *naif*, and his dreams of patriotic derring-do. I was no longer that person at all. I was someone else – older, slower, heavier and far more cynical.

Whoever these people were, they were about to put an end to this version of Richard Brodick, too. There would be no resurrection; I was no believer in rebirth.

I heard the prowler's tyres scrape the edge of the pavement. So, this would be a snatch job, an abduction involving hood and needle and later, an interrogation. Maybe they wouldn't bother; it would mean too much paperwork. Too many questions in committee and disposing of me according to official procedure would leave traces in the files. We liked to keep our failures to ourselves. Damage limitation in this context meant no trial, not even *in camera*, no defence, no appeals.

There would be no headlines to bring the Secret Intelligence Service into disrepute, nothing to dig up after the 50-year rule. I was one of their own and they would deal with the problem in-house. Registry clerks would expunge my entire record, as if I'd never been. *One of MacGregor's chosen few gone rogue*, they'd whisper, *and do you know what? MacGregor dropped the poor bugger like a blazing chip pan, giving him up to the hatchet men before he burned his own fingers.*

I didn't blame him; in his shoes, I'd have done the same. So I braced for a double-tap with a silenced pistol – it would be easy. They'd pin it on the Russians, the Chinese, the Israelis or a drug deal gone wrong. It didn't matter who or what – as long as it seemed plausible and they could plant evidence in the right place. They'd likely seen to that already. I guessed that my body bag was waiting for my remains on the floor of that van. No-one else was watching and if they were, no-one with any brains would admit they saw anything.

In this location, nobody talked to coppers and MacGregor wasn't about to go out on a limb for me, not again, not this time.

Why should he?

Something else occurred to me; if they did have me in their sights, then they'd know the truth about DRAGON, aka Fang, aka Zhang Pusheng, aka Chen Meilin, who was both my star agent and my handler.

I will miss you more than you know, Fang.

Was this pounding heart the way a rabbit felt in its final moments, looking at the farmer squinting along both barrels and curling his finger around the trigger?

Run, rabbit, run.

I could make out the concealed aerial running across the top of the smoked glass windscreen. Puffing out blue diesel fumes, the van coughed like a heavy smoker. No-one got in or out.

They had the park covered.

You're boxed in, pal, trapped.

Breathe.

Running wasn't an option; the moment had passed. It might feel better to at least try, but there was no chance of escape and I knew it – even if my body was in denial, drenched in adrenalin, a powerful rush.

Feet planted apart, left a little out in front, body turned a little to my right, I found my bunch of house keys, and, without thinking, worked them into the palm of my right hand, individual keys protruding between my knuckles. I did something similar with a biro in my left, which I would use to stab exposed flesh – if they got close enough. If I got the chance, I'd go for the throat, eyes and balls and do as much damage as I could – though I was well aware that resistance would be futile, because there could be only one result in the end.

It was stupid. Who was I fooling? I was long out of practice. I'd spent the least 3 years on my lardy arse behind a desk, but maybe fear would fuel the sheer, wild rage of terror that could give me the strength I needed. But for what?

Give it up. You're no James Bond.

No, wait a moment.

They wouldn't kill me – because they'd want to squeeze me dry. They would want everything I'd ever concocted with DRAGON. They'd demand every deception, every lie, every half-truth, every fake intelligence offering, every bent secret. There had been scores, hundreds of instances. It would take months, if not years, to unravel – and for that they'd need me conscious for the debrief. I would hold on to protect her as long as I could, because protecting Fang meant protecting myself.

If only I could have made our final meet, seen her one last time. Whoever said that absence made the heart grow fonder didn't know what the hell he was talking about.

Only then – after all these contrary imaginings had swirled through my head – did I see his silhouette. He trudged along, head down, not looking at anything in particular, preoccupied (or so it seemed) with his own thoughts. He came past the first bike, past the female pillion rider who stood in the entrance, giving both a wide berth, not so much as glancing up. He took his time. He gave no sign of having spotted me or the other members of the waiting team. Were they ours? Or did they belong to the friends across the river?

He tacked against the wind, heading in my direction. His course carried him on between the plane trees, with a trilby pulled down low on his head, hands deep in the pockets of an overcoat that flapped around his legs like a crow's wings. Closer now, he looked ancient. His tweed trousers were baggy, his shoes scuffed.

The image – so carefully cultivated – said this was an old bloke out for a stroll or to buy a packet of fags and a red top from the corner shop.

He lurched this way, then that, unsteady, a lopsided zig-zag. He looked utterly unlike a Whitehall mandarin, more like someone eking out an existence on a state pension, counting every penny, a tramp, an unshaven, incontinent nonentity that most folk wouldn't think to look at.

Spare some change, guv?

Move along. Nothing to see here.

But we knew better, he and I.

He was the legendary C; Angus MacGregor no less, my mentor, immediate superior, the last romantic Jacobite and currently director-general of Her Britannic Majesty's Secret Intelligence Service. SIS was the world's oldest continuously surviving foreign intelligence-gathering organisation, and MacGregor's predecessors went all the way back to the first 'C', the remarkable Mansfield Cumming. Cumming had always been his own man. So had his successors, Sinclair, Menzies … and now MacGregor. Good men, brave men.

He shuffled right past me and the bench, still not looking my way, then slowed, stopped, hesitating as if unsure of his next move, taking a pale hand out of a pocket, patting the coat as if reminding himself of something, checking to make sure that he hadn't forgotten his wallet or cash, looking down to where his feet should be. Then he turned again and, as if having made up his mind, ambled over.

His face was blank and showed no sign of recognition.

Panic over, the sweat on my back cooled, breathing returned to normal.

The motorcyclists were merely members of his close-protection team.

You had me there for a moment, you old devil.

In earlier, better days, he would have emerged alone for a stroll and an informal, off-the-books chat on the Embankment. In warm weather we would have crossed the river and eaten our M&S sandwiches together outside Tate Britain, followed by ice cream as a special treat. At the end of the working day, our business done, I would have gone back to whereverI'd come from, Berlin, Beijing or Beirut – the latter being my place of birth. He would have joined the exodus of office workers and caught his usual train to his suburban home, his wife and cat, his white head bent over the *Times* crossword to avoid eye contact and small talk with the other regulars.

There was none of this close protection rigmarole then; he probably didn't think it necessary even now – firstly because he believed, as I did, that anonymity offered ample security in a metropolis the size of London and it was important not to draw attention to oneself; secondly, because he would have insisted on putting the money to operational use and thirdly, because he detested officiousness of any kind. But this was 1992 and it wasn't up to him; his role was part and parcel of policy, marinated in rapid – and to some – incomprehensible change. As the chief spook of spooks, MacGregor was a member of the *nomenklatura* and like it or not, he had to accept his perks with good grace: his own small army providing 24/7 protection wherever he went, along with an up-armoured Jaguar, armed drivers who knew all about evasive tactics and a Pimlico penthouse with unmarked entrance and lift (for those occasions on which he had to work very late and needed a bed). The clubs of St James and Pall Mall were no longer considered safe for old spies with ultra-top-secret security clearance.

But the Cold War was over. Wasn't it?

His clothes were second hand, the labels removed, and his general air one of neglect and aimlessness. They couldn't do anything about that. It was who he was, and he wasn't about to change, bless him. He'd never aspired to becoming one of the sleek, suave and overfed 40-something civil servants that ruled the Whitehall roost, or thought they did, being outnumbered nowadays by legions of unelected ministerial 'advisors'.

But then I cared nothing for politicians or politics and never had, God rot them all.

I could have kicked myself.

This isn't about you, you paranoid dickhead.

Maybe it was the demise of Roger Peacock, aka GLUTTON, that he wanted to talk about. If so, it seemed that I wasn't going to die quite yet, or wake up manacled to a concrete floor in time for my first thorough beating and a hosing down with icy water.

The dead leaves of the plane trees splashed the ground under our feet in an oleaginous coverlet of orange, yellow and red. The tree-trunks were black with rain, branches poking up in supplication to a sky of uniform grey. The park wasn't pleasant or safe. The homeless, the dealers and their clients all used it. Children from the nearby council flats rarely enjoyed the playground, because thugs had wrecked it and

13

littered the place with condoms and hypodermics. The park itself was run-down, its boundary marked by 8-foot chain link fencing, much of it rotten, sagging with rust and broken in places, providing ratholes for dealers and tarts. If I had incriminated myself by panicking and making a stupid run for it, that's how I would have made it out onto the street – or tried to.

The authorities had torn down the original iron railings at the outset of World War Two, to provide raw material for Spitfires and corvettes, but it turned out to be the wrong type of iron, and had ended up in landfills.

Despite rampant privatisation, the place still looked neglected half a century later, at its worst in winter without its summer camouflage. The Georgian squares, tucked away out of sight, remained though, having been missed by Heinkel bombers, developers, estate agents and both Tory and Labour councillors. (Was there a difference?) I was fortunate enough to live in one.

Traffic rumbled, trains clanked, police and ambulance sirens wailed.

We took our places at opposite ends of a park bench, both facing the South Lambeth Road, like parishioners finding our places on a pew of a Sunday morning, waiting for the minister to begin the service. But we were civil servants, making sure there weren't any fresh pigeon droppings or gobs of chewing gum on which we might otherwise settle our grey-flannelled backsides. MacGregor looked smaller than I remembered and was huddled inside his coat. He had cause to huddle – it might not have been raining at that moment, but it was both damp and bloody cold, at least for London, and someone his age would feel it more than most. Exactly what his age was, I didn't know, except that it was way beyond the normal retirement age for civil servants of espionage, which was 55. Twice ministers had asked him to continue to provide them with a steady hand, with continuity. They needed his telling of truth to power, even if it made them uncomfortable. They respected his intellect and feared his caustic wit. He knew how to handle Whitehall even as the last of the SIS camel drivers and Moscow men were being prodded off the stage. The boss might be old and frail, but he was still tough. C would not twist the intelligence to fit the policy. He left that to the sleazy politicians. And to people like me.

MacGregor was the dad I'd never had – the biological version having been absent and, even on the few occasions he was present, unable to cope with the written and unwritten rules of peace-time and hence always fighting mad with gin. When the madness took him, he'd fight and batter anyone or anything within range of his fists, including my mother and me – and yet still I betrayed this much improved, sober and adopted father almost every day, though he'd shown me nothing but respect and kindness.

It was as if I resented having any kind of bond with another human being. I couldn't bear the responsibility, the possibility that someone might make demands on my time, my loyalty, my affections, that I might have to go out of my way to help someone, that I'd be relied upon to be honest in my dealings.

In all honesty, I couldn't bear that.

I didn't do closeness and I distrusted intimacy.

We both looked around, to the left, to the right, then behind and a little later, doing it all over again. It was habit. MacGregor cleared his own back even now, in his exalted rank of director-general, and carried out his own route surveillance, as I did, every time he headed home or ventured out to buy a paper, with or without the pack of two-legged guard dogs in attendance. He'd note descriptions of people hanging around in a phone box or outside a newsagent's, dog walkers of course, lovers in a clinch in the front seat of a nondescript car, holding each other for a bit too long to be natural. Car registrations. Lights in windows. The beam from a flashlight. The sound of a telephone ringing. He couldn't help himself any more than an old soldier could stop mentally positioning his company's support weapons and his riflemen in slit trenches on the forward and reverse slopes, spotting folds in the ground, among the trees, behind the dry stone wall, as he took the dog out for a stroll. It was a nervous tic for people in our peculiar trade because we were always at war, if only with one another, let alone our many overseas enemies, official and unofficial.

The question was what C wanted (other than my head on a platter), what was so important that it would drag him from his lair with its torn club chairs, Cummings's old clock, dust, peeling linoleum and two-bar electric heater to seek my company out in the open, away from microphones and video cameras and in the cold and rain.

Whatever it was, it had to be both serious and urgent.

3

Fang has written the report by hand in small, crisp characters, the spacing tight, the main points numbered, the vertical lines straight. Its classification is top secret – *jimidu* – and she has stamped the grade across each of the five pages.

The old man reaches across his desk and takes it from her with both hands. He inclines his bald head as if in receipt of a precious gift and places it in front of himself, adjusting the edges with his plump, small hands and fingers like a child's. He doesn't read it, but looks up instead at its author, Fang aka Zhang Pusheng, aka Chen Meilin, aka DRAGON. He doesn't smile, but his eyes seem to her to be friendly enough. There's a liveliness to them despite the dark pouches of wrinkled skin below, framed in round spectacles like the lenses of a swimmer's goggles.

His shiny pate, bushy eyebrows and his short, rotund body remind her of an owl with a startled expression or that of a wise uncle – not that she has an uncle, not a live one, wise or otherwise. This particular 'uncle' wears a dark, Western-style wool suit and white shirt with an open collar.

He gives the impression of benevolence, but Fang knows better.

There's no-one more ruthless or more deadly than this dear old uncle of hers. How else could the 72-year-old have survived so many years as a cadre and risen to his current rank? He's been Fang's immediate superior for 3 years, and she thinks he is the only person she has ever met who makes her afraid. He's no spy, knows nothing about the intelligence business, and that's what makes him so scary. He's Party first and last. Nothing but Party.

Xie Rong, head of *Guoanbu*, China's growing foreign intelligence and counter-intelligence service, gestures with his chin to a hard, upright chair on the other side of his desk. His deputy sits down, back straight, knees together, hands in her lap as he busies himself filling a cup with tea from the big pot on his desk. It's a moment she uses to calm herself, steady her thoughts, slow her heartbeat like a sniper acquiring a target. Xie pushes the cup towards her, leaving a trail of steam.

The tea is the finest Longjing, from Hangzhou. It's also expensive, and Xie is something of a connoisseur. He fills his own cup and reaches for a pack of *Shuangxi* ('Double Happiness') cigarettes. He looks at her, but Fang gives an imperceptible shake of her head. No thanks, boss. Fang makes a mental note to buy him a carton of Marlboro the next time she passes through an international airport. He'll like that.

The office is gloomy and sparsely furnished. It's also cold, despite an ancient iron radiator running along the entire wall under the windows. It clanks or wheezes with the heat forced through its ancient pipes by a coal-fired boiler. Everything else seems to be made of wood, mostly bamboo, dark with age – except for the files in steel cabinets across one wall. A single reading lamp burns on Xie's desk, and dust motes dance in thin shafts of light from between the wooden blinds on the windows running along the opposite side.

An aide shuts the door to the outer office so they have privacy and quiet, silencing the racket of telephones and voices demanding attention.

'You worry me, Department Deputy Zhang. You know why? No? Truly?' He waits, wanting her to show consternation or even fear of him, but her expression remains blank. 'Because you seem to have no vices. People without discernible faults keep me awake at night, you know. Honest people worry me; they are a greater danger to the Party than those who can be bought, don't you agree? I've watched you for years. I've read your file a dozen times. No vices at all. None. How can that be? Are you really so honest?'

His tone is mocking, but under it is a threat all the same. Xie lights his cigarette with a disposable plastic lighter.

He looks at her. She looks back at him.

'You hardly drink, you don't smoke, you don't sleep with the wrong people – none that we know of, anyway – and you don't gamble. No banquets, no parties, no drunkenness. You are such a serious person! What do you do when you aren't working, hmm? Not even addicted to mahjong, like the old folk in my neighbourhood. You're not specu-lating in foreign money or accumulating American dollars and hiding them in the accounts of your friends or under your floorboards. We do check, you know. We follow the activities of all our people because we have to take care of them. You haven't bought yourself a nice condo in New York or leased a villa by the beach in Phuket. You haven't set up your own business on the side like so many. What's the matter with you? You're not interested in fine art or foreign cars. You have stolen no ancient bronzes. You don't even buy foreign jewellery. How is this even possible? Don't you approve of Deng's reforms, hmm? You make a very poor capitalist. No Cartier, no Chanel, no Hermès. You work very long hours. You don't have any fun in your life. You don't understand how a market economy works in a socialist society.' He makes a tut-tutting sound of disapproval with his tongue. 'A good communist like you needs a little re-educating in how to have fun.'

The threat hangs in the air as Xie leans back in his chair and blows smoke at his ceiling, then bursts into laughter; a deep rumble that seems to start somewhere below the table and works its way up to a sudden and short-lived explosion that turns his cheeks red. If this is humour, it's the humour of the camps.

'If I was of a suspicious cast of mind, I'd say you were trying to position yourself to take my place!'

No reaction.

'Okay,' he says in English, regaining control of his expression. He sits upright, pulls himself to the desk again, sighs, puts his plump hands together.

'*Ganxie*. Thank you for this, dear *tongzhi*. There are no copies?'

Calling her 'comrade' is a little old-fashioned. Fang thinks he's being ironic. These days it's used in Party speeches and public announcements, but Fang reflects on the fact that among the young, the term has become something of a joke and people use it as an insult. She will not be the one to bring her boss up to date. Could be he already knows.

Fang reminds herself of a certain cynical saying among civil servants. *Duoshuo duocuo, xiaoshuo xiaocuo, bushuo bucuo*. Speak more, more mistakes; speak little, few mistakes; say nothing, no mistakes.

'No copies, Department Chief Xie. Nothing on computer hard drive.'

He nods in approval, or simple acknowledgement. 'I'll read this with care, but I want to hear it from you, in your own words. Now.

Tell me about this Peacock. What a name ... Peacock. Please begin, Department Deputy Zhang.'

So Fang begins a presentation that she has rehearsed again and again.

This is not a time to show weakness or doubt, let alone fear. If Xie had any notion of what Fang has done – contrary to procedure, contrary to the Party, contrary to her duty as his subordinate – she'd already be in a cell. Or much worse.

'The foreigner named Roger Peacock has been the subject of close surveillance for these past 3 months by the Shanghai Security Bureau which, as everyone here knows, is headed by Du Fu who is, in turn, brother-in-law of Yao Tie, Party Secretary for Shanghai.' That's the nub of it. Fang takes a breath and continues. 'I have learned that Yao himself took an interest in the investigation of Peacock. He did so because his wife, Du Lan, asked her brother to look into Peacock's activities.' Fang believes she has informed her husband of this. 'It turns out that her suspicions were well-founded, though it's not clear what gave rise to them and what it was that made her instigate the investigation. Maybe all she wanted was to send a signal, a warning. Anyway, Du Fu's findings are summarised as an appendix to my report. The inquiry concluded that the *ying gui*, the English devil, was a foreign intelligence agent and one working for his country's Secret Intelligence Service or SIS.'

'But you didn't know this before – through your own agent 2904?'

'No. I don't believe 2904 knew.' She is lying. The number 2904 is *Guoanbu* code for Fang's most productive and most precious agent, Richard Brodick, who has bored his way like a death-watch beetle into the decaying rafters of the counter-revolutionary British spy agency called the Secret Intelligence Service, and whose name in Mandarin is Bo Deli.

21

'My agent would not have withheld this information, had he known. I know how this SIS works – they are very careful to place agents and their handlers together in separate pods so they don't know of one another's existence. They compartmentalise everything, and it has been so ever since the KGB penetrated them some years ago. Because of the damage this caused to the reputation of the British services, there were no defectors to the SIS for more than 24 years. Even their American masters and allies were wary of them and kept their distance. So they tightened their procedures, but the result is that sometimes their left hand is a stranger to their right.'

The truth of it is that 2904 not only informed her, but had given up Peacock – a wonderful gift – and she was to have run him in place and against his existing target without his being made conscious of the fact. That was the agreement, which was part and parcel of their reciprocal relationship and in this instance, it was to show her mastery of counter-intelligence against the British imperialists and to expand her network of foreign deep cover operatives. She was to have reported to Xie that she had turned Peacock, that she was running him in place as agreed, but given what has happened, it's better – indeed, essential – that she says nothing.

'Go on. We have time.'

'Peacock slept with Du Lan. The affair, which she seems to have initiated, was not continuous. Both were frequent travellers. Du has several sexual interests and she has not confined her appetites to this *ying gui*, British devil. Her husband, Yao, has two mistresses we know of. They do not seem to have made any effort to hide their amorous adventures from each other or, indeed, from the investigation. Their marriage remains strong, or so it appears. Perhaps an overriding and shared interest in money and power is enough in their case. And their son, of course.'

Fang is taking a chance with this mention of power and immediately regrets it.

'Peacock advised both Du Lan and Yao on their individual and joint investments and helped both set up companies and organise purchases of property and stocks in the US, Japanese and European markets. This was his cover. Excellent cover – because it was natural. Yao rewarded the English well with generous commissions. He was also English-language tutor to their 14-year-old son during the school holidays. Du Lan would call the Englishman to come to teach, though it's not clear from telephone records obtained by the *Gonganbu* investigation whether this was a pretext for them to meet. The calls were very business-like and brief. A bit like a mistress addressing her servant – sometimes she scolded him, using rough language. He recently helped her buy a condo overlooking Bondi Beach in Australia, as well as a mansion in California. She went out there with Peacock to inspect the Australian property, sign the papers and approve the money transfer from a Hong Kong bank. Separate flights, of course, but they shared a hotel room. They have also met on several occasions at her flat in a prestigious part of Hong Kong Island known as The Peak.'

Fang doesn't mention that Peacock's wife – now widow – has a flat in the same area, on The Peak, and within walking distance of Du's *pied-à-terre*.

Xie takes off his glasses and rubs his eyes.

'Wasn't the wife worried about gossip – her servants, drivers, cooks, hotel staff? What did this Peacock provide in bed that her other lovers didn't? Why did she start this sexual activity? Why take the risk? Was he especially well-endowed? I'm told Westerners are well-equipped in that department. Not that I would know.'

The questions don't faze Fang.

'Because the Englishman had negotiated the contract for the Australian property, which Du Lan then signed. She wanted to celebrate the deal – with champagne and in bed. The one led to the other. To her, it would have been only a bit of fun – recreational sex, the Westerners call it.'

Fang adds an afterthought, in case there are any lingering doubts or Xie imagines that she's speculating. She isn't. 'We have recordings – video and audio – of them together, copies supplied by the Security Bureau at my request.'

Xie helps himself to more tea, looking up at Fang, but she shakes her head. She resumes her tale while her boss lights another cigarette and draws on it, watching the smoke spiral up towards the high wooden ceiling while he listens.

'I believe that Yao failed to share with his wife one important fact, which investigators discovered in their inquiry into Peacock's activities. Yao was exporting large sums of money to Hong Kong and he was then illegally re-importing it as foreign investments, taking advantage of mainland tax breaks, using a variety of banks and accounts in Hong Kong and Macau. He is not alone among our cadres in this practice, as you know. It's very profitable. Both Yao and his wife last year alone made profit in the order of 6,000 per cent on their property purchases and sales in Hainan, thanks to the relaxation of financial regulations in the new economic zones, as well as his Party connections down south. It seems Yao didn't tell her about his Hong Kong tax evasion scheme, possibly because he didn't want her implicated, but also because he might have considered this part of his patriotic activities ...'

She has Xie's full attention now. 'Patriotic – what are you talking about?'

' … on behalf of a certain relevant department, *youguan bumen*, for which he has been working in secret. No doubt he thought his patriotic work would also be excellent cover for his illegal financial dealings. Who knows what he was thinking? The Public Security Ministry doesn't agree. He wasn't secret enough, it seems.'

'Which department – not ours?' For a moment, Xie looks worried.

'The United Front Work Department.'

Xie shakes his head. He looks almost sorrowful. 'Well, well. You'd think he'd have enough on his plate as Party Secretary, wouldn't you, without all this other business? He's not from Shanghai, though, is he? I seem to recall that Yao held a senior Party position in Chengdu before his latest promotion.'

Xie knows this. They're friends, though Xie is now scrabbling about and trying to distance himself from his old Party comrade.

'Correct. He was mayor. But Du Lan and her family are from Shanghai.'

'That explains a lot, given the reputation of Shanghai women.'

Fang wonders why her boss is deflecting the conversation away from Yao's affiliation with the UFWD, the covert agency charged with recruitment and repatriation of overseas Chinese – particularly those with high-tech skills, wealth and influence. She knows what her chief means, though. One slogan of Shanghai men is *gen dang zou, ting tai tai de hua*. Walk with the Party, obey the wife. It's said that Shanghai women control the money and 'train' their men to buy and prepare food, do the housework and look after the children. Shanghai people consider themselves the most sophisticated in mainland China (and regard everyone else as country bumpkins – *tubaozi*

) and therefore hence better at dealing with foreigners, something which Fang – being from the city herself – thinks might well have more than a grain of truth.

Fang has neither husband nor children, and while she likes the idea of family, she's uncertain whether this would be a practical goal, given her character and her obsession with her counter-intelligence work, with getting to the top, with professional success. From time to time she's fantasised about Bo Deli and speculated whether the two of them suit one another and could enjoy a real relationship, something more than their intermittent one-night stands, fun and exciting though they have been. She has even checked their astrological signs and has discovered that their birthdays are only a day apart. Yet she has dismissed the notion as an absurd dream, symptomatic of her being always alone, and in any case, these tempting thoughts are unrealistic on so many levels. It is one thing to sleep with a partner in espionage, another thing to entertain thoughts of lasting affection. It is better not to think about it. She has concluded more than once that intimacy is just a bourgeois weakness of character, a kind of Western contamination, and to be resisted.

'So do we know what Yao Tie is doing for the United Front Department?'

Xie knows. He must do – in which case, why is he asking her? Is this a test of her loyalty? Xie and Yao have met on several occasions. Or is Xie now trying to pretend he doesn't know Yao? But she answers, as she must.

'Because of his Party position and wealth, Yao can do a great deal. The Department identifies recently-retired senior officers of Taiwan's armed forces, as well as those still on active duty but who might be encouraged to retire early, and it gives him a list. He then makes contact through an intermediary and offers them free visits to Shanghai as VIP guests of the city, all expenses paid, and, once they visit, these individuals are offered opportunities – investments, property, business ventures, employment in prestigious institutes, university places for their children, a new car and the usual extras that can make life comfortable. He foots most of the bill out of his own pocket, using dummy offshore companies, and this gains him some credit and it ensures that his own financial affairs escape scrutiny – or at least, it has done so until now. They instructed him to target members of the old guard – originally mainlanders still with family ties here. In return, of course, for helping us to update our knowledge about Taiwan's armed forces and strategy, especially the extent to which the Americans will sell them advanced weaponry – or not – and, most important of all, details of any secret agreement setting out terms on which the Americans would ally themselves with Taiwan in the event of hostilities. These 'advisers' bring with them classified material to qualify for this lavish VIP hospitality and all the privileges they enjoy. An exchange of gifts between close friends.'

'Usual extras?'

'Entertainment.'

'Meaning?'

'Sleeping partners. By the hour, the day, the month, the year – whatever it takes. Even marriage. Recordings are available and, if necessary, images may be sent to the subject's home and workplace if the VIP refuses to cooperate fully or has second thoughts.'

'Beauty trap. *Meiren ji*.'

'It's in case pressure is required to secure the foreign guest's full cooperation.'

'Yao speaks Cantonese?'

'And Japanese. You will know that many older Taiwanese speak Japanese, but few, if any, hold top military posts, so are unlikely to be among Yao's targets for recruitment. They do love Japan, and many older Japanese have strong emotional feelings for Taiwan as a former colony. Yao's language ability would come in useful in any discussions he might have with potential Japanese investors.'

She does not have to tell Xie that more than 200,000 Taiwanese served in Imperial Japanese forces in World War Two and that in 1945 Japanese troops stationed in Taiwan marched in ceremonial white uniforms to the port, where they boarded ships to take them home.

Xie sucks at his tea. 'Which begs the question, what Japan will do when we take the island back? The South China Sea is important to Tokyo. It's only a matter of time, one way or another. How did this Du Lan react when informed that her big-nosed lover, financial adviser and son's tutor was a foreign spy?'

'Investigators say she panicked. It's in the report. She told Yao. She called him several times – she seems to have been in a frantic state, so much so that her husband cut short a trip to Beijing and returned home. They must have worried that the foreigner had discovered not only the extent of their holdings abroad, but also Yao's special work and his illegal tax evasion. Then, 10 days later – 10 days after her brother told her of the investigation's conclusions – she met her foreign lover in a hotel in Beijing municipality at her behest and, after they had spent the night together, she murdered him in his sleep, using a shellfish toxin. To be precise, the toxin of a sea anemone. I received the results of the analysis this morning.'

'And how did you get involved in this matter, Department Deputy Zhang?'

'Well, it's a counter-intelligence matter, Department Chief Xie, and you have given me special responsibility for the 5th Bureau. Colleagues kept me informed of the progress of the Security Bureau's inquiry. When I received the report of Peacock's death, Du Fu and I discussed it and we agreed I should clean up the mess as quickly as possible and suppress the details. At that point, I was unaware of the identity of the suspected killer. At least …' Fang pauses, and then concludes: 'I had no indication then that he was aware, either.'

Xie reaches out and touches the teapot with a finger. 'Still warm enough – sure you won't have another cup?'

Fang leaves Xie's office with every appearance of being calm, even relaxed. She doesn't walk too quickly, or too slowly. She nods at people who greet her. Fang doesn't smile and is careful to show no emotion.

It's only when Fang slumps in the back seat of her official limo that she closes her eyes.

Her own driver is doubtless informing on her. Just to have the job – quite a soft option, all things considered – means he must be reporting in. It might be to Xie Rong or someone else in the *Guoanbu* offices; then again, it might not. It could be military intelligence – PLA2 – or it could be *Gonganbu*, state security.

Everything and anything in the People's Republic of China is secret, unless of course it's published in an official newspaper, magazine or document. A secret is anything the Ministry of Public Security says it is. What a man says to his wife at the breakfast table, or what she says to him in bed. A holiday postcard, a telephone call, a remark overheard in a shopping mall – Fang knows all too well that anything and everything can be regarded as a secret, and that means anyone – Chinese or foreign – can stand accused of betraying state secrets and will be found guilty.

No-one is safe, especially in the fractious Party.

Fang would like to give voice to her pent-up feelings of anger and fear by opening the window, sticking her head out and shouting, cursing or crying – better still, all three. But she has trained herself to be self-disciplined at all times and she can do this because she's held back her emotions as long as she can remember; since childhood and the growing awareness that her family was not what it appeared to be, nor what it was supposed to be. Life is a straitjacket for Fang. The most she can allow herself is to keep her eyes closed, to breathe in and out regularly in an effort to relax and pretend the driver isn't watching her in his rear-view mirror. She must preserve the illusion at all costs.

Is she high-ranking passenger or hostage?

Her mind replays her meeting with Xie. The question now is what he will do about his friend Yao, Shanghai Party Secretary. These two men are more than top Party cadres – they are both old-school Maoists who distinguished themselves – if that's the word – in implementing some of the worst excesses of the Cultural Revolution.

They are comrades in blood-letting and persecution and Yao in particular still has a taste for cruelty – like so many small, inadequate men.

Among the senior cadres, it is no secret that Yao is a staunch opponent of Deng Xiaoping's leadership and his opening up of China to foreign investment, to the modern world, to the temptations – the infectious diseases – of the West. That Yao's wife Du Lan sees herself as a future first lady comes as no surprise to Fang – and for that to happen, Du Lan will have to ensure that her husband Yao becomes president and general secretary. The first obvious opportunity is the next Party congress some months after the Chinese New Year – if

Yao and his ambitious wife can drum up support to force Deng into retirement and to supplant him with their own hard-line faction.

A collective leadership, then, or a tame Party figure who'll do as he's told.

No wonder Du Lan panicked over the discovery that Peacock was a foreign agent.

China's future is at stake.

How will her boss react to her report?

Lying back, forcing her shoulders to relax, monitoring her muscles from her feet up, forcing herself to unwind. Fang concludes there's only one living individual before whom Fang has shown anything like her true feelings and with whom she has ever lowered her guard, if only partially, and that's her agent 2904, Bo Deli.

4

'How are things in the Office?' It wasn't an inspired start to the conversation.

'Chaotic.'

He spat the word out.

We waited for an ambulance, lights pulsing, siren shrieking, racing past to St Thomas's hospital.

'Aye, politicians in a panic, demanding answers to questions they haven't yet asked themselves because they don't know the right questions. Those people are infantile; throwing their teddies in the corner because they can't find the so-called *peace dividend* they were told to expect now the Cold War's supposed to end. There's no gold at the end of this rainbow, not for them, not for any of us.

'They'll strip us to the bone, you'll see. Or try to do away with the Firm altogether.'

I thanked my stars I wasn't still working out of that ugly, overcrowded concrete and glass box that was Century House. Twenty-two storeys of it perched on top of a petrol station on the South Bank, with Formica tables, shabby paintwork and the staff preparing papers demanded by Whitehall's Joint Intelligence Committee, drowning in the minutes of briefings that resolved nothing. It was enough to make anyone grumpy.

Although my berth at UK Station might not provide better accommodation, it was a lot further in spirit, if not distance, from the idiocy of both Whitehall and Westminster. It was my bailiwick, after all. I had a free hand, more or less. Out of sight, out of mind – that was the way we liked it in our 1930s neoclassical, stucco block tucked away in Earl's Court. I wanted it to stay that way, but given what had recently happened in the Gulf, and what was now happening in Beijing and Moscow, to say nothing of the breakup of Yugoslavia, it seemed a forlorn wish.

MacGregor's rant over, he turned to me. 'And how are those nice people running the Communist Party of China? How are the old men reacting to events in Moscow?'

What did I know? I wasn't a bug on the wall of the *Zhongnanhai*, the Chinese version of the Kremlin that was a village, in effect, inhabited by China's ruling class. What could I tell the Director-General that he didn't already know from his sources, official and unofficial, the ceaseless tide of secret mush, much of it from my bailiwick at UK Station? His real question was about how I was reading the situation, how I was responding – not what DRAGON was telling me. No doubt he was also – in an indirect way – raising the death of Roger Peacock, codename GLUTTON.

I knew MacGregor well enough by now to anticipate where this was heading, so I was careful to answer in the collective plural. I advanced my pawns one square at a time, probing my interlocutor's responses as he probed mine. No-one likes to lose an agent, particularly one as effective as GLUTTON.

I evaded the real question and began with the obvious.

'Right from the start in 1980, Solidarity bothered Deng; he had a bee in his proverbial bonnet when it reappeared as the official opposition party in '89. Deng warned of a plague of dissent; he wanted Poland to take a hard line from the start. Of course, he urged tough measures on Moscow. Don't you think he was right in retrospect, from his perspective? But I – we – don't think even Deng, for all his foresight, could have predicted the fall of the Berlin Wall, what, around the same time, two years ago? And then, 4 months ago,' – I thought for a moment: yes, that's right, August – 'the failure of the Moscow coup which everyone watched live on television. The CPC leadership must have been rooting for the insurgents, counting on their success. They had to be, don't you think? Deng is said to have been shocked rigid by the violent death of his dear friend, Romania's last communist dictator, Nicolae Ceauşescu.'

A yellow leaf spiralled down and landed on MacGregor's knee and MacGregor, rather than brush it off, contemplated it.

'Are you saying this Moscow business will kill Deng's reforms, his opening to the West? Shutting down capital inflows, capping exports and limiting growth rate is going to hurt. Not only them. Us, too .'

Like it or not, communist China already underpinned our capitalist consumer paradise. He was referring to Mikhail Gorbachev's resignation, weeks before.

'They'll be looking for scapegoats, I should imagine.'

I was spouting off far too much, a reaction to endorphins now the immediate threat to life and liberty had faded.

MacGregor mumbled into his collar 'The Soviet Union is dying, Richard. The Americans think China will follow suit and implode. Civil war, they say. Widespread unrest and counter-revolution. Bloody mayhem. Famine, the works. But then again, the Chinese aren't at all like the Russians, as we both know.'

So I told him what I thought, and what I thought was what DRAGON had told me.

'They'll crack down, chief. They always do when they feel under threat and these days they're old and scared. For Deng, it will mean his biggest challenge yet from the hardliners. They'll accuse him of being too soft, of being another Gorbachev. Remember what happened in 1989? Tiananmen Square? We thought of it then as students and workers rising up against the Party, which was supposed to represent them.'

I didn't know about MacGregor, but I felt a certain schadenfreude at the disarray in ChiCom senior ranks, still I wondered how DRAGON would emerge from all this, or if she'd emerge at all. My career – my life – depended on it. Hers certainly did.

GLUTTON didn't drink, let alone to excess. Was this her message, buried in the foreign ministry statement? If so, it could only mean one thing: someone had killed Peacock.

In reality, as DRAGON had informed us at the time – and she was right, of course – it had been no rebellion at Tiananmen, but in reality two Party factions at each other's throats. She'd forewarned us, too, about military law imposed 3 months earlier on Tibet, and other outbreaks of unrest throughout China. Yes, students died in Beijing, some under the tracks of army tanks, other protestors shot down by the score. No-one knew how many died. Hundreds, most likely thousands, followed by the mass round-ups. The moderate but irresolute Zhao Ziyang had lost because all he had was the support of the 38th Army Group in Beijing and he had opposed – too late – the use of armed force. The first soldiers deployed were unarmed and very confused. Deng had the rest of the PLA behind him and he had rallied the Party octogenarians. If Zhao had won, China would have turned out to be a different place, though still communist in name. Instead, the emperor won with his iron fist – fending off the liberal wing represented by Zhao on the one hand and the Maoist dinosaurs on the other. He gained time with the blood-letting at Tiananmen – enough time to push through his reforms before age and ill-health brought him down.

'You remember, boss, what Deng is rumoured to have said after the Beijing Massacre?'

'You're about to remind me.'

'He's reported to have said: *sile yiwan, wending shinian*. With 10,000 dead, we will have stability for 10 years.'

'He said that?'

'If he didn't say those exact words, he would have said something like it. He did say in criticism of the hardliners that the colour of the cat didn't matter, so long as it caught mice. Ten thousand dead aren't so many if you remember what he himself has lived through – the war with Japan, the civil war, the horror of Mao's campaigns, the Great Famine in which 36 million people starved to death. The Chinese killed three times as many fellow Chinese as the Japanese, in all their brutality, killed in 15 years of invasion and occupation – and the general estimate is 50 million lives lost in total under Mao. A neat, round figure.'

I told myself I must stop chattering and making speeches. It was just like C to come out and talk to operators like myself rather than shuffle paper, but flattered though I was, opening up to him was always a risk for someone with so much to hide. Why didn't he get back to discussing something specific, such as GLUTTON?

What I craved right then was a cognac and cigarette. Reaction had set in and I was shivering again and trying not to show it.

It wasn't the cold.

'And Deng's challengers? Who are they, Richard? Do you have names? Number Ten wants to know. The White House wants to know. The man himself seems to have disappeared. Is Deng sick? Is he dying? Has he given up and taken to the mountains and the bottle? Or have they forced him into retirement and placed him under house arrest somewhere?'

Had he still been alive, the late GLUTTON, aka Roger Peacock, along with DRAGON, would have come up with chapter and verse.

Looking back, I don't think any of us thought a serious challenge to the emperor was possible, except for GLUTTON, and we would never know now what he thought. Maybe that's why he was dead. We did not know, as we sat in that derelict park, how close we were to confrontation with China, one that could drag in the Americans – not that they needed much encouragement, the gung-ho idiots – the Japanese of course, the Australians … and ourselves scampering along behind, panting, tongue lolling, tail wagging, eager not to be left out but incapable of making much of a difference to anything, but anxious all the same to stay in Washington's good books.

What did MacGregor want?

More important to me, though, was the fact that I was still breathing and that I'd live to lie another day.

That was what mattered.

Screw China. I mattered. Me.

5

'*Hun dan*! Bastard!'

Roger Peacock's wife stands up, her back to the visitor. Susan Ho Ping doesn't want the stranger to see her tears and mascara-streaked cheeks. She faces a window that takes up an entire wall of the living room. There's nothing to see in the dark, except unseasonal rain that lashes the glass as if trying to break in, driven by a gale from an invisible South China Sea.

It's almost midnight. Hong Kong winters are mild and dry – but not this year.

Fang presses on. 'Did you know what he was doing?'

'Of course I fucking knew. I'm not an idiot!' She swings around, no longer caring about the impression she makes, taut with rage and grief, trembling, both hands clenched tight into white-knuckled fists to gain control.

Of the two emotions, rage predominates – or at least it seems that way to Fang, with fear and confusion close behind. 'He went around Hong Kong with her behind the wheel of that ridiculous car of hers, the two of them in full view, the top down, in public, for Chrissakes. Registration LAN 888. So arrogant. Yes, I saw them together, smiling, laughing. Can you believe it? *I saw them*. Have you any idea how that felt? It was so humiliating …' She takes a deep breath. 'He went with her to Australia and California and London and God knows where else. Lan's investment adviser, setting up shell companies, accounts in offshore tax havens. Lan's tax adviser, making them millions. Her son's tutor. Her husband's expert in all matters financial in the capitalist world. He was indispensable, of course he was. Always popping over to the mainland, to Shanghai. That's what her husband told me, you know? Yao. His word, not mine. *Indispensable. A good friend of the family*. Jesus. My husband was fucking her wherever they went and charging them both commission. Creaming off 20 per cent. Of course I knew. I knew it all!'

It wasn't what Fang meant.

'I mean his work, Mrs Peacock.'

'I know what you mean. Don't patronise me. And don't call me that. Call me by my real name.'

'I don't mean offshore investments.'

Through gritted teeth: 'I know what you mean, ok.'

'So, you know who your husband was working for.'

There is silence except for the wind howling around The Peak, a low groan rising to a roar like some enormous animal buffeting the building, before falling away, exhausted, readying itself for a fresh assault. Fang waits. The moment hasn't yet arrived, but she knows it will.

She tries to put herself in this woman's shoes. Fang estimates her at 40 to 45 – a little older than herself, but they're of the same generation. She attempts to imagine what Ms Ho is going through, to feel sympathy for her suffering. Fang has never married, has never lived with any man for more than a few weeks and then only for professional reasons. There has only been one live-in boyfriend, and he proved to be a disaster in every sense. It's not an episode Fang wants to remember if she can help it. She's married to her job – and the Party.

Ho Ping raises her head. 'So – who killed him?'

Fang doesn't hesitate. 'She did.'

'*She* did?'

'Yes. Du Lan killed your husband.'

'In person? She did it herself?'

'She poisoned him.' Immediately the words are out of her mouth, Fang tells herself it is too much information to give someone in her current state of mind. On the other hand, she needs to provide Ho Ping with ample motive to do what has to be done. Fang believes the desire for revenge is strong in most people who've been cheated or robbed.

'Where?'

'A hotel – in north-west Beijing.'

Fang asks a question this time. 'You knew her, didn't you?'

The widow's head snaps back as if Fang has slapped her in the face.

'Knew her? Of course I knew her. I couldn't avoid her, could I? Best of buddies, weren't we? Anything to help dear, swinging-dick Roger. Tennis – always a foursome – barbecues, cocktails in their home, that absurd monstrosity of a house they shared in Shanghai with its 11 bedrooms. That huge basement where smirking little Yao Tie kept all his foreign cars and where they held their outrageous parties. Girl talk in the cloakroom, Bolivian marching powder on a silver salver, martinis before a lunch of crab salad and mayo at the club. Jesus F Christ. We were besties, right? We even went shopping together, can you imagine? Fucking Valentino, Gucci, Balmain, Givenchy. She had the gall to insist on paying with her American Express card. Did I know her ... '

40

'You visited their home often?'

'Do you know what they have in their basement aside from the collection of luxury cars?'

'No – tell me.'

'Right in the centre they had a 12-foot statue on a pedestal – of the Great Leader himself. Mao Zedong, no less, with a Mona Lisa smile. I'm not kidding. Twelve feet tall. And you know something? The kicker?'

Fang shakes her head because it's expected of her.

'It's solid gold, I swear. The Chairman himself, the Great Leader, in solid, 18 karat gold and with a smug expression on his face.'

Now it happens. She sags – laughing, sobbing – and finally collapses on the Anatolian rug, head lowered, a woman broken.

It's the moment that Fang has been waiting for.

She moves closer, whispers. 'I need your help, Mrs Peacock.'

'Don't fucking call me that.'

'Okay. Fine. My apologies. Susan – Susan Ho Ping. I need your help. In return, I'll help you.'

'My help? You've got a nerve. Help – to do what?' She switches from English to Cantonese and takes a glass of water from Fang with shaking hands, gulps it down.

Fang kneels next to her on the rug, takes the glass from her, puts it down on a side table. She answers in Cantonese.

'You want justice, don't you?'

'Justice?' The widow shouts out loud and turns to Fang, teeth bared in a snarl, their faces inches apart. 'You – you talk of justice? I know what you are, what you represent. What can you, of all people, know of justice? What do the state security organs of the People's Republic of China know of justice? You're secret police,

41

I know you are. You're a spy. I have more respect for a Kowloon street walker. You don't care about justice. People like you commit monstrous crimes against your own people and then you cover them up. You're killers. Gangsters. I can say that, here in Hong Kong. I can shout it from the rooftops, tell the media and they'll still print it – for now. We're still free here, you know, though not for much longer. One country, two systems? What a load of balls. I could never say it on the mainland. If I did, I'd end up in a labour camp or dead in a ditch. And you – a communist secret agent here in Hong Kong – want to offer me justice? You want my help? Do you think I'm stupid?'

This isn't going well, but Fang is not the kind to give up.

They're both silent, staring at each other, the one in tears breathing fast and deep, chest heaving as if she's run a race, the other cold and calm. Even the storm outside seems to have relented, pausing for a few moments as if spellbound by this exchange.

Fang keeps her voice low, steady. 'I'm sorry to tell you this, Susan. They were both involved in your husband's murder, and it's likely that her brother supplied the means. You want to get even, don't you? Even if it's not the justice you deserve, you want them to pay, right? Yes? I think you do. You have every right. But then I need your help. Papers, bank accounts, receipts – everything, all of it – every transaction and investment, right down to hotel and credit card receipts. Everything and anything your late husband may have kept in his files, locked up somewhere, here or in England.'

Fang has to push hard, because she needs to be seen to get hold of it before someone else – the Hong Kong police, Brodick's locally-based colleagues – storm in and confiscate the evidence. Or more likely, a *Gonganbu* squad despatched by Du Lan's brother to remove or destroy the evidence, and if necessary, liquidate Susan Ho Ping.

Time is not on Fang's side.

Ms Ho wipes her cheeks with the back of her hand and sniffs. Fang offers her a tissue from a box on the coffee table. Susan is petite, her black hair cut in a bob, her skin so pale it's almost translucent. Whatever scent she's wearing, it's expensive. Fang remembers Peacock on the hotel bed; he seemed so big, a beached whale of a man. Next to him, his wife would have seemed tiny. A whale and a sardine.

'You say you know who it was your husband worked for. We're talking about the British, their special services, right? Have they contacted you? Has anyone been to see you, to offer their official condolences, to assist you? A diplomat, a consular official? A lawyer? Someone claiming to be a journalist? Did they take anything? No? No, I didn't think so.' Fang's voice is soft but insistent. 'Your husband worked undercover for years for Her Majesty's Government. It was dangerous work on the mainland, but he did it. He was very brave. He took many risks for his country. And now? What support are they offering you? Nothing? They don't want to know. Of course they don't. They'll deny ever having known him and they'll deny you the help you need, too. You must know how this business works.'

Ho Ping pulls herself up, using the sofa to get up onto it, leaning forward, arms across her stomach as if in pain.

'What do you want me to do?' And she adds: 'Not that I believe anything you say.'

'I want your husband's papers – all you can find, anyway, before the murderers get their hands on them and destroy the evidence. Now.'

'And then?'

'I want you to vanish – with my help – until things settle and they stop looking. They will look for you. You know that. I'm referring to Du Fu and his friends in the Public Security Ministry. I might ask you to visit the lady in question – with our protection and in Shanghai if necessary. I might need you to tell her the news of your husband's death and to ask for her help.'

'Visit her? Talk to her? My husband's killer?' She shivers, trembling all over. 'Ask her for her help? Are you crazy or sick?'

'Not so crazy if you want to get back at these people. You can do this. I know I can rely on you to play your part. You won't be alone – I'll be with you every step of the way. It might not prove necessary. But if it does, you will play the innocent who knows and suspects nothing. Get close to them. I'll brief you on what to say and what we need.'

Ho Ping takes hold of Fang's arm, digging her nails into the skin. 'You're saying you want me to help you, a communist spy. You people are my husband's enemies – you're Hong Kong's enemies. It's true what the old people say about you; you're communist bandits, *gong fei*. You want me to work for you? Is this a joke? This isn't happening. I must be losing my mind.' The tears and sobs return.

There's no point in denying the obvious.

'To get even, Susan. To hit back. Does it matter who we are, if you can bring them down with our help, see them put on trial, imprisoned, disgraced, stripped of their wealth? Wouldn't it be worth it?'

'I'm going to be sick.'

Fang helps her up, but she pulls away. She runs to the bathroom on bare feet, throws up the lavatory seat, bends over from the

44

waist and vomits. She keeps retching until there's nothing left. Fang stays in the doorway, watching, waiting. She recognises she'll have to stay with Ho Ping tonight, if only as a suicide watch, but it can't be here. It's far too risky. Fang will need to find her a safe place, and fast.

'You're right, Susan. I admit it. You have a right to know. I am from the Ministry of State Security. The *Guoanbu*. But you only have to work with me for a while, days at the most. I'll help you catch the criminals who seduced and then murdered your husband, people who have broken laws not only on the mainland but here in Hong Kong. Greedy people who deserve prison for murder and corruption.'

Well, it's partly true, but it's not the whole truth because the whole truth emerging from this mess is so big it's hard for even Fang to get her head around it.

Ho Ping turns on the tap over the basin, splashes cold water on her face, dabs at it with a towel, wiping away the streaks of mascara. She pushes past the taller Fang, who notices how pale she looks. Ms Ho points to a room off the hall.

'There – that's his study; it's always locked, but I have a key. There's a safe hidden under the big painting behind his desk – it's where Roger keeps his financial papers, records of all his deals. There are three sets of accounts. Three. I know the combination.' She sniffs and wipes the tears off her cheeks as she sorts through a bunch of keys; she finds the right one and, with some difficulty, unlocks the door – it's heavy hardwood, Burmese teak, and Fang helps push it open. The two women take the huge oil painting off the wall, one on each side.

'It's a Pierre Soulages,' says Ho Ping. She's breathless with the effort. 'It's an original. Roger paid 3,000,000 point something Swiss francs for it at Sotheby's in Paris. He was so proud of it, not that I understood what the fuss was. He said it was beautiful, that I should regard it as an investment, that it was a good deal, that it was worth twice that. I still don't like it. I made him keep it in here. Now he's gone, I'll sell it.'

It takes a moment for Fang to realise she means a painter named Soulages. Fang and Ho Ping have something in common, a dislike of abstract painting. This one comprises broad, powerful strokes of black with little apertures of light between them, the thick black strokes vertical like a palisade, glistening like patent leather. It's very masculine. Fang thinks it's ugly – scary also, and she doesn't see the point of putting something so nightmarish up on a wall, let alone pay a fortune for it. How many Chinese families could live for a year on what that painting cost? It's absurd. Obscene.

Fang spends the next hour photographing everything in the safe. It's accounts mostly, with endless columns of figures. There's also a plastic box containing floppy disks, and that's what she wants more than the contracts and account books. She doesn't think the paperwork will be of much use, but it might be helpful in other ways. There are printouts of memoranda and computer messages – electronic mail. It could be the evidence she's looking for, but at the moment, none of it means anything. She needs time to analyse the material, but what's far more important to Fang is that she has taken the first steps in recruiting Hong Kong resident, lecturer and Cantonese widow Susan Ho Ping as her latest informant; an informant Fang intends to cultivate and hone into a weapon. While Fang works with her Minox, working her way through the files, Ho Ping has recovered enough to make them tea. She fills the kettle, then stops, hesitating, head on one side, kettle held in mid-air.

She calls out from the kitchen. 'You hear that?'

'What?'

'We have visitors – and I don't think they're friendly.'

6

MacGregor was sorry to hear about GLUTTON. He showed appropriate concern for someone he'd never met but who had served the cause, whatever that might be. I took a cynical view: keeping the profits from offshore tax havens rolling into the City of London and lubricating shareholder value in the corporate world. Whatever it was, no-one liked to lose an agent and definitely not one as effective and productive as GLUTTON.

'Does he have family? What can we do for them?'

No family of origin, or at least no-one close, and nothing on his file that said otherwise. A Chinese widow, and that was it; a Cantonese woman named Susan Ho Ping, who divided her time between Hong Kong and the Peacock estate in Essex. The Peacocks were upwardly mobile, self-made — new money, not old. Of the two, the wife was better educated and had more style.

Poor man, he shouldn't have had GLUTTON as his code name. I was sure Peacock would have preferred GUARDSMAN or GRENADIER; either would have pleased him no end as the old-fashioned patriot I knew him to be. But agents didn't get to choose their codenames; they were picked alphabetically and, nowadays, digitally – and they shouldn't in any case ever learn what their code names were.

Somehow DRAGON knew hers and approved of it. For hundreds of years, the only people allowed to wear the dragon symbol in China were the emperors – or empresses – because it symbolised force, power, authority. It suited her, and she revelled in the image. And it wasn't a mere image. It was what she wanted to become.

'I saw the official ChiCom statement.'

'Yes, I saw it too, chief.'

'He was one of your best, Richard. He was doing so well. I'm so sorry.'

Aye. I didn't need it rubbed in, though. I'd given GLUTTON up to Fang, and if anyone was responsible for his murder, it was us. Fang was to have run him, of course, and that meant looking after him, not allowing him to be killed. If I hadn't turned him over to her, he might still be alive. She wanted him to continue targeting Yao because we both wanted to find out more about the Shanghai Party Secretary. I needed to know about his so-called patriotic activities and his politics, while DRAGON seemed focused on his finances and tax irregularities.

To be honest, we in SIS knew so little about the CPC leaders – how they lived, their families, their activities, their taste in food and drink, their sex lives – and Yao was one way to penetrate this wall of autocratic power. What we did know could be scrawled on a single postcard, a tribute to the CCP's ability to keep the most mundane aspects of life secret.

The damage caused to UK Station by GLUTTON's loss would be serious. There'd be calls for an internal inquiry. I was the obvious target, if they wanted someone to blame. I'd risen fast out of nowhere, had no friends in high places, MacGregor aside, GLUTTON'S death would bring out the knives of competitors and detractors. GLUTTON was English born and bred and well known in business circles back in London. And he was my head agent. I'd found him, selected him, schooled him, nurtured him and run him, and watched his back, and then traded him on to Fang. Not that he knew about DRAGON's existence or the fact that I copied his reports to her. He had brought us glory at UK Station as a penetration agent because he had the courage and self-confidence to pull it off. Not even MacGregor could save me now, if Fang's successes proved insufficient to protect us both from the fall-out from GLUTTON's death.

So I said, yes, he got close and managed to stay close for 18 months. It's rare, I added, to run someone on denied territory and get in so deep without having been a walk-in to begin with.

'He's an enormous loss, chief.'

'Too close, was he?' MacGregor turned those disconcerting eyes on me again; rheumy eyes, magnified by the thick lenses of his glasses, swarming all over me.

'I wouldn't say so. GLUTTON was doing well. He had the access we wanted, and he kept a grip on it. He was close as a big-nose or *da bizi* could get.' I could hear the defensive note in my own voice.

'Richard. He had access to the wife.'

'Yes, okay, you're right. He was screwing her. I know. That was his mistake, but it doesn't account for his death. Not necessarily.'

MacGregor leaned towards me. 'She was screwing him. There's a difference. But that wasn't the problem. People like that ...'

He left the rest unsaid. I knew what C meant. Or I thought I did; that people of that level of social status and wealth in the new communist China didn't care about infidelity, the occasional

50

indiscretion. To the PRC ruling class – and that's what it was now, a class – Wall Street IPOs and dividends mattered. Foreign investments mattered. A condo in Bali mattered. A townhouse in Belgravia mattered and so did a mansion in the balmy, orange-blossom-scented air of Montecito, California, the purchase of which GLUTTON had recently negotiated on behalf of the wife, his lover. These foreign properties were her family's safety net if it all went FUBAR at home. To wives – *tai-tais* – like her, and many husbands, sex was an itch to be scratched, a pleasant pastime, no more important than a set of tennis. I knew, courtesy of GLUTTON, that she had many itches and did much scratching; so too the husband with his mistress, *er nai* or second milk. And his second girlfriend or third milk, *san nai*. Not for nothing was the wife's favourite set of wheels in Shanghai a silver Maserati with a registration plate that read LAN 888. The number eight was the luckiest number among the Chinese, especially for those seeking wealth, and a registration of three of the lucky digits, bought at auction in Hong Kong, would have cost thousands of dollars and showed that even her grandchildren would never have to earn their own living.

Eight was *ba* which rhymed with *facai*, which meant to be rich.

She lived the dream at home and abroad.

Four, or *si*, was the unluckiest number. It was serious enough for some hotels and apartment blocks to avoid a fourth floor or a room number with that digit.

Chinese people – ordinary folk – were now calling the CCP the 'Party of Princes'. It was almost a given for citizens that their exclusively male leaders had lavish homes abroad, enjoyed the attentions of several girlfriends and avoided paying tax on their ill-gotten fortunes. It was almost expected of them. They were like the British royals – loved despite or because of their tax havens and tax-exempt fortunes, their privileges. That they feathered nests abroad in case they fell out of favour at home was an open secret.

Then I thought of my own situation. Had I been screwing DRAGON or had she been screwing me? I knew the answer to that. Trouble was, I too was itching – for Fang. I missed her smile, her expression when happy about something, the sound of her voice, her laugh, her strength, the scent she wore. Fang had brought some light into my otherwise drab, work-driven existence. Existence was right – it wasn't a life as most people would understand it, not until we'd encountered one another in a Beirut military prison. She'd proved to be good not just for my career, but good for me – period. She was exciting. I enjoyed her company, too – what there was of it. Was that how GLUTTON felt about his sometime lover, or had she been a means to an end?

'Cause of death?'

'Unknown. No doubt DRAGON will tell me.'

'I take it then that this wasn't heart failure, after all.'

Every death was heart failure.

'We don't yet have details.' I decided not to mention what seemed to have been a deliberate message – the lie in the ChiCom statement about excessive drinking.

'But DRAGON wants an urgent meet?'

'She does. I expect this is what it's about.'

'Why not use a temporary case officer, if it's so urgent? She must be used to TCOs by now, and I know you'll have at least one on standby, visa'd up. You've been running her for quite a while – what is it? Almost 7 years? A record for us in mainland China, I believe.'

'For us, yes. A record unmatched by anyone, other than the

intelligence services of the Republic of China. We can't match Taiwan in its ability to penetrate the PRC. She asked for me, chief. DRAGON trusts me. She feels that this is too important for some temporary case officer new to her and her situation. And I'm sure she's right.'

That was a load of old bollocks. I hoped C didn't see through it.

'Did DRAGON know of GLUTTON's existence before his death?'

'Not that I know of, chief, but we'll find out soon enough.'

A lie of little consequence.

Yes, I'd given her GLUTTON on a plate, without his knowledge of course, or rather, I'd identified Roger Peacock as my agent and given her access to his product. According to our agreement, she had agreed to protect her agent, to track GLUTTON more closely than I ever could, and run him in place against Yao Tie, someone who was of interest to us both, if for different reasons. Something, somewhere, had gone wrong at DRAGON's end of our business and that was a big concern. The loss of GLUTTON was bad enough, but I couldn't afford to lose DRAGON as well, in the midst of so much uncertainty.

If I was honest with myself, I had to admit it wasn't only professional. I had what I'd long needed: a successful SIS career, the respect of my peers, financial security, a future. At long last, I felt I belonged somewhere. But what I wanted – as opposed to needed – was something I was almost afraid to admit to myself, let alone anybody else, and it had been brought into sharp focus by GLUTTON's murder and DRAGON's request for an urgent treff.

We were both bad, of course. We were moral cripples, and one was the mirror image of the other.

I not only missed her, but wanted her. That was the trouble; we seldom get what we want and few of us ever understand what we need. I didn't.

Ridiculous? Impossible? Self-destructive?

Yes, of course – it was all three.

One question had been nagging me ever since the death in the Beijing hotel: what had made Du Lan so suspicious that she'd asked her brother to investigate GLUTTON in the first place? Why expose her own family's sordid details to a *Gonganbu* investigation? Had she believed her brother could suppress or redact some of the more outrageous aspects of her affair with a British spy?

MacGregor wouldn't let it go. 'So, Richard, if DRAGON wants to meet, it must be about GLUTTON, wouldn't you say? And if that's the case, then it would suggest that she knows he was one of our assets.'

'I don't want to make assumptions until we meet.'

I didn't spell out the truth of it; never have and never would – regardless of any suspicion anyone might have. At the start, DRAGON had recruited me. We had recruited each other by mutual agreement, in the Lebanese capital of all places – and in the middle of a war and foreign occupation. We had a deal – albeit on her terms. At the time, I had little option, not a sensible one anyhow. She'd lifted me off the street outside my hotel, tossed me into a Lebanese military prison and threatened to sell me on to the Iranians or the Soviets if I refused to accept what was on offer. Yet I owed my swift rise in the Service to Fang, as she owed hers to me. She'd kept her side of the bargain and I had kept mine. I had no reason to feel bitter. The result was that I was running a senior *Guoanbu* officer at the heart of Chinese foreign intelligence, and I was CEO of a secret enterprise set up within UK Station to keep her well supplied with a flow of (often fake) goodies. That kept her happy and safe, a basis upon whichI had built my own considerable reputation and seniority within SIS.

For her part, Fang was running a senior officer at the heart of SIS, and was doing something similar in the 5th Bureau, which was responsible for counter-intelligence. She, too, was a legend in her own lifetime – thanks to me. On the strength of it, Fang had risen to become deputy chief of the *Guoanbu* with special responsibility for counter-intelligence. I was her famous five – Philby, Burgess, Maclean and company – all rolled into one. And yes, we had this on/off affair, not unlike the unfortunate GLUTTON and Du Lan. So far, our relationship had survived and thrived for 8 years even if I had been forced – blackmailed – into it at the start. Neither of us was about to jeopardise it, not over the goings-on in the Kremlin or the sorry fate of GLUTTON, who should have known the risks when he climbed into bed with the wife of the all-powerful Shanghai Party Secretary. Even if his trysts had my whole-hearted (if unofficial) approval at the time.

Of course I had a choice; I couldn't escape that. We all do.

DRAGON and I were joint, equal founders, partners and owners of a secret and profitable global industry specialising in the manufacture of betrayal – and GLUTTON had been one of our several pawns.

But I wanted more, a great deal more. If I knew Fang at all, she did, too.

The Americans had somehow found out about DRAGON, knew of her existence at least, and had tried to take her away from us. Langley had offered to pay the cost of running her jointly, possibly because we'd passed them much of her product, which they had liked a lot once they'd enjoyed a taste. They wanted it all. They wanted control, of course they did. Langley wanted to exploit this asset to the maximum even if it killed her, and the Agency offered safe houses, special communications equipment, enciphered satellite links, fibre optics, executive aircraft, the works. They didn't know if we had one well-placed asset or a network of sub-agents supervised by a head agent. We made sure of that. They promised us a whole new world previously denied to their UK cousins, just for DRAGON's product. They could buy us, like everyone else, and they knew it. Counted on it, in fact. Had we not traded our geographic reach for US dollars, underwriting the cost of our signal intelligence stations worldwide? But if we were honest with ourselves (rare, but not impossible), we knew that running anything with the Agency meant giving it all up to them, bit by bit, and be left holding jack shit other than a bad cheque drawn on an offshore bank registered in the State of Delaware. I told MacGregor that she'd run a mile if she so much as got a whiff of Langley lurking in the neighbourhood, that she'd be lost to both of us. For that reason, it wasn't going to happen. Whitehall and several SIS colleagues didn't appreciate my resistance. They wanted a sale and urged a start to negotiations. Think of the money! I won that battle because MacGregor had my back and had done since my dubious adventures in Pakistan and Afghanistan.

C had made the massive mistake of trusting me.

He was loyal, that was his trouble.

That word again – trust – so prized by the Service, yet so elusive.

I'd got my own back against Langley. I had betrayed the identities of the last three Company agents working on the ChiCom mainland – a naval officer and submariner, a computer analyst and an engineer working in the aviation industry. I'd done it not out of spite, but for good reason: I wanted to make Langley and everyone else in the US intelligence community more dependent than ever on DRAGON's product. Neither DRAGON nor I welcomed competition. Establishing a monopoly on secret intelligence emerging from communist China was something we both wanted. I'd seen the three agents' work in Langley's reports shared with its Five Eyes partners. They were thinly disguised, of course, to protect their identities, but I soon realised where they were likely to be operating, based on the topics they covered, so I'd passed on the likely locations to DRAGON and she'd closed in on them with remarkable speed. In weeks, all three were arrested, interrogated, charged, tried and shot.

Chinese communist law specified 58 offences that carried the death penalty, with treason and foreign espionage topping the list. The number of Chinese citizens put to death every year wasn't known officially, but estimates ranged from 4,000 to 12,000, the highest in the world.

It was a cruel business we were in, to be sure. I told myself the three must have known what they were getting themselves into with the Agency. They knew the risks. We all did. At least they weren't tortured. They were roughed up, perhaps, but because all had close family, they'd confessed almost immediately to save their wives and children from the labour camps – or worse.

Freedom is the recognition of necessity, Friedrich Engels wrote.

So true.

'How did DRAGON contact you this time?'

'The usual, chief. OTP and one of three number stations.'

'So, to recap, Richard. An identifier code, yes? Followed by four digit numbers, setting out a request for an urgent, top priority treff. Right?'

'Right. BLUE PETER. And it was kosher. As always. She's disciplined, unlike some.'

Did he think she'd been turned, doubled?

'When do you go?'

'Tonight. Plane at six.' I checked my watch instinctively.

It was tonight, but the plane wasn't at six but nine. I lied to MacGregor. Lies were protection, not second nature. I didn't lie unnecessarily. I always lied for a reason. It would not be a direct flight and I wouldn't be using my own name. He had no need to know and no reason to want to, but I still had to be careful.

'A night flight, yes?'

'Yeah.'

What was this? Small talk? It was so unlike him.

'I detest night flights. I can never sleep and I feel terrible afterwards with jet-lag, especially when flying east.'

It was the same for me. I always took a decent book, something that would hold my attention and nothing too heavy. A couple of Simenon novels did the trick, especially those set in the south. I enjoyed the descriptions of food and drink, the portrayals of petty criminals and their women. His books plunged the reader into a different way of life drenched in sun, sex and pastis. I could do with all three, and had long ago decided that if I could ever afford it once I escaped from the Service with my pension intact, and possibly a knighthood, I'd move to Provence.

With Fang, of course.

It was a pretty fantasy and hopelessly unrealistic. No matter how hard I tried, I couldn't summon up an image of either of us washing the dishes or changing nappies. It seemed ludicrous.

MacGregor broke in on my daydream. 'You are on no account to venture onto the mainland, d'you hear me, Richard? That's a direct order. I've put it in writing and it will be on your file.'

'I hear you, sir. Of course.'

C would have been going too far if he'd asked where DRAGON and I were going to meet. He knew it. He'd written the gospel on operational security in the Cold War.

'You're getting too long in the tooth for non-official cover, Richard. Your days of NOC assignments are over. When you next work abroad for any length of time, it'll be under diplomatic cover and you'll be declared to the host government. Two postings – three at the very most – and we have to assume an officer is blown, even if he isn't. You know how this works.'

I did.

'You're an executive now. Like it or not, you drive a desk. You manage other people, so get used to it, laddie – no straying into denied territory. You wouldn't survive 5 minutes and we wouldn't be able to help you if you did. They'd take you apart and kill whatever's left of you. You'd be a mine of intel. Even in the unlikely event that they let you live, you'd be a vegetable – to send us a message, no doubt. They've got drugs these days that have the effect of scooping out your brains and frying 'em with paprika. You got that, laddie?'

'Got it, chief.' I looked him in the face when I said it. It was my cross-my-heart sincere look. Then he looked down and flicked the leaf off his knee. We were about done when it started to rain again, pattering on the fallen leaves.

So here was the point of this meeting:

'Ask DRAGON who's up and who's down, will you? Who's in, who's out. Ask her about Deng. What's happened to him? We need the names of his challengers. Ask about these military exercises we've noticed in the south, naval and air combined with troop movements – large-scale and unusual for this time of year. Unusual, too, in that there were no official announcements. Loads of command chatter, all of it encrypted. Not to put too fine a point on it, Richard, what the fuck is going on over there?'

7

The doorbell chimes, over and over, and the repeated banging on the front door makes Susan Ho Ping jump.

'Grab your passport, Susan, and cash, credit cards. Change of underwear. Quickly – go!'

Fang grasps her hand and pulls Susan along as the two women slip out through the utility room and down spiral stairs to the basement, then through the garage. They both hear male voices speaking Mandarin.

'Don't look up at the windows.' Fang leads the way, worried that if Susan were to glance up, her face could reflect the lights in the house and give them away. She tightens her grip on Susan's hand, breaking cover and running through the pool of light around the apartment block into the shadows, pulling her reluctant companion along and then working her way around to the front before another dash behind the visitors' two vehicles – an enormous SUV and a saloon car parked side by side near the main entrance. They make their way into the welcome darkness, then wade through shrubs – their legs and feet are soaking wet – to a line of trees. Fang starts downhill, turning sideways on the slope, planting one foot below the other. Susan copies her movements. This is no time to twist an ankle. She gives up trying to

61

shake herself free of Fang's grasp – she's trembling and Fang, whatever else she might be, seems capable in a crisis. The air feels warm and sticky, and Susan is already sweating. Reaching the first road at the level below and, looking left and right, they run across, out of the glare of streetlights. They pause when they spot the blue lights of police vehicles right below them, and stand motionless, Fang averting her face. Once the police have passed, Fang tugs at Susan's hand again. Then, down they go to the next level as the police turn at the bend right above the spot where they were standing a few seconds before.

At least the rain has stopped, and the storm seems to have passed. The wet vegetation has drenched their clothing, and the mist that swathes The Peak is like drizzle. Fang stops at the rear corner of yet another residential building, keeping to the shade of a service entrance, where they almost crash into a line of rubbish bins.

'Get your breath back. We've still a way to go.'

Ho Ping touches the small bag she has slung around her neck, as if for reassurance. It has her toothbrush, lip balm, a pair of clean knickers, her UK passport, some cash and a debit card.

They hear shouting from the hill behind them, a squeal of car tyres and a detonation, then two more – too loud and sharp to be anything other than gunshots.

The SUV hurtles downhill, lights off, passes by them and vanishes around the corner.

'Move.' Fang drags Susan after her as, once again, they slip and slide downhill. Again they have to stop as a police car races past, downhill this time, siren blaring, in pursuit of the SUV.

They're among clusters of buildings now, tall and drab, windows shuttered against the night, running along an alley and leaping down near-vertical steps, until at last Fang hails a cab.

'I can't,' Susan says. 'I have to stop.'

'No time!' Fang opens a rear door, bundles Ho Ping into the back and follows her.

Almost an hour has passed since they fled Susan Ho Ping's flat and took a taxi to the harbour. Urged on by the merciless Fang, she has no option but to clamber into a skiff in the dark, breathing in a pungent mix of diesel, fish and salt. After a ride of a few minutes – steered by a solitary, featureless figure crouched in the stern – she finds herself on a ramshackle pier. Fang urges her to step across a narrow chasm of blackness to the main deck of a junk. Fang prods and pushes her from behind while a stranger reaches out, seizes her by the wrists and pulls her on board. Ho Ping has always hated deep water, fears it, and in the darkness with its shifting, oleaginous glint under the harbour lights, it terrifies her.

Susan Ho Ping finally falls asleep. The departure from her own home has scared her and the escape has tired her out. She doesn't feel reassured by Fang's insistence that she'll be safe, and that the crew – two men and a woman – are trustworthy, and she doesn't believe that it's only for a night or two. Are they pirates? Thieves? Are they communists like Fang?

As the junk motor's coughs and splutters away from the quayside into Victoria Bay, Fang tells her that the strangers at her door – whoever they were – won't find her and the authorities won't try to look – not once they are out to sea. Around midnight the anchor drops, the chain rattles after it and the junk rolls in the swell. Fang explains these people used to be called *Tanka*, a people apart, sometimes known as the boat people or sea gypsies. They have a distinct culture, their language, too, and have never

63

integrated with the Cantonese, who have historically looked down on them. Fang is sure that Ms Ho must know all this, but she goes on speaking to soothe Susan's nerves. Many now live ashore, Fang says, but a minority still ply their trade as fisher folk and smugglers. They live in Macau and along the southern coast of the Chinese mainland.

Ho Ping doesn't comment, shows no interest, and in time she will succumb to her fatigue, snoring on her back, a sheet pulled up to her chin – like a child.

Their last exchange is about her husband, Roger Peacock.

'Do you miss him?'

Susan looks at Fang, unsure whether to regard her as kidnapper or rescuer.

'He was my husband.'

'Do you mourn him, Susan? Do you grieve for him?'

'What's it to you?'

'I've never married, so I don't know how it feels – to live with someone for a long time and then …'

Ho Ping doesn't answer, but lies back on her pillow and shuts her eyes. Then she says, without turning and with her eyes still shut: 'Are you taking me to the mainland as your prisoner?'

'No. It's too risky now. Later. We'll talk about it – and you're not my prisoner.'

Fang watches Susan Ho Ping sleep from the second bunk in their shared cabin. Her snores are even, measured. Now and again, she mutters under her breath. In the slight swell, the junk rises and falls. It's old, piled with crayfish pots and nets on deck, but kept tidy below. The mattresses and bedding are clean.

Fang listens to the music of Hong Kong, the ubiquitous clacking of mahjong, the occasional shout of victory or burst of laughter from the crew on the main deck until she, too, falls asleep, rocked by the South China Sea.

They have a hazardous journey ahead of them.

8

MacGregor and I went our separate ways in the London rain, he trudged back to Century House, and I to my two-bedroom Victorian terrace near the Oval where I packed a bag – one of those wheelie things with a hard case, small enough to take with me in the aircraft cabin. All I needed were a couple of changes of clothing.

I made an encrypted call to my assistant, Poppy Marsh. I always felt embarrassed asking her to do secretarial stuff, especially as she was a Cambridge First in Modern Languages and fluent in German, Russian, Polish and heaven knew what else, besides being a candidate for the next officer training course at Fort Monckton. I think we both were aware that, if I survived the next decade, I would eventually end up working for her, so I was chary of asking her to undertake errands such as making me coffee, typing up dictation, delving into registry files or booking flights. In time, she'd have her revenge. This time I asked if she would please book me onto an open return flight to Hong Kong via Dubai under my current work name, this very night, and to submit an urgent cash requisition for a couple of thousand US dollars. Please.

Better still, I said, make it two-and-a-half grand, just in case.

Marsh evinced no surprise that her desk-bound boss was, unusually, heading off into the field on his own. She maintained her usual deferential manner in the face of authority. 'Are you fleeing the country permanently, Mr Webster, or is this a romantic break *à deux* at HM's expense?'

David Webster was my work name – and the name in the passport she assumed I'd use because she'd handed it to me earlier in the day at my request.

'*Ganz allein*,' Poppy.'

'Oh, you poor, poor thing. What a terrible waste. Would you like someone to come with you and hold your hand? Or was it something else you wanted held?'

'Are you volunteering?'

In an instant, her voice switched from East End to loud home counties drawl.

'Sorry Dave, old chap, I'm occupied this weekend murdering pheasants and peasants in sunny Berkshire, actually. But Simon – you know handsome Simon, don't you? He's such a dear. Our in-house heavyweight boxing champion, black belt jiu jitsu and unarmed combat specialist? Yeah? He's taken a definite shine to you. Dare I say it, darling, he's got a crush on you. He confided as much to me in the canteen last week, in fact. He's a shy boy, you see. I'm sure he'd be only too keen to hold whatever it is you want holding.'

With that parting shot, Marsh rang off with a scream of ribald laughter.

No respect, the young generation of spies. That was the price I paid for Poppy Marsh's help, but I could live with it, if she could.

* * *

Earlier that day, before meeting C, Poppy Marsh and I had sat in my office drinking coffee and I invited her to join me in watching what I told her was an item supplied by one of our sources in mainland China. I didn't mention DRAGON as the origin.

It appeared to be a copy of an official Chinese video, taken with a handheld camera by a security official, probably *Guoanbu*, but for all I could tell it might have been an officer of the People's Armed Police. This was a vast paramilitary organisation staffed by former soldiers of the PLA that included among its many duties the securing of execution sites.

The video was only a couple of minutes in duration, and it had Chinese characters in the top right hand corner and an official-looking stamp. It was a little shaky and out of focus.

Whoever held the camera began by standing on higher ground, before moving down closer to his or her subject.

Four plain white vehicles – people carriers with their windows painted over – turned off a single lane road onto a rough track surrounded by scrub, a few trees and sandy soil. It could have been just about anywhere, though no buildings were visible, so I assumed that this was a rural or semi-rural location. Somewhere in the south was my guess. The sky was overcast. It was dry and clear. The vans closed up, bouncing and rolling along the uneven track for maybe 50 yards before stopping.

From the lead van emerged three men and, from the front passenger seat, a woman. They looked like civilians in black suits – except for the female, who wore what appeared to be a military uniform, her hair pushed or coiled under her peaked cap. They weren't wearing winter jackets, which strengthened my sense that this was southern China. The camera did not show their faces, only their clothing and

68

the uniform with its insignia and colonel's rank. They stood together, waiting and watching the other three vans. The woman was tall. More men emerged from each van, all identically dressed except for one man in red being taken from each vehicle. Each of these three men wore what looked like red pyjamas and each was held by the arms by the black-clad individuals. The captives seemed to have their hands bound or cuffed behind their backs. They were already wearing blindfolds and their escorts took them – guided them – to a spot a little ahead of the four vehicles and to one side. They lined up, facing the track. Then they were forced, or helped, down onto their knees.

There was no obvious violence – or none I could see.

Poppy said nothing, but she put down her cup and saucer.

The escort retreated a few paces. The woman stepped forward behind the first of the three prisoners. She gave an order – it sounded like an order, but it was muffled and I couldn't make out what she said. Her arm moved and there was a faint crack. She stepped to the next and repeated the process – and again, a third time.

It was quick.

The condemned had toppled forward, one after the other. What must it be like to be the third in line, heart hammering, dry mouth, hearing the first shot, the thump of the body hitting the dirt, then one right next to you? His final breaths, the loud detonation and impact, the body falling …

'Can we enlarge it and run it again?'

'Sure.'

This time I could see the woman's dark navy uniform. It was like that of the People's Police but it had a patch on the right arm, the arm that raised the pistol, which read 国安 or 'State Security'.

'Did you know that they order them to open their mouths?'

Poppy spoke in a mild, conversational tone, as if we were watching a Wimbledon doubles match. She didn't wait for me to respond. 'That way it doesn't make too much of a mess and they can return the remains to the families for burial, provided, of course, the shooter is precise where he places the shot.'

Not him.

She.

No, I didn't know. But I knew of someone who would deliver the *coup de grâce* both with precision and without hesitation.

9

'You can come up on deck,' says Fang. 'No-one's watching.'

Breakfast is a bowl of rice, egg, oyster sauce, a little onion and garlic.

Fang and Ho Ping squat on their heels opposite each other and eat. Withdrawing to the high poop deck, the crew give them plenty of space and don't stare or even look at them. The junk itself – the name is based on the Dutch *jonk* and Spanish *junco* – is around 40 feet in length, with two masts and two square sails. Thanks to the crew's courtesy, they have some privacy. Fang notes there is nothing wrong with Susan's appetite; she uses her chopsticks to clear her bowl in minutes and does so without speaking.

'How do you feel?'

'Better. Thanks.'

'Great. You seem to have slept well.' Fang smiles at her prisoner-come-guest, and her captive hesitates, then returns the smile.

As if embarrassed by this display of empathy, Ho Ping turns her back and gazes out to sea. It is calm, the sea motionless, the sky clear except for a scattering of broken cloud like tufts of pink cotton wool to the north-east. It's a beautiful day. In the far distance is a faint rim of mountains or hills. It's around 18 degrees Celsius – pleasant and in comparison with Beijing's winter freeze, almost balmy.

Fang offers advice. 'You can stay on deck unless we have company. As long as no-one else is in view, you can stay in the open. It's going to be warmer later, and you'll find shade in the deckhouse or below deck. There's a fan in the cabin and you've got a shower. If you see another vessel, go below. The crew will know what to do.'

Susan gazes out to sea. 'Where are we?'

'In Chinese waters. About 5 miles off the mainland coast. I wouldn't try to swim. Even if you made it past the sharks, neither the militia nor coastal defence take to strangers – and the locals won't offer sanctuary.'

The female crew member brings them a teapot and cups. A sturdy, shapely young woman with broad, rough hands and muscular calves, she avoids eye contact with the guests out of respect. She wears loose-fitting blue pants and shirt, patched at the knees and elbows.

Fang pours the tea.

'How long am I going to be here?'

'Four days, 5 at the most, not always in the same place, of course.'

'Why?'

'This is how it's going to be. I am going to ask you a few questions, Susan. About Roger and the people he worked for. When I'm done, it's your turn to ask me anything you want. All right with you?'

'Do I have a choice?

'Not really, no.'

'Then you'd better start, hadn't you?'

'How long were you married?'

'Ten years, give or take a few months.'

'When did he tell you about his secret work?'

Ho Ping doesn't pretend she's unaware of it. 'When it started. Around 3 or 4 years ago, Roger was told to share it with me, that it was better that I knew, so I could support him. By this time we were both frequent visitors to the mainland, sometimes staying for weeks, though it wasn't always easy to get visas.'

'And did you? Support him?'

'Of course.'

Fang feels a breeze, and she turns to see it ruffle the otherwise placid sea

'Was he trained for this special work?'

Ho Ping nods. 'I went with him. It was a kind of holiday at some place on the English coast. It was once a fort. It was only for two weeks so he could squeeze it into his business schedule and I took time off as well.'

'So you work, too, Susan. What do you do?'

'I'm an academic.

'Your subject?'

'Physics.'

'How did you find the training for this special work of his?'

Ho Ping puts her head on one side and ponders. 'It was fun. Some of it was. The report writing and classroom briefings were boring. There was a lot of reading, but I got to pick and choose. I liked the trade craft – you understand what I mean, pursuing people through the streets and supermarkets without being spotted, and being followed and trying to shake them off. Disguises and tricks, like changing hats or jackets while on the move. Why am I telling you this?'

Fang ignores the question. 'Your husband's successful, right? I mean with money.'

'Sure.'

'And his relations with Yao and his wife contributed to that.'

'Of course. But he was successful before he met them, right? Roger didn't need their money, though I suppose it has made quite a difference to our lifestyle over the years.'

'No children?'

'No. We said we'd wait and then somehow we never got around to deciding to start a family. Roger and I were always so busy and he travelled a lot. As you know.' Susan turns her head away; she's weeping and trying not to show it. Fang pretends not to notice.

'Did you help him with his special work?'

'No. I would have if he'd asked me to.'

'You never set up dead-letter drops or cleared them?'

'No.'

'You didn't carry out route surveillance – clearing his back or housing someone?'

'You mean by housing following someone to see where they lived? No.'

'You weren't a courier? You weren't trained in cryptographic work? In radio?'

'No.'

'So you're clean, then, you're on no-one's radar.'

'I guess I must be. As far as I'm aware.'

'That's good. It's helpful.'

The crew have jumped to their feet and are working, hauling up the anchor, then the red sails. They don't start the diesel engine. Because they are fixed with bamboo battens, the sails are easy to raise, like lifting a rectangular blind. The crew heaves away on the sheets, two men on the mainsail, the woman raising the smaller one at the stern.

They work fast, arm over arm in tandem, grunting with the effort. The woman is the one giving the orders.

'Tell me about their son.'

'Nothing to tell. He's a typical teenager. Morose at times, sulky, quite bright, polite to guests, but with the sense of entitlement that all these kids with very wealthy parents seem to have. He'll never want for anything, so long as the system continues the way it is now, and he knows that. You know what I mean, don't you? Corrupt, materialistic, with a very rich elite contemptuous of the poor. So I guess you could say he's spoiled. If I had to sum him up in two words, I'd say he was like his mother: needy and greedy.'

The water slaps the bows in a rhythm as the junk starts to move. They're headed away from the coast and further out to sea.

'How's his English?'

'Good. Pretty much fluent, I would say, but with an accent.'

'And Mandarin.'

'Of course, it's his mother's tongue.'

'Does he get on with his father?'

'My impression – and Roger's – is that they see little of each other, and the father doesn't seem able to talk to his son. The mother spoils him, like all Chinese mothers, and she takes great interest in his school work. She gets very angry if he fails to achieve high marks. They seem very close. She dotes on him, but drives him hard, too.'

'Just a couple of things more, if you don't mind. Tell me more about the Yao family – if you would, please. Who wears the trousers? Is it Yao …"

Ms Ho interrupts. 'No. *She* does. She's in charge of everything, and I mean everything – everything that matters. Yao's a bureaucrat. He's weak – despite his first name, which means 'steel' and is typical

75

of his generation. He's the flamboyant type, loves to show off how rich he's become. Her husband likes parties, he likes to drink, to surround himself with pretty young women, to tell stupid jokes, to show off. He likes cars. Yao likes expensive clothes and shoes. Swiss watches are his thing – he has quite a collection. I guess he likes the power he has as Party Secretary because in Shanghai everyone defers to him. A little emperor in his own back yard. It's a pretty big back yard. Not that he knows what to do with it, except dish out favours and make people indebted so she can make use of them later. We have the saying that I'm sure you've heard – that when someone becomes an official, even his chickens go to heaven. Yao is a big official and has a lot of chickens and he wants everyone to recognise that he has the best ones. But when it comes to decisions, it's the wife who decides, who tells him what to do. And he obeys.'

'And how do they behave towards each other?'

'I don't have any idea how they are in private. Even in public she tells him off, criticises him, orders him about. At big gatherings, she puts on a show of being affectionate – holding his arm, kissing his cheek, speaking in respectful terms. But it's not real.'

The sea is picking up, the junk's prow rising and falling as they head southeast.

'And their home in Shanghai?'

'It's huge – a mansion, a veritable castle, surrounded by several acres of garden, most of it lawn, with two tennis courts and an Olympic-size swimming pool. Yao doesn't swim – I don't think he does. But she does. And the boy.'

Fang wants detail and Ho Ping obliges. She accounts for it all. The servants, the security detail, the reception rooms, the corridors, the bedrooms all en suite, the grand staircase, the kitchen and pantry, the vast basement with its gold statue of the Great Leader and the imported cars. They talk as the sun rises overhead and Fang feels it burn into her hair – what a contrast with Beijing's deep cold! They retreat into the deckhouse, which they have to share with one crewman who has the helm. Everything seems made of wood, varnished. Fang guesses it's teak, perhaps mahogany.

'Thank you, Susan. Now it's your turn to ask me questions.'

Ho Ping never gets the chance, though.

All three crew are peering out to sea in a westerly direction. The rim of land has vanished. Fang jumps up and goes out on deck. Ho Ping follows.

'What is it? What are they looking at?'

The skipper has better eyesight than either of the passengers. She approaches Fang and stands beside her, more than a head shorter, but broader and more muscular. 'Fast patrol boat from mainland,' she says in Cantonese.

Neither Fang nor Ho Ping can see anything except the sea sparkling in the sunlight. Above their heads, the sails are full and the junk moves at a steady, if slow, pace, the hull slapping the wavelets in a steady beat. It takes a few seconds for their eyes to adjust. Fang thinks she sees something at last, a speck, a black dot – no, it's bigger than that – a smudge, nothing more. It gets larger, and she sees a flicker of white; as the craft builds up speed, it creates a bow wave.

Susan Ho Ping has one hand to her mouth.

'Oh, my god,' she blurts out. 'What is it? What do we do?'

Fang doesn't respond. She has one hand up, shielding her eyes.

She ducks back into the deckhouse, grabs a large straw hat like an inverted bowl, and claps it on her own head. Fang reappears on the open deck, tying a cord under her chin to keep it in place and her features in shadow.

'Coming this way,' says the captain. Her tone is matter-of-fact. 'Here in 5, 6 minutes. We won't start the engine or they'll think we're trying to run.' She looks at Ho Ping and then says, again in Cantonese. 'People's Liberation Army Navy, PLAN.'

She tries out her English. 'They saw us on radar. They look for you, yes?'

10

I didn't travel as David Webster, and I didn't take the Emirates flight from Heathrow to Dubai and on to Bangkok. I cancelled Poppy's booking. Instead, I delved into my personal stash of valid passports and came up with my favourite. Dexter Fisher, 'Dex' to his non-existent friends, a name so absurd to be almost real. A resident of bucolic Clonakilty in the Republic, he was co-founder of an electronics company in nearby Cork. It still boasted a live telephone number and a functioning answerphone. I booked and paid for another flight, using Fisher's American Express, one way from Paris to Hong Kong, business class. That would pop up on Century House screens, but I reckoned on having a week clear before anyone in accounts noticed the sale, by which time it wouldn't matter. With any luck, the book-keepers would nod it through without query in any case.

I paid cash for the London–Frankfurt–Paris legs. Both economy class; the first on my own behalf, the second in dear old Webster's name. It would throw a little dust in the eyes of anyone checking my travel arrangements because I'd only used young Dex and his passport once before – and that had been a two-day trip to Oslo 3 years earlier. Poppy Marsh might take all of 30 minutes to work it out, but then

Ms Marsh was more adept than most and she wasn't someone I was concerned about. Not then, anyhow. I told myself she had better things to do with her time than checking up on her immediate superior by tracking his previous legends and travel arrangements.

I had ample time to think about my assignment. I hadn't seen DRAGON in person for almost a year, and I was anxious about how she was, whether my *Guoanbu* adversary, collaborator, fellow traitor and occasional lover had changed in any way. Did she miss me? No – what was I thinking? Sentimental attachment wasn't high on the list of qualities prized by well-drilled Chinese communist spies.

I missed her, though. I had wet dreams about her; even after 12 months I still got a hard-on just a micro-second into thinking about her. I could always picture her narrow feet, her wrists, her neat ears, her curtain of black hair, her lacy black briefs, her smile like sunrise, the tantalising scent of her skin. Did she have someone else in her bed – or beds – by now? A succession of lovers? Why wouldn't she? It would be natural enough, and I would be foolish to feel envy, but foolishness was never an obstacle in my undisciplined life. It was true – I did feel jealous. Why would she stay celibate in my absence? Had I done so? No, of course not. In any case, if my own experience of Fang was any indication, for her sex was something in her tool box of espionage – and that's how it should be.

DRAGON was so much more than an occasional lover, though; she was the source of my professional success. She had gained me my current role as chief of UK Station. That, among other things, was responsible for running penetration agents in what were often referred to as hard target or denied territories. That's to say, those 'hard' countries where recruiting and running agents was hazardous and almost impossible: the Soviet Union, or what was left of that decaying empire, and its crumbling colonial possessions in eastern Europe. North Korea, of course, and China, the assertive Asia–Pacific superpower on the *qui vive* for enemies and rivals. We recruited agents offshore, in third countries, where clandestine activities were easier, and then ran them back on their home turf, but once again using third countries for the occasional treff. Any one of half a dozen TCOs handled DRAGON's material on my behalf. They were never in direct contact with DRAGON, they had no idea who she was – I hoped they didn't, at least – and she didn't know them, either, by name or appearance. To them, she was a chalk mark on a park bench, a loose brick, a hollow in a monkey puzzle tree, a parcel flung through a car window, a towel tied to a balcony railing, a hat on the back seat of a car. Anonymous.

Guessing aside, all they would know was that they were helping to 'run' an asset on behalf of UK Station.

I had plenty of time to think about Fang in European departure lounges that night, through to the early hours. In so doing – over far too much bad coffee and too many overpriced G&Ts – I realised how ridiculous my momentary panic in Vauxhall Park had been that afternoon, for the obvious reason – obvious to me now – that I was iron-clad against suspicion, a veritable dreadnought of espionage. I could do no wrong in the eyes of MacGregor and the Firm. I would have plenty of warning of my demise, if it ever came to that. I couldn't claim the credit; my immunity wasn't my own doing – it was DRAGON's achievement. If it hadn't been for her, I'd still be working under diplomatic cover as a third secretary (commercial) in the Democratic Republic of the Congo or somewhere equally salubrious. I had her to thank for not only my promotion to a senior executive grade, but also for the wall of security behind which I could operate not only as her handler, but also as her deep cover agent close to the top of my own service.

For everything she provided as my agent, I had to match as her agent. Secret for secret. Nothing came free in the lives of traitors.

The turning point in both our fortunes, I realised, had been the Gulf War, so-called 'Operation Desert Storm', which had begun this past August with the Iraqi invasion of Kuwait. That short war made DRAGON's reputation in London – and my own.

But we must go back a wee bit. During the 8-year Iran–Iraq war, which ended with a ceasefire in 1988, China's PLA2 – military intelligence – had obtained from its Iranian counterparts an Iraqi version of the Soviet T–72 tank. So DRAGON had informed us when the Middle East had been her bailiwick. The Soviets had circumvented the UN terms of embargo by supplying their Iraqi friends with the tanks in the form of kits, which the Iraqis then assembled. We knew, again thanks to DRAGON, that Chinese military intelligence reported to the Central Military Commission that the Iraqi version of the T–72 was more advanced than anything in the Chinese arsenal. In speed, mobility and firepower, as well as its low profile and its reactive armour, it was decades ahead of anything in the ChiCom tank divisions. It wasn't perfect, but then no battle tank is, under all conditions. Its three-man (or woman) crew had to be slight of stature in its cramped and confined space, for the automatic loader had a tendency to grab an unwary gunner and push him or her into the breach if he or she didn't watch out.

For the Chinese communists, the T-72 wasn't the worst of it. PLA2 officers watched aghast as the US-led coalition proceeded to slice through Iraqi armour during Operation Desert Storm. The coalition forces used real-time satellite intelligence, known as JSTARS, streamed down to tactical level, to the armoured battlegroup commanders, coupled with successive waves of pin-point air strikes in a 48-hour war.

In Beijing there followed a stream of reports to the Chinese leadership emphasising the need for urgent reform, something Deng Xiaoping himself had long demanded. DRAGON supplied us with these reports, too, and the measures taken – the drastic cut-backs in manpower, the radical reduction in army divisions, the massive increase in R&D spending and, in her latest drop, a detailed account of re-armament, including negotiations to buy the Soviet FLANKER, the Sukhoi-27 fighter, from Moscow as well as Israeli help in developing in-flight refuelling.

These reports of military reform, all 223 of them, along with appendices, maps and photographs, formed an immense printed compilation the size and weight of a single volume of the *Shorter OED*. Unlike the Oxford dictionary, it was classified top secret with a tight distribution list of 33 that included the top ranks at Langley, the Pentagon and the White House to say nothing of our own Ministry of Defence, defence intelligence, the chiefs of staff and the Foreign Office.

Number Ten wanted only the idiot's guide, a two-page summary with bullet points, heavily redacted. What a surprise.

This was her masterpiece, her legacy, and it was all human intelligence. I had no idea how much of it was fake or doctored. Not all. Let's say a goodly portion, 25 per cent. There was no point in trying to figure it out; one way or another, it was a work of immense ingenuity and a worthy monument to our secret partnership. DRAGON was a star, and it followed that I was, too. Such creativity – indeed, a monument to our twin betrayals – so much so, that my well-connected Poppy Marsh had told me (in a sly tone as she delivered my morning coffee) only the previous week that there were whispers circulating in Whitehall corridors that I was about to be fingered to head one of the Firm's seven directorates. Controller Asia Pacific seemed the likeliest. According to her, the confidential *nihil obstat* process had already begun. Was she teasing me? It could be, knowing her, so I tried to dismiss the notion. DRAGON would love it, of course she would. Her UK agent at the pinnacle of the Firm would have access to everything available to the Five Eyes services and it would mean another promotion for her, too, this time all the way to the very top.

Forget Wall Street – we would be masters of the universe.

So my panic in the park had been nothing but a sudden and irrational onset of paranoia.

Once on my way, I was careful. In Paris and Frankfurt, I watched my fellow passengers. As I scanned *Newsweek*, I glanced about for anyone who, like me, chose the same transit lounges and followed – or led the way – onto my connecting flights. People who might vanish into the bathroom and emerge a minute or two later with a different coat, or wearing a hat or scarf when before they had none. I looked for travellers who lingered too long at the newsagent, using the rotating stands of cards and airport thrillers as cover to peek out at the rest of us. The same went for public telephones; push in a few coins, pretend to call a number, keep the receiver to one's ear, then turn and look around for the target as if keeping an eye on family or wife. Talk, laugh. Add a smile, a wink or a wave. I was supposed to know all the tricks and what to look for – it was what I'd have done, had I been keeping someone under surveillance. Once on board the KLM and Lufthansa flights, I tried to memorise the faces of passengers and their seat numbers around me; those across the aisle, those in the row immediately in front and two rows back, building up physical descriptions and repeating them to myself. People mapping. A human topography of espionage.

Stop it. Stop being so bloody paranoid.

Relax.

At the start of the Paris flight, I gave up my seat without a murmur of protest to an elderly and well-dressed Frenchwoman who demanded it with a scowl. She seemed grumpy, I thought, because she said neither please nor thank you – but the flight attendant said she needed easy access to the 'facilities', and I was happy to have her place by the window.

My companion on the Frankfurt run was a youth around 22 or 23 with bad skin, long curly hair, a Metallica tee shirt and a red-and-white baseball cap worn back-to-front. He drank bottles of pilsner in rapid succession and listened to … well, heavy metal – that's what it sounded like, at least – through his earphones, all while stamping his smelly trainers. Even the flight attendants – hardened graduates of human misbehaviour – looked at me with pity. I was careful to keep an eye on him, and of course on my wheeled suitcase or whatever it was called, snug in the overhead locker. The lad was so unlike a professional that I thought he might be one, if only because he seemed to be overdoing the performance of delayed adolescence.

I almost missed my Cathay Pacific flight to Hong Kong because I fell asleep on a long, comfortable couch in the club lounge at Dubai airport. I asked the staff to make sure I was awake when the flight was called, but the people behind the desk had changed shifts and I had to run for the plane with moments to spare, dragging my wheelie after me, hurtling on board, waving my boarding pass and collapsing into my seat. Business class was at least more comfortable than economy, and I threw back the glass of champagne I was offered and accepted another. For me, though, the thrill was going to be the landing at Hong Kong's Kai Tak airport – rated the sixth most dangerous airport in the world.

The runway, at the east end of Kowloon Bay, was surrounded by water on three sides, and overlooked by mountains on the fourth. Victoria Bay lay to the south. The pilot had to bring the plane down to below 600 feet and make a sharp, 47-degree turn for the short and tight final run. I loved that part, the sudden plunge and the abrupt turn, made all the more dramatic by the gasps and yelps from other passengers. I relished the sudden G-force as the huge plane seemed to stand on wing, only to swing back into place. We passed right over Mong Kok's Bishop Hill. It was one of the most crowded neighbourhoods on earth with clusters of high-rise apartment blocks – concrete human anthills, each rooftop festooned with its own jungle of television aerials.

I was entering alien territory, like moving into woods without a compass. I would be out of my depth, my safety dependent on the goodwill, indifference or hostility of people I didn't know at all. It was what MacGregor had told me *not* to do, but at least I wasn't on the mainland.

11

The sailors know the drill.

As soon as Ho Ping is below decks, two crewmen put the hatch in place, cover it with the chart table, and toss creels and rope on top of the hatch, which in any case resembles the decking. It's a standard operating procedure and they've practised it many times. Someone would have to know the hatch is there. Or get down on their knees and examine the deck's varnished hardwood planks to discover the almost seamless fit.

The junk is divided into several compartments, both the forward and after hatches being left open in case the visitors demand a search.

Fang hopes it won't come to an inspection for several reasons, one being the presence of her guest and another the radio transceiver hidden in the planking of the forward hold, the *China Sea* being one of her number stations, the one she uses for sending her OTP signals to Bo De li.

They drop their two red sails and the junk rocks in the slightest of swells.

What the crew and Fang know is that although the *China Sea* has red sails, showing that it's a vessel based in Hong Kong, it is also registered with the PRC maritime authorities – but only Fang knows that its registration – 795S, painted near the prow – marks it down as a boat under the control of the Ministry of State Security.

The *China Sea* began life 30 years before, moving cargo from place to place along the coast, and enjoyed a second incarnation as a shrimper. A typhoon sank her in 1978. After being submerged for 3 months, she was resurrected. Once restored at great expense, she returned to duty as a tourist boat. Her owners used her to ferry wealthy Cantonese and foreign tourists on trips by the hour or day around Hong Kong and its islands. The owners went broke, and a small and little known company – a *Guoanbu* front called Happy Tourist Star Enterprises – came to the rescue. It bought *China Sea* for cash and kept her moored alongside dozens of other fishing junks in Victoria harbour.

This is not Fang's first trip on board. She's dropped agents off in Hong Kong and spirited others away before the British authorities could lay their hands on them.

Fang recognises the approaching vessel as an elderly Type 062 gunboat, classified by NATO as the Shanghai 11 class, 135 tons, with an unimpressive top speed of 28 knots – thanks to its 900-horsepower diesel electric engine. She knows it by sight because of the distinctive armament – twin 37mm cannon fore and aft.

The *China Sea*'s crew members wave. The PLAN sailors don't respond, but to Fang's relief, there's no sign of a boarding party mustering on deck.

The gunboat slows, circles the *China Sea* and comes within hailing distance, its engine coughing and spluttering before moving away. Fang sees people on the bridge inspecting them through binoculars. Fang also notes that the covers are in place on the muzzles of the twin cannon.

Even though the gunboat's crew is on side, she still doesn't want them to identify her.

She keeps her straw hat on, her face in shadow, and hangs back behind the others.

Chinese bureaucracy, even in the rarified world of foreign intelligence, is never free of rivalry. Xie Rong has his detractors and Fang is his deputy. She's associated with him and his career even if she doesn't share his views on political issues. It's a fact that the more successful a high-ranking official is, and the higher he or she climbs, the more enemies gather. It's also the case that any official will know the ranks below, but will never know the hierarchy above.

To be spotted at sea off the mainland – photographed – in a *Guoanbu* vessel from Hong Kong? Not a good idea at all. There'd be too many questions.

They're in the clear, for now at least.

12

We met up on a Kowloon pavement. We didn't talk about the weather because that's an English habit. Generally, the Chinese much prefer to chat about food instead. Perhaps that's because English weather is foul and Chinese food, at least during the great upheavals that have punctuated thousands of years of China's history, has all too often been in short supply. It's also something of an art form. Floods, droughts, conquests, revolutions and civil wars have left their mark on food, language and the national character.

'Have you eaten?'

'No – what about you?'

'No? Well then in that case, we must have lunch.'

Major Ma was tall, thin and swarthy, his silvery hair combed straight back from his forehead and tied in a pigtail. I had no idea how old he was. My guess would be in his seventies. He had the knobbliest fingers I'd ever seen, and they played on the melamine table top as if on a keyboard. The rest of him stayed still. He didn't smile. Ma held his chin up and, once seated, stared straight ahead towards the door, as if expecting someone else to join us. The Major maintained this posture without so much as glancing in my direction as we talked.

'You know what my name means, don't you, Mr Fisher? It means "horse".. "Ma" is not a common name here in Hong Kong. You will also know how much the Chinese, especially we Cantonese, like to make fun of people's names – particularly those of our employers and rulers. It helps reduce the stress of working for people who earn so much more than we do and enjoy luxury lifestyles, to say nothing of power and influence. So you can imagine what some people say about me, though I'm not a wealthy colonial. To them, behind my back, I'm Big Horse, Slow Horse, even Smelly Horse – oh, and we mustn't forget the favourite, *Ma liu* – Horse Piss.'

I was meant to laugh, and I did.

'We had an Englishman here a few years back, the chief secretary, Philip Haddon-Cave. You recall the name? Very astute, very effective, but he had an unfortunate manner. He came across to us ordinary people as a typical colonial ruler, stiff-necked and pompous. His nickname was *xia deng ji* in Mandarin, *ha dang gai* in Cantonese. This means low-class chicken, or prostitute. I think his Chinese staff and those who had to mention him on television had difficulty keeping a straight face, do you see? It helps Hong Kong people tolerate colonial rule if they can mock the rulers.'

Did Major Ma think of himself as 'ordinary'?

With this light-hearted, self-deprecating monologue, my host broke the ice and put me at my ease. Someone brought me an English-language menu. We sat at a large, round table at the back of a branch of Café de Coral – '*dajiale*' or 'everyone happy'. It was one of the most popular restaurant chains in Hong Kong, with a reputation for wholesome food and exemplary service. There was no alcohol, and I tried to persuade myself that it was better that way. I wondered if my choice – chicken with sticky rice ('glutinous rice'

91

was how it was described on the menu) along with black mushrooms and Chinese sausage – would cause offence. Despite his profession, Major Ma was said to be a leading light of one of Taiwan's Cha'n Buddhist organisations and Chinese Buddhists, if I wasn't mistaken, were vegetarian.

'We tend to call people by animal names, Mr Fisher. Mao used to call Cantonese people *huang pi gou*, imperialist running dogs, and he called you Europeans *bai pi zhu* or white-skinned pigs. All the more insulting when in fact the Cantonese are the smartest and most open-minded people in China – they started to emigrate in the 17th century and this helped give us a knowledge of the world, of languages, and helped build global networks. My family is Cantonese, so I took the insult to heart.'

Our food arrived. Major Ma didn't seem to notice or care that this barbarian was eating meat, after all. What I knew about him could be written on the back of a postcard. He was an intelligence operative of many years' standing. He had networks in the colony and extending to Macau, Taiwan and into the mainland – it was for that reason that he was said to receive a generous retainer from Langley, and no doubt others I didn't know about. But he was happy to chat to most Westerners in the same line of work who took the trouble to contact him and invite themselves to lunch. He always had something to offer. We did seek his help with specific tasks from time to time. That was it. I knew nothing of his rank, but that it must have originated in the war, fighting against or with, the Japanese, or perhaps it had been his KMT rank in the civil war against the communists. The answer would be somewhere in a file in Century House, gathering dust.

'We all want independence, Mr Fisher. Make no mistake. Once the

92

drink flows, you will hear people speak of it. Not just an independent Hong Kong, but an independent Taiwan, an independent Tibet, an independent Xinjiang – and of course Guangdong, the richest Chinese province of all. On its own, it would have a GDP bigger than most European states. Its capital would be Guangzhou – or maybe it should be here. What a dream! Of course you have to ask yourself where China's borders are – they seem rather blurred and porous, but then Chinese national identity is like water – it finds its way into all manner of places.'

His voice dropped as he leaned towards me, chopsticks held in those amazing fingers paused in mid-air. 'And as you know, the British authorities despise our local pro-democracy activists. Officials don't listen to what they have to say. They treat our young idealists with contempt. They don't conceal it, either. Instead, your Special Branch spies on them, taps their phones, follows them, tries to recruit them as informers. The British don't want to upset the mainland, so they do this dirty work for Beijing in the vain hope of winning concessions. It's the behaviour of a coward.'

Ouch. I wasn't about to argue, though; it sounded about right and in keeping with the colonial mentality of my countrymen.

'So, Mr Fisher, what can I tell you?'

I noticed that now and again he would turn his head towards one or other of three young men of military age sitting near the door, as if reassuring himself of their presence. All three wore baggy, short-sleeved shirts outside their dark pants – baggy enough to conceal weapons, I thought. There was a similar pair at a table over to our left, clean-shaven, with short, military-style haircuts.

'I'm here very for a meeting, but I wanted to check in with you and to see if there are any developments – any unusual activity by the mainlanders and their security and intelligence agencies – that I should know about. Anything in the last few days.'

The only meeting I had planned was with Major Ma and I had set it up as an excuse, should Century House ask why I had visited the island. The Hong Kong trip was a rather time-consuming and expensive diversion from my true destination, and Major Ma was central to my thin and hasty cover story.

Our plates vanished, and tea arrived.

'It depends on what you consider unusual, Mr Fisher. There's always something going on. The Chinese mainland security and intelligence agencies are expanding here all the time. It's getting crowded, and the process seems to have accelerated over the last couple of weeks. The strategy is to settle thousands of Han Chinese here, to displace the Cantonese and replace our language with Mandarin. They are going to swallow Hong Kong – as you say, lock, stock and barrel. New bridges and roads, of course, to tie the island and mainland together. But that's in the future. Three days ago a team of *Gonganbu* people crossed over, nine all told – and all male. You know what I mean by that – the Public Security Ministry. Four came by air on two separate flights from Shanghai, the rest overland via the New Territories.'

'Is that unusual?'

'I think so. They were in a hurry and had a specific goal.'

'Which was?'

'Perhaps it was a coincidence, but two days ago – the day of their arrival – a home on The Peak was broken into. That's very unusual. Nothing valuable was taken, and there were plenty of valuables if they had cared to do so. Pictures and ceramics. Antiques. There was even a small Qing teacup which, if auctioned here, would fetch millions. Oh, and a wonderful work by the earliest and greatest calligraphist, Wang Xizhe, that makes my mouth water thinking about it. It must be beyond price! According to the police report, the wall safe in the study had been opened, but by force or not, I do not know. Nothing there except commercial papers, account books and bank statements. Some of which they took and left the rest strewn about the floor.'

'What about the occupants?'

'No sign of them.'

'So?'

'According to the police report, a neighbour raised the alarm, alerted by noisy activity in the neighbouring property – somebody using acetylene torches or moving the furniture. Could have been a detonation if they blew the safe rather than cut it open. Anyway, the police were quick to arrive, given it's a wealthy area favoured by foreign taipans. Someone fired shots, and the burglars got away, unscathed. There was only one casualty among the police, a flesh wound and nothing serious. One wonders whether it was worth the invaders' trouble.'

'There's a link … ?'

'You tell me, Mr Fisher.'

'Who is the owner of the property?'

'Ah. That's where it gets interesting. Do you know of her? She's Cantonese, married to an English businessman. He was reported to have died about a week ago in a Beijing hotel. The cause of death was given as heart failure, triggered by excessive drinking. Name of Peacock. Does it mean anything to you, Mr Fisher? A Roger Peacock, financial adviser to some important people and quite successful – hence his wife's flat on The Peak. She's a science lecturer named Susan – Susan Ho Ping. She's Cantonese, too.'

I shook my head, pursed my lips and adopted my standard 'not interested' expression.

Major Ma knew rather more about my interests than I would have wished.

'The *Gongangbu* team split up again and left the very next day for Shanghai, their task completed – whatever it was.'

'You have very good sources, Major.'

'I should. It's my job to have excellent sources, Mr Fisher, and I've been keeping my ear to the ground for quite some time. Half a century. After 12 years here, I regard Hong Kong as my home – though of course I'm a citizen of the Republic of China, and the Taiwan government pays me my wages. I go back to Taiwan once or twice a year. It's very restful because the authorities haven't destroyed Chinese culture. It's the way the mainland used to be before the communist bandits, *gong fei*, seized power. So we try to keep our eyes open and, as you English say, our wits about us. Our survival depends on it. Are you staying long?'

'I have a flight in the morning.'

'You're staying overnight in a hotel?'

'Yes, but I haven't booked anything yet.'

'Oh, I almost forgot. There's one more development I should mention. While the mainlanders were ransacking the flat, someone else who might be of interest turned up at Kai Tak, on a routine China Air flight from Beijing. She's the communists' chief spy hunter. Do you know her – by her reputation, which is considerable?'

I felt myself tense up and forced my shoulders to slacken, opening my hands and resting them on the tabletop.

'What name does she use?'

'Let's see … hmm.' His fingers beat a rapid tattoo while Ma stared

96

straight ahead. 'Oh, yes, Chen. Chen Meilin. Of course, that's not her real name. Zhang Pushing is another. She's been here before, some years ago, accredited to Xinhua as a so-called special correspondent. For a while, she was a trouble-shooter in the Middle East. Arms transfers, bribing politicians and recruiting agents of influence seemed to be her interests back then. Does her work name mean anything to you?'

'No, I can't say it does.'

When in doubt, deny everything.

'I understand she holds the official rank of colonel in military intelligence and we also believe that she's deputy chief of the *Guoanbu* as head of its 5th Bureau under Xie Rong. The 5th is responsible for counter-intelligence. Her reputation is as someone who is both effective and ruthless. She's credited with having uncovered a French spy ring in Beijing a while back. Did you know? A few weeks ago, her people rounded up three alleged CIA agents, and she shot them herself, the video of the execution being compulsory viewing for all *Guoanbu* officers both in China and in embassies abroad. Are you shocked, Mr Fisher? Her message to her colleagues. How do you say? *Pour encourager les autres*? We say, in Mandarin, *shaji xiahou*, which, roughly translated, means kill the chicken to scare the monkey. The lady has managed to kill many chickens and scare many, many monkeys. She's well thought of in Beijing and is still young – early forties, they say. She must have good connections, *guanxi*. For someone so young – and female.'

'Any idea what she might be after in Hong Kong?'

'We asked ourselves that very same question, and we wondered whether there was any connection with the public security ministry's activity that same night. I thought you might enlighten me.'

'I'm sorry, Major, I can't. It's news to me.'

More lies on the part of Richard Brodick. It was second nature by now. There were so many, I was starting to find it hard to keep track of them. But as a practised liar, I could tell that Major Ma was lying, too. There had to be a reason for his trying too hard to display anti-communist views.

'Well, as I say, she has quite a reputation as a spy hunter. She must be after something or someone here, don't you think?'

I took out my wallet as the bill arrived.

'No, put your money away, Mr Fisher. I insist. You are my guest. Now, I have a vacant safe house. It's a three-bedroomed flat in Ming Wei Gardens with a view from the balcony over Deep Water Bay. Do you know the address? The apartment is empty most of the time. You could stay there. We keep an eye on the building and it's serviced. It's swept weekly so you don't have to worry about eavesdroppers. The fridge has the basics. It's safer for you.'

How did he know I was at risk?

Ma seemed to know my thoughts. 'We both know you're too senior and too well known, Mr Fisher. Hotels aren't secure for people in our trade, especially foreigners of your rank. You would attract attention of the wrong kind. Too many hotel staff come from the mainland. Informants, paid and unpaid, voluntary and involuntary. Caution is advisable, especially with Chen Meilin in town – and given your status and the fate of your countryman, Mr Peacock.'

What did he know of my rank and status?

'What would you suggest?'

'You will be my guest tonight. You will be safe, and we will deliver you to the airport in good time for your flight. It's the least I can do. I will sleep better for knowing my guest is safe. My motives are selfish – I don't want to sweep up any broken crockery, if you take my meaning. Housework was never my strong point.'

The youth at the nearest table came over and leaned down as Major Ma issued instructions in rapid, whispered Cantonese. That done, he beckoned with a long forefinger and another aide jumped up and approached us, holding something behind his back and then handing it over to the major who gripped it in his right hand.

Major Ma stood, and I followed.

'I'll see you to your apartment, Mr Fisher. We can have a drink – a real drink this time – and then I will leave you in peace. What time is your flight tomorrow?'

I realised he was holding a white stick. Major Ma was blind or partially sighted. I was sure that detail wasn't in his SIS file. It did say, though, that Ma was Hong Kong station commander for Taiwan's National Security Bureau or NSB, and that he was a good friend of the NSB's current director-general, Song Hsin-lien. All of which made him a formidable force in the complex world of east Asian intelligence.

We were on the same side, after all, even if Taiwan was being squeezed by the ChiCom python and had been penetrated by its communist foes.

There was a bottle of Jameson on the dining table along with two cut-glass tumblers. Major Ma knew my likes and dislikes, or so it seemed – in this case, a penchant for whiskey.

I played mother and poured out two generous doubles.

'If you want ice or water, you'll find them in the kitchen,' Ma said. I didn't.

At his suggestion, we went out onto the balcony. I unlocked and slid back the glass door. A jungle-clad hill fell to the water – an inlet that looked very deep and calm and reflected the green from the surrounding hills. There was some traffic on the road right below us, but it wasn't loud enough to spoil the sense of peace or the view. I savoured the potent scent of topical vegetation and seawater. A pale mist covered the sky, and the temperature seemed mild. There was no wind.

We sat on two comfortable outdoor chairs and sipped our drinks.

'I didn't tell you everything about the incident on The Peak.'

'Oh?'

'Two women were seen leaving the property on foot in something of a hurry as the burglars arrived. There was a thunderstorm that night – heavy downpours, high winds – it isn't supposed to rain in winter. It's conjecture, but it seems one woman was Susan Ho Ping, the flat owner. She left her car in her garage at the apartment, no doubt because she wanted to avoid detection and she wasn't taking any luggage. There wasn't time. I don't have a description of her companion, unfortunately, other than that she too was a woman, also Chinese, and rather tall.'

My host was well-informed, but there was nothing that was particularly sensitive.

'Since then there have been no sightings of Ms Ho, and as for Chen Meilin, I regret to say we have no idea where she is. We've lost contact. She could have gone to ground at Xinhua, which acts as a sort of embassy here for the Chinese communists and is their primary intelligence base. Yet we did not see her entering the premises. Our people haven't spotted her leaving by any of the official Hong Kong exit points. So one can only speculate – are they still together, working in tandem, lying low somewhere, out of sight? If they were together. Which makes me wonder about Chen's involvement and her relationship with He. Is her presence linked to the murder of the Englishman, Peacock, 9 days ago?'

I didn't speak, but waited to hear him out. It wasn't going to flush me out of cover, and it wasn't enough to get a response. I wasn't about to confirm or deny anything.

'And then, of course, there's your appearance, Mr Fisher. You are most welcome, of course, and I'm delighted to make your acquaintance, but is this another coincidence? Was it by chance that you contacted me with all this going on? Forgive me, please, but as one professional to another, I know your name isn't Fisher, and I'm informed that you command something impressive called UK Station, an organisation inside British intelligence that specialises in running deep cover agents in denied territories, including the Chinese mainland. And that's why I thought it best to ensure that a senior SIS officer should be safe, at least while on my turf. We wouldn't want anything to happen to you, especially as you seem to travel below the waterline, or so it seems. Otherwise, you would have stayed with your British friends.'

'I'm grateful. Thank you.'

'Are you here because of what happened to Mr Peacock?'

'No, I'm not.'

'Is Ms Ho Ping the subject, or one of your subjects, of interest here in Hong Kong?'

'No.'

'And this woman, Chen, or Zhang? Is she someone you know of, or have come across at some point?'

'No, she isn't.' Did Ma expect me to tell all for a meal, a dram or two of whiskey and a night in one of his safe houses?

I tipped up my glass and swallowed the last of the Jameson.

101

'There is something you might help me with.'

I let him wait, setting down my glass and shifting in my seat.

'There seem to be some unusual movements of the 41st and 42nd Army Groups in Guangzhou – the divisions in Guanxi and Guangdong – unusual in that there have been no announcements that I know of about winter or spring manoeuvres. Also 16th and 23rd Army Groups in Shenyang. Do you know anything about this?'

Major Ma stared straight ahead, motionless.

A full minute passed before he answered.

'Yes, Mr Fisher. You are correct. These are unusual. Two of the mainland's seven military districts, both in the south, have been placed on alert. All leave is cancelled and no official reason has been given. Air, ground and naval forces are involved. I'm sure London must be aware, thanks to their signal intelligence stations here.'

I would not be drawn on so sensitive an issue. Nine years before, the GCHQ station at Little Sai Wan had closed and was replaced by a more modern facility code named DEMOS-1 at Chung Hom Kok on the southern side of the island. It monitored satellite communications, and sported five enormous dishes set up on a narrow ridge of rock overlooking the South China Sea. Chinese communist intelligence services took a very close interest in the facility. The SIGINT presence continued to expand with DEMOS-4, built on a cliff edge and snatching telemetry data from China's missile tests – not least those of the submarine-launched ballistic missiles that formed part of Beijing's retaliatory strike capability. And all this expansion happened at great cost while knowing that in a few years – in 1997 – we would have to withdraw. Why bother? For the simple reason that the Americans relied on us for China coverage and paid top dollar for our services.

So I asked Ma about the manoeuvres. 'Do you know why?'

'I could speculate.'

'Please do.'

'Infantry reserves in Beijing have also been activated. I would say it all points to an imminent power struggle, wouldn't you? And I should add that Hong Kong must play some part in their calculations. How do you say? A bargaining chip?'

'Could be it's an exercise, after all.'

Major Ma smiled his serene smile. It was his turn to put down his empty glass; he rose to his feet, found his stick and tapped his way across the parquet flooring to the door.

'Thank you for this, Major. For your kind hospitality and the helpful conversation. It's much appreciated and I've enjoyed meeting you.'

Another of his young men stood in the corridor, hands folded in front of him, alert and like a trained soldier, he avoided looking at either of us.

'My pleasure, Mr Fisher. Goodnight – and I wish you a safe journey.'

I went back to the balcony and savoured more of Major Ma's Irish. I told myself it would help me sleep. Courteous, helpful, hospitable, likeable and experienced – the Major was all that. I didn't trust him, though, any more than he trusted me, and that was not at all. He wore his politics on his sleeve. I was tempted to contact London, using my new and portable transceiver, but I decided it wouldn't be wise. I couldn't be certain of my security, even if they *had* swept the place. If there was video monitoring, whoever was responsible – the Taiwanese or anyone else – might record my keystrokes.

Well played, Fang. Yet another clever move on your part. I was almost taken in by your colleague's impersonation of Major Ma. He tried too hard, though.

13

Fang's team – her *dui* – is waiting for her at Bangkok's Don Mueang Airport, the oldest commercial airport in Asia and currently the second busiest. There are five *Guoanbu* members all told, including the team leader or *duizhang* named Yang Bai. She's a woman of slight build with a shock of black hair cut very short. Were it not for her heart-shaped face and soft features, she could have been mistaken for a male teen. But, as Fang knows, Yang is anything but soft.

The two women meet up in arrivals – neither says anything. They don't shake hands. Yang falls into step next to Fang as they head to the exit. It's pretty much the end of the high season for foreign tourists. The departures section seems more crowded – winters are short and as the temperature rises in Thailand, breaching the 30-degree Celsius level, it is too hot for most Europeans and Americans. It's almost the end of the school holidays, too, though the obese couple in front of them, waddling along in what looks like brand new summer clothing in bright yellows and pinks and weighed down by enormous cases bristling with labels, are among those taking advantage of discounted package deals as the hotels and resorts start to empty.

The two women leave the cool air-conditioned atmosphere behind and move out into the steamy exterior, still side by side. Fang is a head taller than Yang. They both wear flat black shoes with straps over the tops of their feet – lightweight, flexible and perfect for the tropical climate – and for running.

'Small team – *shao dui* – as you wanted.'

'They will have to do everything, Yang Bai.'

'Not a problem, Deputy Chief. They know.'

'Bai, you will be the supervisor, *jiandu*.'

Yang acknowledges the order with a curt nod, but she's pleased by that and possibly by Fang's use of her first name.

Ever since Thailand's army commander, General Suchinda Kraprayoon, overthrew the democratic – but very corrupt – civilian government a year ago, tensions have been rising. Thai security agencies have become far more pervasive and intrusive.

They're able to speed up to a normal walking pace to the exit as the two tourists move aside to join a larger group of oversized visitors. 'You will supervise your watchers, *jianshi deren*. I want a daily sweep of the hotel rooms and the safe house until this is over. Is the *ying gui* – British devil – behaving himself?'

'He gives us no trouble.'

'What's the *waibin*'s routine?'

'Breakfast in his room at 0800. At 0900, a 6-minute ride on the back of one of our scooters to the Plaza Lagoon complex, then two hours swimming in the club pool, always under observation, followed by lunch in the same complex. He's left alone to eat, but we observe from outside. We bring him back the same way – sometimes by car, sometimes scooter – but change the route. He usually takes a nap in his room, then has a few beers and a club sandwich or salad on the

roof and, if he wants, a dip into the small pool they have up there.
Asleep before midnight. A nice life.'

'Does he talk much?'

'No.'

'Complaints? Questions?'

'He's the perfect guest. Silent, which is how we like it.'

'He's talked to no other foreigners or guests?'

'None.'

'Phone calls?'

'We have disconnected his room phone. We have video and audio 24/7.'

'Does he ask about anyone … his wife?'

'Never has. He asked for some English-language books, which we have provided from Kinokuniya bookshop. Mostly crime fiction. He likes an author named Deighton. Len Deighton.'

This particular part of the exercise is going better than expected.

The team has three taxis waiting – two yellow Toyota Corollas and one red, all three of them in the bright, customary livery of Bangkok cabs, plastered with ads, registered with the authorities and owned by a small company maintained by the *Guoanbu*'s Bangkok Station, located in the enormous Chinese embassy compound on Ratchadaphisek Road.

Yang explains: 'One of our people is back at the hotel minding the *waibin*. One car will go now and pick up our colleague and take him to the safe house, where we have someone keeping an eye on the place. The route is clear.'

That leaves Yang and one remaining colleague to drive the two other taxis into town. Fang nods a greeting of sorts at the two male team members, settles in the back of the red taxi while Bai takes the wheel. She doesn't want to talk to the team. That's Yang's task. They're her people. Fang wants to delegate security, transport and communications so she can focus on the 'guest' – and her forthcoming treff with her top agent, 2904; aka Bo Deli, aka Richard Brodick.

But first, there's a conversation she needs to have.

'Where to now, deputy department chief?' Yang looks at Fang in the rear-view mirror.

'Safe house.'

They take the expressway, but after 10 minutes or so, the last Toyota breaks away to collect Fang's fellow officer. The second car is right behind Bai's, riding shotgun. It provides a backup and extra security in case anything untoward should happen. Fang knows Bai wouldn't want to be responsible if their taxi broke down or there was an accident that left Fang stranded.

They're soon in the northern district of Bangkok known as Ladprao, a built-up area of the expanding capital. Thirty years before, the streets were unpaved and buffalo from neighbouring farmland wandered around. Now it's crowded with shops, high-rise offices, malls and hotels and always in the grip of slow-moving traffic. Thailand is a consumer paradise for those who can afford it – but it's obvious to Fang, gazing out at the streets, that most people are still too poor to qualify.

Not that everything is perfect back in the communist paradise of the People's Republic – far from it. Fang recalls an adage she's heard more than once on a Beijing street: *xinxin kuku sishinian, yizhao huidao jiefang qian*, or '40 years of sweat and pain, then one morning we went back to the era before Liberation'.

The 'Liberation' having taken place in 1949.

They turn off Chokchai 4 Road into *Soi* 54. The shops and food stalls peter out and Fang finds herself moving through a quiet residential suburb – a private housing estate, in fact – dating back to the 1960s, comprising bungalows with corrugated iron or asbestos roofs and tiny gardens. Larger, more modern properties have replaced some of these. The safe house is one; it's a new, two-storey building with a balcony on the first floor, a carport, several mango trees and a lawn. Recently built, according to Yang, and owned by a Thai woman who only a few months ago died of cancer. Her *farang* husband, a German, soon left Thailand with their daughter and now he rents it out. It has a spacious, relaxed feel about it. The walls are built of double Q-con bricks, plastered and then painted a Mediterranean yellow. The roof tiles are pale grey, and the windows and doors are located so they never face the direct sun.

A member of the team opens the tall gates and they drive in.

'He's waiting for you inside.'

The man who gets up off the sofa and comes forward to greet Fang in the living room is tall, dark, with silver hair combed straight back and tied in a pony tail.

They both smile – they appear pleased to see each other.

Fang is the first to speak. 'It's good to see you again. I'm sorry we missed each other in Hong Kong.'

'But it was necessary, Deputy Chief, given the circumstances.'

They sit on opposite sides of the dining table at the far end of the large room, which is white, with a cream tiled floor. It's cooler inside than out, and the plain colour scheme gives it a light, calm feel.

Fang is impatient and has no liking for small talk. 'Well, did it work?'

'I believe so, yes.'

'He accepted that you were Major Ma.'

'Let's face it, most foreigners can't really tell us apart unless they

108

live among us for a time. I'm the right age, the right height, my hair is white – all I had to do was add a white stick and act as if I was blind – so yes, your big-nose bought it. I don't think Mr Fisher, as he calls himself, will have seen a picture of Major Ma and even if he has, it will be an old one and nothing more than a faded passport image. And of course, I made the right counter-revolutionary remarks befitting a Taiwan intelligence officer.' He shrugs and smiles again at Fang, pleased to see her, his expression suggesting that he'd like to chat about old times.

Fang isn't having any of it.

'You confirmed the troop movements?'

'I did. He asked me. I didn't have to bring up the subject. I don't think he knew about the reserves called to duty in Beijing. Or the heightened activity at the two submarine bases on Hainan Island.'

'And the potential threat to Hong Kong …'

'He took the point.'

'And the break-in we arranged?'

'As you instructed. He made out that he knew nothing about it or the people involved.'

'You took good care of him?'

'Yes, of course. He stayed in the flat at Ming Wai Gardens for the night. We had a couple of drinks – I made sure he had his favourite whiskey. Our people took him to the airport the next morning. There were no problems. He's professional and I found him to be agreeable, but wary – we both were – but he seems to have accepted that I was who I said I was, along with confirmation of the military activity. I hope he doesn't meet the real Major Ma any time soon.

'I'd ask who this man Fisher is, but that would be inappropriate, even between friends.'

'Yes, it would. Bad security.'

Fang has achieved her aim. Instead of Brodick quoting DRAGON as the sole source of any report on PLA movements, he will be able to attribute the material to a second source – a senior, named officer of Taiwan intelligence. The corroboration would give his intelligence more weight in London's Joint Intelligence Committee. London would have to take it seriously and so would Washington, the primary target.

'I enjoyed the assignment, I must say. It got me out of the office and coming here has been most welcome, too. Thank you, Deputy Chief.'

'Thank you.'

That Fang was once his subordinate as a junior PLA2 officer in Hong Kong 20 years ago does not, in her view, equate to friendship, nor does their association entitle either of them to indulge in indiscretions, especially in the case of Bo Deli.

Fang walks him outside to one of the taxis, and thanks him again – without shaking hands.

The fake Major Ma has left, and within a couple of days will return to working under his usual intelligence cover as a senior special correspondent accredited to Xinhua, operating out of the news agency's Hong Kong headquarters. He'll have his hair cut, and the silver will grow out and revert to the customary black.

Fang feels the air of expectancy on the part of her team. Everyone's on edge. They know Fang is expecting to meet an important asset, and she hopes that's all they know. It's conceivable that Yang might have picked up his code number, 2904, but nothing more. They're on their feet, waiting for Fang, fidgeting, eager to start. Even Yang is shifting her weight from one athletic leg to the other. They have no idea how important this Bo Deli is, not just to Fang and her career, but to the Central Military Commission back in Beijing.

The most important technical secret he's betrayed to Fang consists of a series of top secret US documents relating to underwater tests. They are summed up in a single word: cavitation, the formation of vapour bubbles within a liquid at low pressure, which occurs when the liquid speeds up to high velocities.

Thanks to Brodick, Fang now knows that cavitation produces extensive erosion of the rotating blades, more noise from the resultant knocking and vibrations, and a significant reduction in efficiency. For the submarine hunter, the noise alone can not only locate the submerged boat with precision, but also identify it by the characteristics peculiar to its individual cavitation.

Cavitation has been a subject for scientific research since the beginning of the 18th century and international conferences are held on the topic every few years, spawning dozens of research papers on theory. These are devoured by the world's submariners and marine architects. But what's relevant for Fang is that for Beijing's navy headquarters, submarine development is massively important.

The PLAN's order of battle includes over 60 submarines, most of which are elderly Soviet Whiskey and Romeo class diesel–electric boats, built under licence in Chinese yards but suitable only for coastal defence. Ballistic missile submarines include the Type 092, carrying 12 launch tubes for the JL-1 missile with its range limited to regional targets. But the newer Type 094 is far more advanced, and capable of firing the JL-2 with a range of 8,000 km and equipped with three or four MRVS – multiple, independently targetable warheads. From locations close to China's own waters, 092 boats are capable of launching a retaliatory nuclear

111

strike against targets on the US mainland – a huge step forward for Beijing's war planners.

What Fang knows, and what she thinks Brodick *doesn't* know, is that the SSN or nuclear attack submarine (Chinese designation 09-111, NATO reporting name Shang class) represents a technological leap forward. The PLAN top brass regard it as China's answer to the Soviet Victor 111 SSN (Soviet designation *Shchuka*), because the Red admirals believe it capable of projecting Chinese naval force into the western Pacific, threatening US carrier groups and escorting China's latest SLBMs to their potential launch sites. And it's ready to launch, following years of development.

The Central Military Commission received Brodick's reports on classified cavitation research with delight. The Commission chairman himself sent Fang a personal commendation for her work in stealing such vital intelligence from the CCP's foes.

But of course Fang's co-conspirator, Bo Deli aka Richard Brodick, may entertain the notion – as so many Westerners do – that China lacks both the machines and machinists to provide the industrial means of turning these US research, design and test documents into the stealthy, multiple blade propellors that equip US and British submarines. It's a typical case of underestimating what China can achieve.

A wonderful intelligence coup, but of no immediate benefit to China.

Fang wonders if that notion helps Brodick rationalise his betrayal – that, and the fact the technology is American and not British.

She knows that if this is the case, he's deluding himself – because the 09-111 indeed does have a variable pitch, seven-blade propellor, thanks in part to Brodick's revelations – making it as quiet as the Victor 111 as well as the US Navy's improved Los Angeles class SSNs.

At 110 metres and displacing 7,000 tons submerged, the new PLAN SSN boasts a vertical launch system for anti-ship missiles as well as cruise missiles.

In short, it's a formidable and very modern beast.

If the 09-111 has been modified thanks to espionage, so too was the Victor 111 – indeed, US sailors have nicknamed the Russian boat 'Walker' after the Soviet spy of that name who did so much to help the Soviets catch up in sub technology.

Maybe they'll call the next Chinese class 'Bo Deli'.

Fang stops day-dreaming and turns to the team. 'Let's go to collect him, shall we?'

The gates open, the taxis roll out onto the street.

There will be three of the team members involved. Yang proposes one will remain to track the *waibin* in the hotel and another will secure the gates of the safe house and keep an eye on the premises. Fang agrees that three will suffice, and with her along to identify the asset, she tells herself four should be more than enough.

She doesn't show it, of course, but Fang is both excited and apprehensive.

How will he react when she shows him detailed plans of the 09-111?

Has Bo Deli grown fat, expanded his waistline, lost his hair? Is he married? Does he have kids? Will Fang feel the same way? Will she want him with the crazy, physical urgency she did in a Beirut at war with itself?

Or was that the place and time, the whiff of danger and death all around them that gave their love-making an extra edge? Fucking a newly-recruited British intelligence officer amid a civil war had something to do with it, of course. Will he want her with the same abandon? Will he like her being on top? Or has whatever it was

113

they had then, died? If the answer is that yes, they do still thirst for each other, then how on earth will they steal time together under the noses of Yang Bai and her *dui*?

The questions keep coming.

How will Bo Deli react when she introduces him to her hotel guest and Brodick realises what she's done? Will he agree to her plan? Will he help, or try to stop her? If it's the latter, what is she prepared to do in response? She picks an English term – will she kill the goose that lays the proverbial golden egg?

14

They were onto me right from the start. As I climbed into the cab, I turned and saw another pull out and follow. It hadn't been queuing in the taxi rank, but parked further back on the opposite side, close to arrivals. I saw two people on board, and a minute later, a couple of motorcycles joined us.

I wasn't imagining it. They didn't try to conceal themselves. if they had, they would have waited a little longer. Either they didn't care, or they wanted me to know.

My driver turned his head. 'Where to, boss?'

I didn't answer at once, because I was too busy watching the watchers in their Toyota Corolla.

It was a problem. I would not try to shake them off – that would be too obvious. I would have to lose them, but in a way that would seem that they'd lost me through their own incompetence, not that I'd tried to rid myself of them. One elementary rule of espionage is never to shake off a tail unless it's an emergency or cannot be avoided – unless, of course, there's an unusual need to identify oneself as an intelligence operative. The priority has to be protecting the agent or source.

Were they Fang's people? They could be anybody, anybody who

knew I was SIS and a senior officer on that flight to Bangkok and heading for a meeting with my top agent.

That knowledge was more worrying than the identity of the people tagging me. Above all, I had to protect Fang, my agent, and also my *Guoanbu* case officer.

They might be a CIA team, if only because Langley had long sought to discover the identity of my Chinese source. The Agency wanted to take over the reins, and this might be one way.

Maybe they were Taiwanese NSB operatives. Or they could be Thai counter-intelligence operating on their own behalf – or for a third party. With the Thais, it was about money more than anything else. Ask a Thai why he or she is praying to the Buddha and they'll more often than not say for luck, for wealth.

The driver of my cab might well be one of them, whoever they were.

The motorcyclist on his red 125cc Honda was well ahead, keeping his eye on us in his mirrors. His companion, on a dusty blue Suzuki, was holding back two or three cars behind. He closed up on secondary roads or in heavy traffic at the lights, weaving around and among other motorcycles and scooters. He was good at it, except for one thing. His helmet was distinctive – a dirty, battered white – and it stood out, which didn't seem very professional on his part.

This little procession winding its way into the city reminded me that Fang had chosen Bangkok for our treff for practical reasons. First, it wasn't too far for her to travel. Second, there were a couple of hundred thousand of her fellow citizens living or working in Thailand. That meant plenty of sea room for a deep-sea fish like her to move around undetected. Then again, there were even more indigenous Thai Chinese – numbering in the millions – who controlled much of Thailand's commerce and industry, from tiny shops to vast industries.

There had been a time when US-backed military dictators in Thailand whipped up anti-Chinese sentiment, using anti-Chinese pogroms to consolidate their grip on power. It would be harder to do nowadays. Thais and Chinese were so well integrated by marriage that it was difficult to distinguish one from the other after generations of miscegenation. The Chinese were more admired than envied for their entrepreneurial skills, or so I thought.

Another good reason: the PRC embassy compound in Bangkok was huge, no doubt with a well-staffed *Guoanbu* Station housed in an extensive annexe. Fang could draw on any resources she needed and she was senior enough as head of the 5th Bureau to do so without having to explain herself.

Chinese foreign intelligence had their work cut out in Thailand. The Americans flew spy missions from northern Thailand into North Korea and Chinese airspace. The NSA had their SIGINT stations up north, watching Chinese and North Korean communications and monitoring missile telemetry. CIA and NSA activity would top the list of *Guoanbu* and PLA2 priorities. Second, Washington supplied Thailand with weaponry and training. Beijing would want to monitor that. A north-east Maoist insurgency was no longer supported by Beijing, but would be of interest. So too, a Moslem insurgency in the south, a long border with Myanmar – especially with armed ethnic groups fighting the Myanmar authorities (and with one organisation, using China's border as a haven) – and the flood of drugs entering Thailand from so-called jungle factories along the frontiers.

The *Guoanbu* lights would burn late into the night.

I gave the driver the address not of my true destination, but of a brothel known to our local Station. It was known to many people, including foreign embassies and corporations. The Thai military dictator's sister-in-law owned it. She had three similar properties in the Lotus Park chain, each said to have a stable of approximately 400 female employees. Two were in Bangkok and one was in northern Chang Mai. The driver didn't turn a hair; he would have been used to *farangs* arriving by air and wanting the 'wash and brush' they couldn't buy at home, with local law enforcement paid to look the other way.

White Lotus was a palatial building, red despite the name, complete with fake turrets and towers. Well-tended lawns and ponds surrounded it, and below the name emblazoned in gold letters across the front wall was a smaller neon sign in a tasteful script that read *luxury massage* nestling in white lotus petals. Without the signage, it might have been a movie set for a palace in Jaipur. Its sister whorehouses were Blue Lotus, in downtown Bangkok, and Red Lotus, up north.

The lotus was an important Buddhist symbol, for although rooted in mud, its flowers emerged pristine above the muck. Purity of mind and spirit, despite being rooted in the filth of materialism. How fitting for a whorehouse.

A uniformed flunkey stepped forward and opened the door of the taxi as I paid the driver. I took my trolley bag with me. The flunkey wanted to help, but I shook him off and used the exchange to glance back at the highway. My watchers were all there – I hadn't imagined it. The taxi with its two occupants had stopped near the turnoff to the 'massage parlour', while the two motorcyclists had spaced themselves out along the road fronting the building. So they were going to wait for me to emerge.

Good for them. It'd be a long wait in the sun.

The air conditioning struck like an ice shower, freezing the sweat on my back. The foyer was huge and carpeted in florid swirls. It resembled one of those immense casinos in Las Vegas – only without the one-armed bandits. Inside were three heavily-built men in dark suits and ties with short haircuts, their backs to the walls, wearing impassive expressions and plastic earpieces, alert but at ease like soldiers on parade. Doubtless private security, involving ex-cops or serving police officers moonlighting to augment their pitiful wages. They took no notice of me. I suspected they had orders not to stare at customers.

The long reception desk across my front was of black marble and decorated with flower arrangements. Three uniformed women stood behind it in a row, smiles in place, like hotel receptionists, in black suits, white shirts, wearing bow ties and name badges.

Above them was the inevitable portrait of the king in a gilt frame.

'Welcome, sir'. Another young woman had appeared, but I didn't see or hear her approach. She bowed and put her palms together in a *wai*, a gesture of respect which I immediately and without thinking returned. With a broad smile that showed her perfect teeth she turned away. 'Please follow me.'

Her name badge read *concierge*. It reminded me of the days when ushers showed cinema-goers to their seats.

This was no Odeon.

A dark corridor opened up to what I could only describe as an atrium. A vast glass wall took the place of a cinema screen. It ranged from floor to the high ceiling and curved around the sides. It was not unlike an aquarium, but there were no fish. The lady gestured – would I please take a seat on the amphitheatre facing it, the stepped levels cushioned in red velvet.

She asked if I wanted a drink. It was on the house. I didn't, but I wanted to play for time. I asked for tonic water with ice and lemon. I seemed to be almost alone, except for a couple of foreigners sitting on the far side, drinking beer. I thought I overheard snatches of

Spanish. It was early afternoon, so hardly surprising that business was slack.

Shoals, not of fish but young women, glided into view. Some wore swimsuits, others shorts and halter tops, some underwear, one or two even swept by in long gowns that opened down the front. Each held a white card on which there was a large black number. They sat, sprawled, knelt, lounged. They chatted to one another or stared out – at me, it seemed, but it wasn't clear if they could see out. One or two waved. Some pouted, pointed at themselves and mouthed what I imagine was 'you like?' and 'you want?' Most looked bored.

There must have been 30 of them or thereabouts, presumably representing the slow afternoon shift, paraded on command at the arrival of customers. They were all young, slim or curvy, and all pretty, though that might have been a matter of make-up and lighting.

All I needed to do was call out the digits of anyone I took a shine to. Trouble was, I took a shine to them all. So I picked a number at random, hesitating long enough to make it appear that I had given the matter some consideration. I also wanted any watchers outside to wilt in the heat and give up waiting for the fornicating *farang*. I sipped my drink and inspected the sweet Thai faces before me.

I made my decision. 'Fourteen!'

The young woman with a fringe, neat bob and angelic features holding the placard with that number rose to her feet. She said something to her friends, glanced at the aquarium glass with a smile, offered a *wai* to her invisible client, and in moments appeared before me.

'Come, please.'

She took me by the hand and led me to what appeared to be a hotel room. Painted or papered in magnolia and a dusky pink, it was comfortably, if anonymously, furnished with an en suite bathroom off the entrance. The girl, who I thought was in her twenties, began her routine by closing the door. Then she ran a bath, testing the temperature with her fingers and pouring in bath salts or something of the sort. Returning to the room where I sat, she stood in front of me, so I rose to meet her and she – who can't have been over five-one – undressed me. She began with my shirt buttons, and told me her name was Kanda – it was not her real name, of course. She asked me about mine. I said it was Drew.

'Nice to meet you, Drew.'

Next, my belt. I tossed my clothes on the bed, but she insisted on hanging them up in the wardrobe. All part of the inclusive service. Once I was naked – and erect – she led me to the bath, which was by now steaming and full. She tested the water one last time, and I climbed in. It was pretty hot, and I sank down, enjoying it, notwith-standing my erection, which now protruded above the surface of the bubbles like a submarine periscope scouting for enemy vessels in a choppy sea.

Kanda stripped and joined me in the bath. 'It feels good, yes?' She took no notice of my priapic state. No doubt Kanda had seen all that before, countless times. She took a large yellow sponge and washed me, starting with my face and neck. This was part of the well-rehearsed drill, predicated no doubt on the assumption that the act of sex itself would last a couple of minutes at the most.

This was industrial, production line prostitution.

'You like?'

'Sure.'

'You like me?'

'You're beautiful, Kanda.'

She was, too.

She was washing my balls at this point – well, she was fondling them underwater and pretending to wash them, I should say.

'You want Kanda?'

Well, of course I did. Who wouldn't? There were two problems, though. The first was that I wasn't there to fuck a pretty young whore. I was there to evade my followers, whoever they were. Then again, Kanda could have been my daughter or a younger sister. That thought put a dampener on my push-button male lust. I told myself there were villages in the impoverished north and northeast of Thailand that had grown prosperous by sending generations of young females to bars and brothels across the country. Their families built modern homes with all modern appliances on the proceeds, along with cars and televisions and the rest of it. There were others I'd read about who were sold to gangs and supplied to brothels along the county's southern border with Malaysia that were virtual prisons, surrounded by barbed wire and guarded by thugs with automatic weapons – establishments owned by criminal groups that were crude and brutal and which catered for the cross-border trade in which the women were expected to service dozens of clients every day.

I told myself I wasn't responsible for this state of affairs. That didn't make it right, though.

Foreigners were only a fraction of the Thai sex industry, although it was the part that attracted most publicity. It was Thais themselves who formed the bulk of customers in a vast industry. When local men got together for a drink and meal after work, their wives knew it wouldn't end there – their husbands would go on to a nightclub or whorehouse where professional tarts or enthusiastic amateurs would round off the night out.

That didn't make it right, either.

By now, Kanda had me out of the bath and dried me with a big towel. She took me to the bed, her fingers entwined with mine. She lay down, back against the pillows, stretched out her arms.

'Kanda wants Drew.'

'I'm sorry, no.'

I sat on the bed but made no move towards her.

She sat up, with surprise, alarm, and irritation in her expression. 'You don't like?'

'Kanda, you're great. You're beautiful. But no sex. I can't. I'm married, you see.'

I divorced years before – as if any of that mattered.

Poor Kanda. She'd followed her standard operating procedure to the letter. She'd performed brilliantly up to this point. But failure didn't come to it. My marriage didn't, either. It appalled her. My refusal could mean losing her job, being chucked out, even fined or beaten. God alone knew what the repercussions would be for her. It mystified her – and she was angry. Most who fucked her would be married. It would never have occurred to her that she'd be refused because of a client's marriage.

The entire process had so far taken under 30 minutes.

I got up, went to the cupboard where my clothes were, grabbed my wallet and paid her the standard 900 baht fee – a whisker under 10 quid.

She dressed, and left the room only to return with the receipt. She wasn't smiling and didn't look me in the eye. I had my pants and shirt on by this time. I gave her another 1,000, a big tip by the standards of the place, curled her fingers around it, put a finger to my lips.

She knew what I meant.

123

'For you, Kanda. Thank you.'

'You good man,' she whispered. 'Wife lucky.'

We went out together. The concierge was waiting for us with her Colgate smile. 'Was everything to your satisfaction?' No doubt she used a spreadsheet in her office to work out the precise cost, profit and timing involved in servicing clients.

'It was brilliant. Kanda is special. She gave me a good time.'

'Thank you so much.'

Wais all round.

'Oh, I have a favour to ask. Can I avoid going out the front? Do you have a back door?'

'Of course, sir. This way.'

'Could you call a taxi, please?'

'No trouble, sir. Please take a seat. Would you like another drink – on the house?'

Kanda had already vanished, a little better off than before we met.

I stood on the elevator, which was rising towards the top floor of the Central Plaza shopping mall at the end of the Ladprao Road in Chatuchak district, feeling fresh thanks to Kanda's bubble bath. Ahead of me were two *katoeys*, lady-boys as they are called in Thailand, both well over 6 feet, very slim and impeccable in their make-up and clothing. Behind me clustered a group of high school students in uniform with short skirts, giggling and teasing one another and behind them, a couple in their thirties with a toddler in a pushchair.

The Thais loved shopping malls, old and new – and new ones, each grander than its predecessors, were going up all the time. They were air-conditioned, providing relief from the high temperatures and humidity outside. They were bright, spacious temples to consumerism. The

Thai middle classes had taken to fashion, brand names and high-tech goodies with immense enthusiasm. Malls were aspirational, places to see and be seen, to watch other people, to meet friends over coffee – a growing addiction – and of course, to shop with all the names with which we are all so familiar; from Calvin Klein to Zara, from Sony to Philips, Apple and Samsung. There were fashion shows, too, and a boy or girl band would put on a display to advertise a new model of luxury car with sales staff on hand to offer easy repayment and discounts. There were cinemas, play areas for children, skating or running circuits and dozens of eateries and bars scattered about as well as a food hall, usually in the basement, boasting such foreign delicacies as marmite and haggis as well as wines from California and the Périgord. Malls offered a fake lifestyle, a world of pretence, an escape.

Walking around, mirroring in the windows, riding up and down the elevators like a *farang* tourist looking lost and bemused, I felt sure I was in the clear.

All I had to do now was buy an iced coffee at the Krispy Kreme kiosk – *Home of the Original Glazed Donut Since 1937* – and take a seat—and wait, staying calm by watching the shoppers below me.

In a matter of minutes, I would meet my agent and case officer, Fang.

15

Fang turns at the knock on the hotel room door. Yang opens it.

Bo Deli walks in, his manner cautious, looking around to make sure there's no-one lurking behind the door or in the bathroom.

'It's you at last,' he says, smiling. It's a tentative smile, she thinks, even nervous. What's he afraid of? What's he so worried about?

Fang responds in English. 'Pleasant trip, was it?'

He looks at Fang, then around at the spartan double room.

'Not bad, not bad at all.' Does he mean the room, or his voyage?

Fang nods at Yang. 'Wait downstairs. I'll call reception when I need you.'

Yang closes the door behind her.

'Tell me, Richard. I can't help but ask. I'm intrigued. Did you enjoy your bubble bath at the White Lotus?'

He's changed little, Fang decides. A little more weight, the beginnings of a paunch, but nothing that a less sedentary occupation, more exercise and less alcohol couldn't solve.

Her question seems to take him by surprise, but he doesn't seem to be at all embarrassed and that's disappointing. She's making fun of him, but she also wants him on the back foot.

'They were your people, then?'

'Who else would they be?'

'I don't know. They could have been anyone. Americans. Russians. It was the only way I thought I could lose them without being obvious.'

'You didn't lose them, though, did you? We spoke to – what was her name again? Kanda? Beautiful, very young – so I'm told. Seems you were sexually abstemious and generous with your tip. I'm surprised you didn't make full use of the facilities. Most men would have. It's very popular with foreign businessmen.'

'I hope you didn't get her into any kind of trouble.'

'You've grown sentimental, Richard. Why would we give her any trouble? Kanda spoke well of you. Said you were a *farang* gentleman. Maybe the first she's met.'

'Is this room …?'

'We've had it swept. Yours also.'

They stand 2 metres apart and look at each other.

She feels it still. It hasn't evaporated, after all. That surge of desire is still present. The feeling is more durable than she has expected, the sensation so physical and instinctive that it surprises her. It's painful, like being stabbed. The emotion almost unnerves her, so she takes a step back. No, it doesn't matter that he's unshaven, that his face is ashen after his long flight, that his khaki chinos and short-sleeved polo shirt are crumpled. He might stink of the whore's fragrance, too.

None of it matters. She doesn't understand why she feels the way she does. Is it the risk? Is it the forbidden nature of it that she finds so attractive?

'We have lots to talk about; we might as well start.'

'I agree.'

'But first, Richard, there's someone I want you to meet.'

'Someone I know?'

'You do know him; rather well, in fact.'

Fang strides over to the bedside phone, glad to break the spell. She lifts the receiver, listens for the dial tone, calls 9 and adds a room number. She turns and looks at Brodick, inspecting him, as she speaks into the receiver.

'He's here now. Why don't you come on up?'

The Khwamsukh – the term means happiness – isn't a hotel but an international youth hostel. It's located well away from the usual tourist haunts in the Thai capital, down a quiet *soi* in Ladprao with shop houses on either side and set back from the street. An inconspicuous five-storey building, a fountain out front dribbling water into a trough of tropical plants and tiny fish, glass doors opening to a small lobby and reception desk on the ground floor, a self-service kitchen and small dining area on the mezzanine, a tiny lift, 28 rooms on the remaining floors and a plunge pool with wooden decking and garden complete with palm trees on the roof. That's it.

It's inexpensive, clean and basic. The concrete structure is painted white throughout, with beige tiles on the floors. The only decorations are a mirror in every room, a carved wooden headboard above each bed and a red coverlet that looks like silk but is polyester. There's a television in each room, but there are no overseas channels. Sports teams and students visiting the capital from other parts of the country favour it. Foreigners turn up from time to time, young families on a budget, the independent variety of travellers who do their homework, are careful with their money and don't mind staying well away from the action.

Fang turns on the television and turns up the volume. There's a local football match on, and the sounds of the players and crowd will, she thinks, muffle any conversation.

Someone knocks three times. This time, Fang opens the door.

'My dear chap,' booms a male voice. 'Great to see you.'

The visitor is tall, somewhat obese. He's wearing baggy blue shorts, a short-sleeved Hawaiian shirt and flip-flops. He comes in and grabs Brodick's hand in both of his, pumping it up and down and grinning. Fang slips behind the new arrival and shuts the door behind him.

'I … I thought you were …'

For once, Brodick looks flabbergasted. Fang notices that he's suddenly even paler.

'You thought I was dead, old boy. Stone cold. Murdered. Then cremated. Sorry about that. The inconvenience, I mean. Must have caused some trouble back home, I shouldn't wonder, eh? Chaps running around Century House in a panic, I dare say, what? Had no alternative – isn't that so, princess?' He turns to Fang, as if seeking corroboration. Fang doesn't appreciate the 'princess', but this is not the time to object.

Roger Peacock winks, lowers his voice. 'We couldn't tell a soul. You must realise that.'

Fang gives an order. 'Sit down. Both of you.' She's worried Bo Deli might collapse.

Peacock shrugs, mutters something under his breath about 'she who must be obeyed'.

She takes the end of the double bed, sitting between them like a referee. The two men occupy the only two wooden chairs and face each other. Fang sees curiosity, suspicion and concern in Brodick's expression.

129

'What the hell's been going on, Roger? I thought you'd died in a Beijing hotel. We all thought so. Murdered, indeed – with a cock-and-bull statement put out by the foreign ministry about a heart attack after a skinful. The last bit must have been a message, because I know you don't drink.'

Brodick glances at Fang and away again. She doesn't respond. Peacock beams, opens his enormous hands. 'As you see, I'm alive and well and firing on all cylinders – and glad to be out of it, I can tell you. Thanks to our mutual friend here. She even ordered my cremation. I heard her on the phone, but she substituted some other poor soul's mortal remains.'

'Will someone tell me what the fuck is going on?'

Fang sees the anger and frustration in Bo Deli's expression.

'Fasten your seatbelt, chum.' Peacock rubs his hands together. 'We're going to tell you a story that will make your hair stand on end.'

Fang is pleased that her agent has used the pronoun *we*.

Fang lets Peacock do the talking. She's heard it all before and, in any case, the *waibin* doesn't have the full picture, only his own rather narrow view of things – and that's OK because Fang will fill in the gaps later, should it prove necessary. She's also interested in Bo Deli's reaction to what Peacock has to say.

When he's finished, Bo Deli rubs his face with his hands the way a cat uses its paws, as if he's washing – a gesture that suggests that he's not sure he believes any of it, or it's that he's tired out by all this jabbering.

'And your wife, Roger? Susan. Susan Ho Ping. Is she still at the Hong Kong flat or back in the UK?'

'Fang is looking after her.' He stares down at his feet.

'Is that right?' Brodick turns to her.

'She's safe, Richard. Out of reach of anyone who might do her harm.'

'Sorry, Roger, to ask this, but may I ask if she – Susan – believes that you've been killed?'

Fang answers. 'She does, yes. I had to tell her.'

'How is she taking it?'

This has become a conversation between Brodick and Fang.

'Ms Ho was upset. Angry.' Fang glances at Peacock.

'Was she aware that Roger was close to Yao Tie's wife?'

'Du Lan? Yes. Susan knew about the relationship. She was upset about that, too.'

It's the turn of Fang and Peacock to exchange looks. Brodick is almost done – for now.

'What of Du Lan? What's happened to her?'

Fang answered. 'She's in *Guoanbu* custody – you might call it house arrest. She's under investigation for treason and for Roger's murder.'

Peacock interrupts. 'But she won't go on trial, will she? You promised she wouldn't.'

Fang smiles. 'You care for her that much? I promised nothing, Roger. I don't make promises. No–one goes to trial in the People's Republic and is found innocent. You must have noticed – you've been in China long enough and often enough. If Du Lan were to be charged and brought before the judges, you know she'd be found guilty, and in her case, it would mean death. You know this. It's not a question of promises.'

'But you're not going to – it's for a murder that never happened.'

'The authorities don't know that. It all depends on the brother, Du Fu. Remember him – head of Shanghai Security Bureau? I told you before – if he co-operates, then Du Lan will have nothing to worry about.'

'And will he – co-operate?'

'What do *you* think he'll do, Roger? What would you do in his place? He doesn't have much choice now, does he? Not if he cares for his sister. And she doesn't have a choice, either, if she cares for her brother. As a matter of fact, she's already talking.'

It's odd, watching the two foreigners together. At one point, while Fang has moved away into the corridor to talk to Yang Bai, she glimpses Peacock lean forward in his chair and she hears him ask Bo Deli, his voice lowered yet still audible: 'Is she working for you, chief, or are you working for her?' It seems to be both question and taunt, or an example of the peculiar humour enjoyed by the English. Fang doesn't hear the reply because Yang is demanding her attention.

Fang resumes her seat on the bed and sets out the sequence of events.

When Du Fu submitted his agency's report on Peacock, identifying him as a British spy, it was, as a matter of routine, flagged for the attention of the *Guoanbu* and its 5th Bureau, because Fang's fief handles counter-intelligence. It crossed her desk, and she called Du Fu to ask if he planned to arrest the foreign spy. Du pointed out that Peacock wasn't in Shanghai but in Beijing, as far as he was aware, and he was keen not to alert Peacock for fear he'd flee the country.

Fang offered her department's help, but Du would have none of it. His sister, Du Lan, would take care of it, he insisted. She was on

132

her way to the capital. Fang asked him what the plan was, saying Peacock should be arrested as quickly as possible. She told him she would be happy to help pick up Peacock and any fellow conspirators in Beijing's foreign community. The 5th Bureau would do all it could to assist.

Du brushed the offer aside, saying it was all under control.

Fang acted. She sensed what Du Fu and his sister were up to. She contacted Peacock, who told her he'd spoken to the lady in question, who'd told him in no uncertain terms not to go anywhere but to wait for her. He told Fang he expected his visitor at his hotel late that night. It was obvious that he was referring to Du Lan, Yao Tie's wife.

The visitor would not arrive before 11.00 p.m., so Fang had time to prepare. She went to the Friendship Hotel and briefed Peacock. She contacted a senior police detective – a trusted *Guoanbu* 'friend' that she'd used before – to ensure no-one entered or left Peacock's room until she – Fang – arrived early the next morning.

Du Lan was stopped before she entered the hotel premises. Plainclothes *Guoanbu* operatives boarded her SUV and, escorted by another *Guoanbu* vehicle, drove to a safe house where Du Lan was told she had been placed under arrest. A hypodermic and what turned out to be the toxin were found in her possession. Fang turned up later and explained the true nature of the situation to her.

Peacock interrupted. 'How did she take it?'

'She was furious, as you might expect. It was quite a performance. She shouted and screamed, kicked and clawed my people, made many threats, denied everything, accused us of kidnapping, said we didn't know who we were messing with, that her husband was a powerful Party figure with important contacts, that he controlled Shanghai and much else besides. We gave her

133

nothing to eat or drink that night and it was freezing. She asked for a blanket. We refused. She wanted to use the toilet. My officers refused that, as well.'

Peacock shook his head. 'That's rather mean.'

'When she understood the seriousness of her position and realised the game was up for both her and her husband, her tune changed. Du Lan asked to speak to her brother, who she said was head of the Shanghai Public Security Bureau. This, too, was refused. She admitted she had planned to kill Mr Peacock after her brother informed her that the Englishman had been exposed as a spy – to protect herself, her brother and her husband, along with the family's wealth. Du Lan denied they had anything to do with it. She claimed it was all her own doing.'

Brodick had a question. 'What did you get from her?'

'Everything. She gave it all up.'

'In return for what?'

The question from Bo Deli surprises Fang. It's obvious. He knows how this works. Isn't it the same everywhere?

'Her life.'

'That's it?'

What does he expect?

Bo Deli replies: 'Her money, her foreign bank accounts, the property she bought with Roger's help?'

Fang's smile is chilly. She doesn't need to spell it out.

Bo Deli presses on. 'And what does she say in return for her life?'

'She has given us the names and the timing.'

'That seems pretty straightforward, then. All you have to do is turn this over to your chief and let him decide. That's what he's there for.'

134

'If only it were that simple, Richard. My boss, Xie Rong, is on the list. He's one of the Eight. I can't trust anyone in the Party.'

No-one speaks. Both Peacock and Brodick get it. Fang can almost see the implications sink in, the cogs turning as Bo Deli wrestles with it. Yes, they're thinking to themselves, there's going to be an attempted coup, the insurgents backed by a large section of the PLA and the People's Armed Police.

If they succeed, Deng will fall – and with him, his reforms.

Even if he rides this out, the Party will split. There might well be unrest, even fighting. The global financial system will take a hit. The Party will be damaged – unless it takes effective action to stop the conspiracy in its tracks.

Fang watches them; do these Westerners want this to happen? And if they don't, are they willing to risk their own lives? It's not their struggle, they're foreigners after all, they're not even Party supporters. Why should these two spies care what happens to mainland China and the Chinese Communist Party? What will their paymasters in London order them to do? Perhaps such an upheaval in the Party could damage, or slow, the PRC's advance to number one position in the global economy. The PRC accounted for 2 per cent of the world GDP in 1980, it's already at 20 per cent in '92 and rising fast. This political turmoil could set the country's growth back decades.

Isn't that what the counter-revolutionaries in Washington and London would want?

The room is so quiet Fang can hear own breathing. Aside from the hum of the central air conditioning, the only sounds are from outside – the cars on the main street, Thai voices and laughter in the alley below, the shouts of children happy to be on their way home from school and kicking a football about. How wonderful it must be to lead a simple life of total ignorance. How innocent. What bliss.

16

What I'd learned would have to be boiled down to bare essentials with minimal commentary, and I was wondering how the Firm was going to react – if they'd react at all.

There wasn't much time. I hurried to my room one floor below, using the stairs and meeting no-one on the way. The three of us had agreed to reconvene by the rooftop pool at sunset, provided Yang Bai gave the all-clear and we'd be alone for the next session. I had an hour to write it all up and send my reports.

First things first. I laid out my gear across the double bed. Technology had moved on, and this time there would be no TITHE transceiver, the type I'd used in Beirut back in '84 when I first met Fang. It was far too bulky to be carried through airports. This time I was trying out something new – new to me, anyway – a satellite telex. It lacked the speed of TITHE's high-speed burst transmissions, but it had other advantages. It came in two soft, black faux leather cases containing a small keyboard and screen, a clip-on encryption unit and a hard antenna which could be set up on a wall or window to capture the satellite signal. The whole thing was lightweight. All I had to do was type out my report, press *encrypt* and once the satellite signal had been locked onto, press *send*. Then wait half a minute for the 'sent' signal and a little later, a 'received' acknowledgement.

It was state-of-the-art for 1991 and the entire apparatus – in the two saddlebag-style pouches – could fit in a standard briefcase or Bergen.

Satellite telephones were available, of course, and they could send and receive voice and data, but the apparatus was very large and visible; it would need at least three people to load it onto a pickup or Land Rover Defender. I'd ruled out such a device as not being portable. The parabolic antenna, once deployed and unfolded, stood out a mile and would only invite curiosity.

First, I tested the satellite signal from the windowsill. It was strong.

My first message was the shortest.

SECRET. UK EYES ONLY. IMMEDIATE.

DRAGON DEBRIEF BEGUN

010484–54–658UK

Off it went and a minute later I had the precious acknowledgement.

The second would raise an eyebrow, but would be nothing compared to the surprise of the next serials.

SECRET. UK EYES ONLY/FLASH.

GLUTTON ALIVE AND WELL.

1. GLUTTON is alive and well and was interviewed in the presence

of DRAGON, who prevented the former's attempted murder and arranged the asset's exfiltration and relocation to Thailand.

2. PRC authorities advised GLUTTON deceased following submission by DRAGON of (fake) DNA & blood sample and report of GLUTTON's murder and cremation. DRAGON submitted a secret report to *GUOANBU* chief XIE RONG to this effect.

3. GLUTTON murder was planned/attempted by DU LAN, GLUTTON'S lover and wife of YAO TIE, Shanghai Party Secretary, with the help of her brother, DU FU, head of Shanghai Security Bureau (*GONGANBU*). Also, according to DRAGON, DU FU provided his sister with shellfish toxin for the assassination.

4. The decision to kill GLUTTON taken by DU LAN & DU FU after Public Security Ministry (*GONGANBU*) investigation concluded GLUTTON was a UK intel operative. They advised YAO of this and the plan to murder GLUTTON. They chose assassination in preference to arrest because GLUTTON knew too much about YAO's illegal finances.

5. DRAGON currently holds DU LAN in custody on the mainland. Precise *GUOANBU* location not yet known.

6. DRAGON reports that during interrogation, DU LAN identified her husband YAO TIE as a key figure in plot to unseat DENG XIAOPING at forthcoming PARTY CONGRESS following the CHINESE NEW YEAR. YAO financed the plot, buying support and/or silence of key cadres with funds gained through 'flipping'

land sales on HAINAN ISLAND and illegal tax evasion i.e. by exporting profits and re-importing them by classifying the imported money as foreign investments hence free of PRC tax.

7. DRAGON reports DU FU willing to cooperate to save sister's life by providing details of the planned coup involving PLA and PAP formations.

8. DRAGON reports current PLA/PAP manoeuvres, reserve unit mobilisation and a higher alert status of two southern military districts are part of preparations for DENG ouster. Ref. report of interview with MAJOR MA of NSB.

9. DRAGON says coup leaders known as THE EIGHT ELDERS are opposed to Deng reforms, both political and economic. DRAGON says they aim to curtail international contacts and speed 'unification' of the mainland and Hong Kong as well as TAIWAN/REPUBLIC OF CHINA (ROC), if necessary by force, along with greater domestic repression, incl. greater restrictions on free speech/media.

COMMENT:

Would appreciate earliest advice on whether to stand aside or assist DRAGON in attempting to disrupt alleged plot.

010484–54–658UK

It was nearly sunset. Two more signals to go.

SECRET. UK EYES ONLY. IMMEDIATE.

GLUTTON'S PARTNER HELD INCOMMUNICADO/IN PROTECTIVE CUSTODY.

DRAGON'S *GUOANBU* PERSONNEL HOLD GLUTTON'S WIFE SUSAN HO PING IN PROTECTIVE CUSTODY AFTER LATTER'S HKG HOME RAIDED BY SUSPECTED SHANGHAI-BASED *GONGANBU* PERSONNEL.

LATTER WERE ALLEGEDLY TRYING TO STEAL FINANCIAL RECORDS OBTAINED BY GLUTTON PERTAINING TO YAO TIE'S PAYMENTS TO ALLEGED COUP PLOTTERS.

ONE HKG POLICE OFFICER SUSTAINED FLESH WOUND IN BRIEF EXCHANGE OF FIRE. RAIDERS BELIEVED TO HAVE RETURNED TO MAINLAND. NO ARRESTS REPORTED IN HKG.

SOURCES: DRAGON AND MAJOR MA (NSB).

010484–54–658UK

And the last one for today – and the most important. It would be enough to keep Century House occupied for some time, and while I thought I'd mastered the intricacies of Chinese family and given names, these did give me a headache. It certainly wasn't bed-time reading. I had recited names and appointments over and over again in an effort to remember them:

141

EIGHT 'ELDERS' OR PARTY 'PRINCES' NAMED IN PLOT
TO OUST DENG:

SOURCES: DRAGON/GLUTTON

1. YAO TIE. Believed born 1924. The youngest and wealthiest of the
'Party Princes'. Currently Shanghai Party Secretary, former Chengdu
mayor. Former leader of one of the most rabid groups of Red Guards
during the Cultural Revolution. Flamboyant, of weak character, enjoys
a reputation for displays of wealth, such as a penchant for wearing
BRIONI suits and high-end Swiss watches, but defers to his wife DU
LAN in decision-making. (See appendix with photograph of YAO
sporting a PATEK PHILIPPE wristwatch in public, valued at approx.
50k USD new). DU LAN has reportedly set her sights on being First
Lady and is viewed as the driving force behind YAO's ambition to
supplant DENG. YAO has made millions of US dollars by exporting
and then re-importing profits from land deals as foreign investments
through accounts and banks established with GLUTTON's help,
thereby evading PRC mainland tax. Corruption is a capital crime.
GLUTTON has obtained YAO's bank details showing offshore/
mainland transfers and real estate profits from HAINAN property
purchases and sales. Clandestine payments to senior cadres reported
having begun on 6 July 1990.

2. WU XIAN. Believed born 1912. Deputy Chairman of the
CENTRAL MILITARY COMMISSION, hence one of the
most influential senior Party cadres after DENG. A hardliner,

he supported the TIANANMEN crackdown, only to state it did not go far enough. A keen advocate of military intervention over the TAIWAN/ROC question. According to figures obtained by GLUTTON, WU has received in total 1.2 million USD or equivalent in payments and gifts to members of the WU family, from cars to university scholarships, from YAO-associated accounts. Eleven money transfers were recorded, varying in amount and frequency.

3. JIANG YUNJI. General commanding PLA THIRD ARMY and hence of all land-based strategic nuclear missiles. Thought to have been born in QINCHENG circa 1915. No details known of personal life. Service in the civil war and war against Japan, followed by a series of senior military posts that placed him close to MAO. Thought to be associated with WU XIAN and a recipient of YAO funds amounting to 760k USD from offshore accounts linked to YAO. There have been 33 payments since July. Has suffered from intermittent ill-health during the past decade but details not known.

4. GU YUDONG. Born 1916. PLA general and commander of the GENERAL POLITICAL LIAISON DEPARTMENT (*ZONGZHENG LIANLUOBO*), a separate and rival military intelligence organisation to PLA2 (the latter is the 2nd Department of the army general staff or *ER BU*). Party hardliner on HONG KONG, MACAO, TAIWAN (ROC) unification. Served in Party intelligence service known as the CCP CENTRAL INVESTIGATION DEPARTMENT (*ZHONGYANG DIAOCHABU*) and associated with the notorious sadist and 'Party hangman' KANG SHENG as one of his loyal subordinates in the 1940s. DRAGON believes GU has a large, extended family living in CHANGCHUN. Recipient of

420k USD in funds from YAO accounts, most from HONG KONG banks. Seventeen payments in all.

5. XIE RONG. Current minister heading *GUOANBU* and DRAGON's immediate superior. Born SHANDONG 1921. Active hardliner during Cultural Revolution and an associate of YAO in the 1960s–1980s. Current position regarded as political rather than professional as XIE has little prior experience as an intelligence officer. Most of his positions have been related to Party organisation. A conservative critic of DENG. Six payments from YAO-linked accounts totalling 142k USD over 5 months.

6. LUO MAI. Born circa 1920 in SHENYANG. Current head of the UNITED FRONT WORK DEPARTMENT OR UFWD (*ZHONGGONG ZHONGYANG TONGYI ZHANXIAN GONGZUO BU*), an organisation that aims to influence international opinion and in particular targeting pro-Taiwanese Chinese (*HUAQIAOH*) to persuade them to change sides and back Beijing. Crediting with having landed some big fish in the past. LUO MAI may be a nom de guerre – but his organisation has, according to GLUTTON's files, received in excess of 2.3 million USD or equivalent from YAO-related accounts recorded as 37 'voluntary donations' from overseas Chinese supporters but all traced to YAO-related offshore accounts and laundered in some cases though brass plate companies registered in Panama, the British Virgin Islands and the US state of Delaware.

7. LING QIWEI. Until recently head of the INTERNATIONAL LIAISON DEPARTMENT OF THE COMMUNIST PARTY or ILD (*ZHONGLIANBU*), responsible for liaison with overseas

communist parties and national liberation movements. Now retired, he is still regarded as influential in senior Party circles and wields considerable influence as an adviser to top cadres. Personal views not known, but a recipient of 40 'donations' amounting to over 1.8 million USD from YAO-related offshore accounts.

8. ZHOU LIJUN. LIEUTENANT-GENERAL. Born circa 1919. Assistant to the DEPUTY CENTRAL MILITARY COMMISSION. Officer commanding Southeast Military District. Specialist in amphibious warfare. Notable within his bailiwick are two ARMY GROUPS, the 41ST and 42ND headquartered in GUANGZHOU, and which includes several 'rapid reaction' formations. Associate of JIANG YUNJI, PLA 3rd ARMY commander. Active service in war against JAPAN, civil war. Backed armed military intervention to crush dissent in 1989. Supported DENG against 'moderates' but critical of the leadership for failing to take quicker, tougher action to quell unrest. Received nine payments totalling 450k USD from YAO-associated offshore accounts since November 1991.

COMMENT: The 'Eight Elders' identified by GLUTTON and DRAGON have an obvious intelligence, security and military profile. They have received 7.872 million USD in illegal funds from YAO-linked offshore accounts and DRAGON is confident some of this will be distributed and used to buy the loyalty and/or silence of cadres.

T010484–54–658UK

The stakes were big enough for DRAGON to risk all. London didn't matter, not anymore. The world's greatest empire was long gone.

What did matter to Beijing – and Fang – was Washington. Only Washington had the power, the status, the allies, the bases and the military clout to do anything about this. Washington had to be Fang's target. The US 7th Fleet was one thing. Our sole Royal Navy frigate parked off Hong Kong island was, well, a sad joke – along with the garrison, a single battalion of Gurkhas protecting UK installations on Hong Kong territory.

It also reminded me of our history lectures at Fort Monckton during the new officers' training course in '83. They drummed it into us newbies that the Secret Intelligence Service was, above all else, and in contrast to Langley, a human intelligence or HUMINT agency. We gathered intelligence from people. Further, it was shaped by the demands and requests from other Whitehall departments. We might put up ideas and suggest projects, but SIS was a creature of others' wishes, hence the role of Requirements, which funnelled these requests to the Service, and Production, which managed the results and channelled them to our 'customers'.

What was needed above all was patience, resources to carry out the long term tasks and focused political direction – all three of which were lacking in 1990s Britain. We didn't rush off to do whatever we liked in the name of Queen and Country – or the FTSE 100.

This conspiracy to oust Deng appeared genuine, but it could be the kind of intelligence the Firm's usual customers in Whitehall would ignore. On countless occasions, Century House's customers had complained they weren't getting enough of this or that – not enough on merchant shipping passing through the Baltic, perhaps, or the types of aircraft parked on Czech airfields. Whatever it was, we'd haul out copies of the stuff we'd provided only to show how many times our Whitehall consumers – whether they be the Department of

Trade or the Ministry of Defence – had ignored the reports because they'd failed to understand what they represented. The complaint would then become 'why haven't you given us an intelligence assessment, in that case?'

It was never the job of SIS to analyse or assess intelligence. We were there to present facts we'd gathered, often at great risk, from our secret sources. If we allowed ourselves to be pushed into the business of interpreting intelligence, we'd become little more than a political think-tank, providing customers with what they wanted to believe, as opposed to what they needed to know – even if they didn't have the smarts to understand the latter.

I could imagine some over-qualified chinless wonder on the China desk at the Foreign Office reading my secret report on the Eight Elders, shrugging and saying to himself or herself that there was nothing the UK could do about it, and then shredding it and adding printouts of the electronic messages to that day's burn bag.

It was all too likely. The one hope was that C would read it and understand its importance at once and make a few calls – one being to the Permanent Under Secretary at the FO to draw his attention to it, another a call to Number 10 and the PM's Permanent Secretary to flag it, and maybe to his opposite numbers at Langley and the NSA.

It was time to head up to the roof, where we planned to gather for further conversation, this time with something to eat and a few beers.

But now I had another thought.

I had asked for advice – orders – on whether we should attempt to foil the plot or stand aside.

Back in the 1920s, SIS under its first C, Mansfield Cumming, had been deluged with fake intelligence from groups of Russian emigrés in European capitals – many of them former intelligence and military officers of an anti-communist bent – penetrated and indeed in one or two cases, started, orchestrated and run by the Soviet OGPU, the Joint State Political Directorate, the Cheka's successor and forerunner of the NKVD and KGB. The Trust was the most notorious emigré organisation, set up by the OGPU to destroy Russian opposition. Some of the material SIS received was forged, some of it sold to several other European agencies. One such agent worked for the Germans, the French, and the Poles. It had been quite a profitable industry for both forgers and fake agents. For a while SIS had been deceived, if only partially.

It was also the case that at a very early stage of the Firm's development, it had found itself torn between demands for political operations and the more traditional role of intelligence gathering. This too could be traced back to the 1920s and the brave and spirited actions of 29-year-old Lieutenant Augustus Agar, later awarded a VC and DSO for employing flat-bottomed motor torpedo boats based at the Terijoki Yacht Club on the Gulf of Finland to sink Russian warships, including two Soviet battleships and a heavy cruiser – even though we weren't at war with Russia. The trouble with these 'special operations' was that they made the infiltration and exfiltration of SIS agents along the Baltic coast – close to the Soviet base at Kronstad, whose defences, including minefields, the enterprising Agar had repeatedly penetrated – all but impossible. One such SIS agent, the successful and gifted undercover operator Paul Dukes, later knighted for his exceptional service, could not escape by boat because the Soviets were on high alert after Agar's explosive activities, and had had to make his way out of the Soviet Union and back to the UK via Latvia.

Bangs in the night and spying did not sit well together, as SIS and its sister organisation, the Special Operations Executive, were to discover to their cost in World War Two.

Spies needed quiet to do their work. Normality was their best cover.

And a third thought occurred to me as I dismantled and concealed my telex gear, placed some key components in the room safe, locked my room door and headed along the corridor and up the stairs to the roof. The reports I had transmitted to London might indeed prompt a 'special operation', the nature of which might be anticipated by Fang and her masters in Beijing – and one they'd use as a provocation.

Wait a moment. Leaving my gear in a room that might be searched was pretty stupid. It would be better to hide it in plain sight. I took it down to the lobby and asked the receptionist if they had a safe or at least a secure cupboard to lock away my cash and passport, then added my apparatus – it was less likely to attract the attention of searchers interested in me and my possessions.

Maybe that's what Fang wanted – SIS to launch an operation that would be compromised, revealing an imperialist provocation, and would provide the ChiComs with justification for a crackdown, then a PLA assault on Hong Kong, Taiwan, or both.

Shit.

I felt sick. I stopped and leaned against the wall, resting and listening for any footsteps, doors opening and closing, voices, at the same time trying to make sense of the chaos in my head yet somehow remain objective.

All was quiet – except in my head.

Objective – how could I be? I was sleeping with the enemy – when I got the chance – and working for the enemy.

Did I see things straight – or had Fang reduced me to a blind, cunt-struck fool?

Was I strolling into a *Guoanbu* ambush?

No, I was seeing phantoms. Major Ma had corroborated much of it – if he *was* Major Ma, which I doubted. And if Ma was an imposter concocted by Fang, it was nevertheless an impersonation that suited my purposes. The old men on Fang's list of plotters were real enough. I recognised some faces and most of the names. They existed.

There was one thing lacking from my report on the Eight Elders, and that was the name of whomever it was the conspirators planned to put in Deng's place.

17

What's the matter? Bo Deli doesn't look at all well as he trudges up the last steps and emerges onto the roof.

He looks haggard, worn out.

Fang doesn't want to stare – she glances at him and looks away. The eyes give away his state of mind, she tells herself, and his are inflamed, with dark, puffy smudges below. It's sheer fatigue and also worry at being tagged by strangers in a foreign county, and now surrounded – protected – by her people. No, it can't be easy. She reckons his edginess is natural enough; it must be the effects of jet lag and the need for a night's rest.

A large passenger plane floats past in the darkening sky some way to the north, lights blinking, moving west to east and preparing to land. The sky is turning a vivid gold and pink in the west – glorious with the setting sun and so much pollution.

Fang has a dozen Chang bottled beers on ice and she watches her helpers, led by Yang, drag the rough wooden tables together and set out the takeaways and plastic cutlery. The squad melts away, leaving Fang, Peacock and Bo Deli alone – but a squawk from Yang's walkie-talkie tells Fang that she is still there, invisible, standing well back in the stairwell in case Fang needs her.

In the small pool, Peacock floats on his back, his belly uppermost, his sunburned face Buddha-like in its impassivity, staring up at the darkening sky. When Brodick appears and walks around the decking, Peacock stands upright in the water, runs a hand across his head and makes for the poolside, pulling himself up and puffing with the effort. His face looks brick red from exposure to the sun.

'Good to see you, old man.'

Bo Deli doesn't respond. He slips off his jacket – Fang sees he's wearing a very crumpled and off-white tropical suit. Smart, but then again, he looks as if he's slept in it.

Fang has spent enough time in Peacock's company to know she doesn't like the agent Brodick has handed over, making her, in effect, Bo Deli's head agent. Not that a case officer has to like an agent, but it helps. She finds him loud, and his efforts to build a wall of extrovert tomfoolery both exhausting and unconvincing. She doesn't trust him, though she has to give him credit for his financial work on the Eight Elders. He took good care, too, to leave papers in the Hong Kong safe for the raiders to find. They're supposed to think they have all the data, and that will suffice. Peacock copied everything onto two sets of floppy discs, one set now in Fang's possession, the other kept for Bo Deli.

All things considered, a peculiar dual loyalty has developed.

She wonders how Peacock feels about it.

Who does he think runs the show now – Brodick or Fang?

The issue comes up a few minutes later as Fang instructs Yang to organise her squad into two shifts, working 4 hours on, 4 off, and dividing them up between hostel and safe house. The latter is where they will rest when off-duty. While she's conversing with Yang in a low undertone, Brodick and Peacock have taken up positions facing each other, sat on sun loungers on the far side of the pool, under the branches of a magnolia tree in a large white planter, their heads close together. The magnolia looks forlorn, bereft of flowers and with few leaves. No-one bothers to water it and the rising heat can't help much.

'So tell me,' she hears Peacock ask in a low voice, his tone mocking, 'I have to ask you again. I'm not joking. Which of you is the boss? Are you working for her, Richard, or is she working for you?'

Brodick, who's facing away from the pool and Fang, replies at once, but Fang can't make out what he says. She thinks – though she's unsure – that this is not something he wants to talk about now, in this place. The word 'inappropriate' comes up. Peacock isn't offended or deterred, though, and he speaks again and Fang overhears him say that not everything is on the discs. There's something else, and he'll give Brodick a note about it.

Once again Brodick mutters something, but more insistent – something along the lines of 'will you shut the fuck up'.

Bo Deli stands up, irritated.

Of course, the two Westerners will stick together. She wonders if she should ask Bai to organise a room search. Is Peacock hiding something from her? If so, Fang wants to know what it is. Peacock's in no position to play mind games. Will Bo Deli share whatever it is? He should. Fang doesn't feel entirely in control, and it bothers her.

They set the food out. Room service – which relies on a local eatery across the road – doesn't offer much choice. But it'll have to suffice. The beers are disappearing fast, judging by the cluster of empties, and thanks to Peacock's prodigious thirst.

Yang nods at Fang, who acknowledges the gesture – two members of the squad will be on duty, one outside hotel reception, the other in the street, watching comings and goings from the driver's seat of one of the *Guoanbu* taxis. Darkness is upon them, and the mosquitoes are out in force, and they seem to target Peacock's scalp. The Englishman defends himself by slapping on a pungent mosquito repellent he bought earlier at one of the Seven Eleven convenience stores.

They eat, with no attempt on anyone's part to make conversation. Fang notes that Peacock jabs at his rice with a fork. He's playing with his food and doesn't seem interested at all in eating, while Brodick, sitting on his own now, a paper plate in front of him, is wolfing down his pad Thai with chopsticks. He hasn't finished his first beer to Peacock's three. Fang contents herself with Lipton's iced tea – she tells herself she needs to stay alert. Someone has to, after all.

As the daylight seeps away, the lights on the roof go on.

There are no other guests up there. They have the place to themselves.

Brodick collects the empty bottles and Fang piles up the used food containers and utensils when Yang Bai reappears. She stands waiting for Fang to go to her before speaking in Mandarin. She doesn't want the foreigners to hear.

'Surveillance.'

'Where?'

'Pickup parked in the street, a red Toyota Hilux. Driver and two passengers on board – one passenger got out and came into the lobby, a Thai national by the look of him, and he asked about room availability. He's settled himself in an armchair with a view of the front door and lift, his back to the stairs, reading tourist brochures. The stranger told reception in Thai that he was waiting for his wife. He doesn't seem to have booked a room and didn't answer when the receptionist asked if he was planning on staying.'

'You checked the vehicle registration?'

'It checks out. It's one of theirs and is on the list.'

Through an asset in the Royal Thai Police – a badly paid force and one notoriously corrupt, partly because of the lousy wages – the *Guoanbu* have got hold of a list of all registration numbers of civilian vehicles – non-diplomatic plates – assigned to the CIA station in Bangkok, along with those of the Agency's sub-station in the northern city of Chiang Mai.

'Have you swept the area?'

'As we speak.'

'There have to be more of them.'

'I think so, yes. Two more, at the very least.'

'We follow the plan.'

Fang looks and sounds calm, but she isn't. This is an emergency, and although it's one she expected and planned for, it's still an unwelcome intrusion when she needs it least. Peacock is travelling under his own name and with his UK passport and has entered Thailand on a standard 30-day tourist visa obtained on arrival. There is no reason that Fang can see why he would appear on the Agency's radar. If Peacock should make any sudden moves – an unexpected departure from the hotel, for example – he will only draw attention to himself. So Peacock will play the innocent, and afterwards remain in the hotel with strict instructions – though Fang doubts whether Peacock will ever obey any instruction he doesn't like – to keep to his room or the pool area and avoid contact with any third party.

One of Yang's squad will have to forget about getting any sleep tonight and remain on duty in the hostel's vicinity to monitor Peacock and any interest shown in him by the CIA assets, if that's what they are.

Brodick and Fang, along with the rest of her people, will try to get out unobserved and make their way to the safe house.

155

If that was all there was to it, Fang wouldn't be worried. But she's uneasy. Somehow the Americans seem to know about Brodick – and herself – placing them not just in Thailand, but at this precise location. But how has this happened? Have they been tipped off? Is there a leak?

If Langley knows where she is and uses local, i.e. Thai, assets to keep tabs on her and Brodick, it must mean that eventually Thailand's National Intelligence Agency (NIA) will know, too. The NIA handles the country's security and counter-intelligence. It works with the Americans. There'll be eyes on them wherever they go.

Although she hasn't wanted to admit it to herself, she's been looking forward to being alone with Bo Deli. She has missed him, wanted him, despite her own better judgement – whatever the reason and the weakness it implies in her character and ideological integrity. It's the forbidden nature of it that appeals.

Right now, any chance of getting together in private seems non-existent, but perhaps that's a good thing.

Yang's hand-held radio clicks twice.

'There's a police checkpoint now on the main road, around the corner some 10 metres from the turn. Unofficial. Three uniformed Thai cops waving down cars and shaking down the drivers for cash. Usual thing.'

'It's too much of a coincidence.'

'Agreed.'

'Anything further up the other end of the *soi*?'

'Nothing so far, chief.'

'We must move. Now.'

Simple plans are almost always best.

The first *Guoanbu* taxi parked in the *soi* starts up, switches on its headlights, and moves forward and then turns, reverses, the driver deliberate in taking his time, blocking the street and ensuring the pickup can't move forward or up to the hostel. The second taxi appears from the opposite direction, stops right outside the hostel and the driver gets out, saunters into the lobby and up to the reception desk and asks for a Mister Peacock. He ignores the watcher slumped in the armchair. The receptionist calls Peacock's room. Peacock answers that he'll be downstairs in a minute or two.

The driver of the pickup sticks his head out of the driver's window and shouts at the first taxi driver, telling him in Thai to move, to get out of the way. The latter ignores him. As Peacock appears, walks out with the driver and gets into the back seat of the second taxi, Fang and Brodick slip down the stairs to the mezzanine floor. At the rear of the little self–catering kitchenette is a second, narrow flight of service steps leading down to the rear of the car port. They hurry down, but do so quietly.

At the bottom there's a narrow exit – a cement footpath behind the hostel and shadowed in darkness under the broad leaves of banana plants like ragged battle pennants blocking out the ambient light of moon and stars – that takes them to the main road, and they emerge beyond the informal police checkpoint. The cops don't see them because they are too busy helping themselves; they have stopped two motorists and have their hands inside the drivers' windows – as is the local custom – so that they can't be spotted by witnesses or caught on video taking the bribes of 10-, 20- or 100-baht notes in the sodium glare of the street lights.

Yang is up on the hostel roof, watching the proceedings.

Peacock is driven off. He's not followed, or doesn't seem to be. At the end of the *soi*, the driver turns right, away from the checkpoint. He will take Peacock to the nearest mall where – if he is tagged – he'll lead his pursuers a dance on foot among the shops for a few minutes before buying something – anything – then returning to the waiting taxi to be driven back to the hostel. The object is to divide any watchers and expose them.

Their second *Guoanbu* taxi – approaching from the opposite direction and facing the police – picks up Fang and Brodick, turns full circle in the street and carries them to the safe house.

When the Toyota pickup tries to follow, it's too late. The trail has gone cold. Both taxis seem to have vanished, and the reason is simple – the safe house is only a few blocks away from the hostel, just off *soi* 33, and one of the taxis is already parked inside the property's gates.

The second drops Peacock off at the hostel without incident.

Fang thinks her ploy has worked, but there's still the nagging sense that they haven't accounted for the full complement of Langley's local watchers. There should have been at least five of them in their team.

Yang Bai reports she is now on foot and headed to the safe house.

Crickets saw away in the trees in their thousands, bullfrogs croak in the shrubbery and unseen creatures scratch and scrabble over the tiled roof – an entire world is awake with the onset of night. The latter are squirrels, tree rats or lizards – or all three – in pursuit of one another, along with geckos running about on the interior ceilings and walls and a variety of snakes in the trees.

Fang doesn't care for snakes. Yang has told her she spotted a python climbing one of the fruit trees out back – an adolescent and nearly grown, she said. At least it wasn't a cobra.

By standing outside on the first-floor balcony, shadowed from the moonlight by the roof's overhang, Fang can see down the length of the residential street. All is quiet. There's no-one out there on foot now that Bai has arrived, and no cars are moving. The houses are shuttered and few lights show. It's a quiet neighbourhood and there are none of the shophouses that stay open late.

There's no sign of any watchers.

Peacock went straight up to his hotel room and a little later, his light went off. Fang is relieved; she thinks he's the kind of foreigner to grab any opportunity, once off the leash, to head for the newest bar and strike up conversation with strangers, especially bar girls.

Langley's Thai watcher, lingering in reception, had little alternative but to leave his post once the reception desk shut, as the receptionist put off the lights and then withdrew to the hostel office, locking the internal door behind her to catch a couple of hours' sleep on a couch before returning to her text books.

The last thing Fang hears on her radio is that the red Hilux has not returned to its position outside the hostel.

Thailand is second only to the United States in the number of pickups bought each year; locally-assembled Japanese models are the most popular. Random thoughts like these pursue one another through her mind, rather like the nocturnal animals of the gardens scampering overhead and rustling in the branches of the green mango trees around the house. An unidentified and unseen bird utters a repetitive shriek of one note every few seconds and it seems very close. Downstairs, Yang's team talk quietly, and Fang has an urge to tell them off, to order them to sleep, but reminds herself that she's delegated responsibility to Yang, the squad leader. She must stop interfering.

And Bo Deli? Does he believe Peacock's intelligence? Does he also believe the names of the Eight Elders along with the financial details obtained from his association with Yao Tie? Does Bo Deli buy the notion of an imminent coup attempt from within the Party? Will Century House accept whatever Bo Deli has signalled to London? How long will it take for London to share its intelligence with Washington?

There isn't much time left. Days.

Fang knows she lacks the information to determine, or even guess, how the British will react. It's always possible they'll do nothing, and order Bo Deli to sit back and observe.

His people at Century House are intelligence collectors, not geared up for special operations like the American CIA. Don't the foreigners understand the size and ferocity of the storm that's approaching at speed? Don't they see the dangers for Hong Kong and Taiwan – even if they don't especially care what happens to the mainland Chinese?

It's not the British she's counting on, though. London doesn't matter. It's the messenger. She's hoping the ineffectual British will inform their US masters – and soon. Washington will give the British a nudge and Bo Deli will receive his marching orders. Or so she hopes.

Main thing now, she tells herself, is to get Peacock and his wife Susan Ho Ping on flights back to the UK. The *Gonganbu* should by now have stopped looking for her in Hong Kong and she can go ashore. With Du Lan and Du Fu singing away, Fang has given up her plan to use Ho Ping as bait to lure Yao, his wife, and her brother out into the open.

Fang leans forward, elbows on the iron railing, but almost nods off, so she straightens up and walks back and forth along the balcony's entire length to stay awake. The temperature has dropped to what Fang estimates to be a tolerable 28 degrees Celsius, but the mosquitoes are still attacking – clouds of them.

Bo Deli hasn't put on the air-conditioning. He's helped himself to the master bedroom, its king-size bed and en suite. Selfish bastard. Does he think he outranks her? She also notes that he hasn't waited for her but has gone straight to sleep, not that she blames him. He needs it. She knows he's asleep because now and then, as she slips back and forth along the balcony, from the French doors of the master bedroom she hears a grunt, a murmur or a brief burst of snoring through the glass.

Fang would have loved to have been able to talk about the dilemma she faces, and what she intends to do about it – but it will have to wait until morning.

She whispers his name out loud. *Richard.*

Yang's people have the ground floor and a shower room to themselves. Fang will take one of the smaller bedrooms on the first floor. She'll use the family bathroom to clean up.

Fang knows she can't count on Bo Deli's help. Maybe his, but not that of his employers. What could they do anyway, even if they had the resolve? She might have to do what needs to be done alone and the chances of getting away with it – alive – and without help are not good.

Not good at all.

Do you dream of me, Richard, the way I dream of you?

18

Someone woke me at 0410. Dragged me awake would be more accurate – it was as if that someone hauled me out of a deep subterranean cavern and I didn't like it at all. I wanted to sink back into the comfort of sleep, but Fang wasn't having it.

She pulled away my sheet, shook me by the shoulder.

'The police are coming.'

Police? What police? Where was I? I looked about me, resentful at being woken, remembering the bedroom, the safe house. I pushed myself up, swung my legs over the side of the bed, touched the fake oak flooring with the soles of my feet, still dazed as if drugged or hung over.

'Move, Richard. They've been to the hostel, searched your room and mine, woken up the receptionist and questioned her.'

I was wide awake now – well, sort of.

'Who have?'

Fang was being patient, all things considered. 'Police, Richard. Thai police. Several uniforms, two in plain clothes – maybe police, maybe not. Maybe they're your CIA friends.'

Not mine, love. Downstairs, someone was dragging open the front gates and first one of the taxis, then the second, started up and I heard them move out onto the street.

'Did they search the office and the storeroom?'

'Our rooms – yours and mine. They checked the registration book and asked where we were. They're on their way here, according to one of Yang Bai's people. They seem to know we're here. Have you got something locked away back in the office?'

I ignored the question. 'And Peacock?'

I was sufficiently awake to scramble into my clothes. Fast.

I'd have liked a cold shower.

'Peacock's in his room. Seems they weren't interested in him. They checked his passport and visa at reception, that's all. They didn't speak to him, if that's what worries you.'

That, at least, was good news.

'Where are we going?'

She avoided answering. 'They'll likely stop our taxis, ask the drivers for their papers and demand cash, too. It should buy us a little more time. Now hurry.'

The police in Thailand were armed as a matter of course; it was quite a macho gun culture, but they had to buy their own, with the help of loans because the price was sometimes a fortnight's wages. Some acquired inexpensive Spanish-made .38 revolvers, others preferred fashionable 9mm SiG Sauers from Austria or Glock semi-automatics. I'd even seen a massive .357 on one officer's belt. They loved big American guns. They'd watched *Dirty Harry* too often, obviously.

As for ripping off motorists, it was standard practice. Taxis were regarded as fair game. In fact, police stations were profit centres, and the big pay-offs went to senior officers. Dirty money trickled up, not down. A colonel, for example, lucky enough to be posted near one of Thailand's borders, could be expected to be a dollar millionaire in 5 years. If he was a general and willing to take kick-backs from both prostitution and the drug gangs, he'd be a multi-millionaire in half that time. It was the way things were.

At the end of the cul-de-sac was a 10-foot-tall breeze block wall, not plastered or painted, neither pretty nor particularly robust. It wouldn't have taken many monsoons or summers of extreme heart to crack it in several places. It ran along the rear boundary of the safe house – and neighbouring houses, as well – because it marked the edge of the private housing estate. Beyond it lay an open field of grass, several acres in extent, part of someone's private property and occupied by a small herd of goats. I could smell them. I've always liked goat's cheese, and they stank just like that. A series of shaded lights ran along the perimeter, but the lights were dim and the field itself was dark. Over on the far side was a private driveway marked by the subdued lighting and – several hundred yards away – a multi-storey, flat-roofed building that Fang said belonged to the owner's family in the form of several apartments, one on each level, each with its own balcony. The owner had the penthouse on top, his children and other relations were housed below.

We went out the back, through the kitchen.

Crossing over to the wall under the screen of fruit trees, a distance of 5 metres, we stopped. Someone had hidden a tall bamboo ladder at the foot of it, and Bai and Fang lifted it so it rested against the topmost blocks. It was sturdy, made of bamboo poles of the kind often used by the Thai construction industry for scaffolding. Bamboo was as durable and strong as metal, but much lighter and more flexible.

We went up, one by one, scrambled over and dropped down the other side, landing in tall grass and dried leaves. My jump wasn't athletic and I was glad no-one else in SIS saw my performance. I lost my balance and fell over; I didn't want to think of the snakes, spiders and other creepy-crawlies I'd disturb as I toppled with a thump next to Yang, who'd gone first. One of Bai's 'soldiers' was last – pulling the ladder over so it fell back against the foot of the wall. Without it, they'd have difficulty following us.

I was pouring with sweat. It might be the early hours, but it must have been over 29 degrees Centigrade and humid.

Then we ran – staggered, in my case – keeping to the perimeter and the trees and out of the starlight. I glanced back; the invaders' flashlights threw beams around the house and then inside.

In seconds I was drenched – by the wet grass and my own sweat. Yang had – remarkably, I thought – already marked out an escape route. She led us not to the driveway and the gate as I expected, but off to the right, to a hole torn or cut in the fencing of a neighbouring house. The two-storey building seemed very dark, shuttered, as if the residents were absent. I hoped they were. She held back the broken fencing so we could scramble through on our hands and knees without getting our clothing snarled up in it. One barb did find me, though – it tore my shirt and gouged my back. I felt the sting of it and felt what I imagined was warm blood mingling with sweat and trickling down my spine.

She seemed to know what I was thinking.

'No dog, okay?' Yang looked me in the eye, slapped my shoulder in a what I took to be a gesture of reassurance. 'Go – run!'

So I did.

The *Guoanbu* taxis were waiting for us in the *soi* beyond the house, and we piled on board.

* * *

165

We returned to the hostel. It seemed odd, given that the police and whoever it was who paid them to look for Fang and I must still be watching out for us, but as Fang explained, they wouldn't expect us to return. She was probably right. I had good reason to do so anyway – I needed to get hold of my comms.

The streets were empty. On the way, I discovered two leeches on my legs. One fat, livid slug on each calf. I asked if anyone had a light, and with the aid of a disposable lighter provided by the *Guoanbu* driver, I bent down behind the front seat and proceeded to burn them off. The windows were open, but the sizzle and stink of burning hair filled the taxi. I wasn't sure if it was true what people said, that if you pulled them off, they'd leave their heads behind and the bite would turn septic. They were plump with my blood and they dropped to the floor, curling up in response to the pain I'd inflicted. I resisted the temptation to stamp on these bloated creatures only because of the mess they'd make of the floor of the taxi.

'What are you doing?' Fang turned to look.

'Getting rid of my leeches.'

She made a face. 'That's disgusting.'

'The leeches, or my method of getting rid of them?'

'Both.'

Only then did she discover she had one in one of her trainers, and she uttered a yelp of horror. Fang was tough, but she was a city woman, after all.

Yang jumped out of the second taxi and went ahead, scouted out the lobby and exchanged a few words with the receptionist who was awake after the police raid and who looked both frightened and annoyed, the annoyance at being woken directed at us.

'I didn't think you'd come back,' she said, speaking to me in English.

166

'Why not? I have to settle the bill and I have a few of my things locked in your office.'

'You want them now?'

She wanted us gone, bill or no bill. I couldn't blame her.

'Please. If you don't mind.' I said it with a smile. My ingratiating manner seemed to work, for she got the key and unlocked the office door and waited until I'd got my gear, then locked up behind me.

I was relieved she didn't comment on my odd appearance, or that of the others. I must have looked filthy. I smelled that way, too.

She accepted dollars and worked out what I owed. I gave her a decent tip.

She was very young, 19 or so, and a student at one of Bangkok's most sought after universities, Kasetsart. She was studying forensic science, so Fang had informed me earlier. Her older brothers had already graduated in law and dentistry. Her parents were both doctors, high-achieving members of Thailand's growing middle class. Some text books lay open on the reception desk. If she could stay awake for at least part of the night, her shift must provide her with a few hours of study. No wonder she looked annoyed.

Outside, the red pickup had gone and no-one still sat in reception. If we still had watchers, they were invisible. We seemed to be in the clear, at least for the time being, but we had to assume we were blown and so was the *Guoanbu* safe house.

Time for a lukewarm shower, a change of clothing. I had the bedroom air-con on low, crawled between the sheets, wearing a pair of boxers and a white singlet, and lay on my back. I switched off the bedside light. But any hope of returning to sleep for a couple of hours was dashed almost immediately by a persistent tapping at my door.

I kept the chain on the door when I opened it – in case I was going to have to escape via the window and down the drainpipe. I needn't have worried.

It was Fang. She wasn't alone.

Peacock sat on the edge of my bed. He was a big man and, for a moment, I thought the whole thing would tip over.

'Make yourself at home,' I told him, though of course he already had.

Fang was pacing up and down, nervous. She peered out of the window, cupping her hands on the glass pane to see out into the street. When she wasn't doing that, she was looking at her watch.

Peacock held out another floppy disc. 'This is better than paper. I hope London can make sense of this. It's a list of payments by Yao to overseas accounts; your lady friend here and I think they belong to sympathisers with some influence in the media – people who will present the coup as something positive and a matter of China's internal affairs, nobody's business but their own. Useful idiots. Members of parliament, journalists, editors, people in Westminster and inside the Beltway who'll try to offset the storm of criticism when it happens with their own disinformation – supplied by Beijing. Paid hacks.'

'Won't work,' I said.

'No, you may be right, it won't. But they'll try to muddy the water and if we can identify the recipients, it'll give us an idea of who their playmates are in London and Washington. Americans for the most part, then six accounts in Germany and five in the UK, three French and two Spanish recipients. One Canadian. All told, 23 payments, but all we have are the account numbers and sort codes.'

'It's time, Roger.' Fang made it sound like an order.

Peacock clambered to his feet, and the bed righted itself. 'Look,

Richard, I am sorry about all this. It's a mess, I know. But I'm no longer any use to either of you here. Susan's already on a flight back home so it's best I leave, too. Fang here agrees – she has booked me on a flight leaving in 3 hours.'

'You'll have a lot of explaining to do. To Susan.'

'Don't I know it.'

'And don't apologise to me. You've done great work. Nothing short of heroic. I'm sorry it's over – from our point of view and yours. You did brilliantly, Roger. You did. You won the lottery in intelligence terms. You know that, don't you? It's one hell of an achievement. You should get a medal. I'll try to make sure you do.'

'I'm sorry, too,' Fang added. She looked and sounded as if she meant it.

I turned to Fang. 'Do you mind if I have a few words with Roger – alone?'

She looked at me, then at Roger, and made for the door. I could tell she didn't like it one bit. 'A few words, okay? I'll be right outside.'

When she'd gone, I said, 'I hope you can patch things up with Susan.'

I confess that I said it not out of genuine sympathy – I wanted to see GLUTTON's reaction. If his marriage fell apart – if it hadn't already – things could get very nasty. There was nothing a London tabloid liked better than a messy divorce mixed up with spies and a multi-millionaire's wife. Unless it included a royal or two, of course – and it usually did.

And I'd lied to him. They would meet him on arrival and he would be a guest of the Firm for quite a while. I thought so, anyway. He wouldn't have a choice. He had plenty of enemies. If his materials on the ChiCom leadership and its plan to oust Deng were accurate, Beijing would go out of its way to find the source and shut it down. So would Yao Tie and brother-in-law Du Fu of the Shanghai Security Bureau.

'What do I say about ...' Peacock tipped his head towards the door. 'If London asks?'

'Tell them the truth, Roger.'

'Which is what?'

'That the Chinese intelligence officer you know as Fang or Chen Meilin intervened and saved your life by faking your death and cremation, that she wrote a report for her superiors naming Du Lan, wife of Shanghai Party boss and millionaire Yao Tai, as the killer.'

'That's all she told her people? What about the payments, the conspiracy to unseat Deng? Hasn't she mentioned any of that?'

'I don't believe so, no. Not yet. You can also say she got you out of the country, brought you to Thailand and provided you with protection until she could get you on a plane home, and your wife on another flight out of Hong Kong.'

'And you?'

'What about me?'

He looked embarrassed. 'You and Fang. What do I say about your relationship?'

'What relationship, Roger? You know fuck all. Nothing. Aside from her being my best agent. She brought us the crown jewels long before you came along, but the less you know about that, the better. She's helped you do it again, this time with the Eight Elders, as well as saving your life. And remember – I've been running her for a lot longer than I've known you. Right?'

'Right, chief.' He looked awkward, and so he bloody should be for suspecting that I was Fang's agent.

170

Which, of course, I was.

'London will tell you what we all know: that you've done a terrific job for us. They'll congratulate you, ask if there's anything you need and they'll want to discuss your future – but only after you've taken a break and sorted out your issues with Susan.' I didn't mention any debrief. There would be one – I hoped it would fall to me to preside over it and give Peacock a glowing report and a free pass. That should put to bed any doubts he still had, and any doubts I might have, about his intelligence relationship with Fang.

'It's over. My marriage, I mean. Along with my business on the mainland.'

'I'm sorry if that's the case. It was all in the line of duty. You can tell Susan that much and it's true, isn't it?'

He didn't respond. It wouldn't make any difference, whatever he said. It was too late for explanations. Businessmen didn't make good agents, even though they had access to the people who mattered and could travel – but those advantages aside, the difficulty was that they tended to recoil from the damage espionage could do to their business. GLUTTON had been so much better than that, and now he was paying the price.

We shook hands and I opened the door.

As soon as GLUTTON left with Fang – her parting shot was a glance over her shoulder at me and the rather obvious observation – 'we need to talk' – I locked my door again and set up my satellite link.

There was a message, both *most secret* and *urgent* for me, and from no less a figure than C himself – even though there wasn't any green ink to identify him.

010484–54–658UK

SECRET. UK EYES ONLY. FLASH.

A. PROVIDE ALL POSSIBLE DETAILS ESPECIALLY TIMING.

B. ADVISE PLAN ASAP.

C. YOU WILL AVOID DIRECT ACTION IN PERSON.

D. YOU WILL RESTRICT YOUR MOVEMENTS TO THIRD COUNTRIES.

E. ADVISE PROSPECTS FOR SUCCESS/FAILURE.

I had been in this business long enough to know what it meant.

I was on my own.

Yang drove me to Bangkok's main railway station, Hua Lamphong. She didn't speak. We were both knackered. I knew I was, and it took little imagination to assume that she was more so; always on call, her duties both many and endless, a boss and a subordinate of a most demanding Fang. And more – she was a loyal and conscientious cadre. She would see me as a bourgeois imperialist and a counter-revolutionary big-nose. A loathsome creature and a pain in the arse, and she'd have hated having to babysit me and GLUTTON. No matter how tough, no matter how well trained and motivated, this must take its toll. I noticed that en route she used her mirrors almost all the time, employing that universal trick of spies to detect a tag by slowing down and speeding up – yet doing so without drawing attention to herself. She was a thorough professional. On arrival, she didn't park but kept the engine running, turned in her seat and with one hand opened my door. She didn't speak, but I knew what that meant: get the hell out.

Yang watched me haul myself and my possessions out of the silver Honda Civic and she drove away at once, without a farewell or smile, almost running over my feet in her hurry. The *Guoanbu* taxis had been retired – doubtless returned to the *Guoanbu* station compound to have their registrations changed on the assumption they'd been made by Langley's foot-soldiers. I'd retired Fisher too, for the same reason, at least for this stage of the journey, and once again settled myself into Webster's cover. That was the name on the rather good fake of a UK passport in my pocket, and on the second class rail ticket in my sweaty hand. Mr Webster was known in several places, but not Thailand. Mr Fisher would no doubt re-emerge when it was my turn to fly out of Don Mueang, homeward-bound this time.

My destination was 4 hours away by train, half that by road. Bai and Fang might drive, or they could split up – that would be the sensible option – and use the air-conditioned buses that played loud and incomprehensible – incomprehensible to me, that is – Thai movies, more or less preventing anyone disinclined to watch from having a nap. The buses were cheap, fast and comfortable as well as providing a couple of breaks en route.

They would be there before me, whatever method they chose.

I had time to buy an iced coffee before boarding Train 43, the first of 11 trains that day, a 'special express' departing at 0750.

Hua Hin was my goal, a small but expanding resort on the vast crescent of palm-fringed sand on the Gulf of Thailand. Once a fishing village, its popularity grew from the 1920s onwards among Thais who could afford weekend breaks, because of its proximity to the capital.

The monarchy helped seal its respectability by building palaces in the area. It then became popular for water sports, and it wasn't long before 'developers' snapped up swathes of the flat, low-lying farmland and began throwing up ugly hotels and high-rise condos in brutalist concrete for well-to-do locals and hard currency *farangs*.

I watched the early morning mist burn off the landscape of rice paddies and Buddhist temples sliding by. Storks stood on one leg as the train rattled past. It was so relaxing that I soon fell asleep.

Some time later, I woke with a start – I'd drooled out of the corner of my mouth and down the front of my shirt.

The man standing in front of me was talking at me. Whatever he'd said, I'd missed it. He was short and tanned and younger than I. No doubt fitter – smarter, too, in a well-cut and off-white linen suit, along with Ray-Bans. He gave me what I read as a smile – although it was perhaps more smirk of contempt than smile.

'Hey, buddy. You were snoring like a locomotive. Lucky there are few passengers, or they might have thrown you out of that window you're leaning your head against.'

I hated him already. I left my head where it was.

It took a while to get the words out of a parched mouth. 'Who the fuck are you?'

My lack of good manners didn't faze him in the least.

'Mind if I join you?'

'I'd say not, but it looks as if you already have.'

He'd shrugged off his coat, folded it and sat down opposite, pinching his trouser creases and shooting his cuffs and all the while he showed me his perfect teeth.

'Jeff Green.' He repeated the name in case I didn't get it the first time. 'Jeff Green – that's Jeff with a J – and Green the Third'. With a manicured nail, he flicked a card onto the table between us, missing a small puddle of cold coffee and my empty coffee cup. Maybe Jeff Green the Third had practised his party trick. I didn't look at his card and hoped he was disappointed that I didn't show how impressed I was. I doubted Green was his real name.

I closed my eyes again, hoping he had a walk-on part in a bad dream.

'Guess I wasn't expecting such a senior SIS executive to venture off the range all on his own.'

'You guessed wrong, Mr Green. You've got the wrong man. Anyhow, who says I'm alone? I've got the Guards Armoured raring to go and waiting in the next carriage.'

My head felt like a soft boiled egg sliced open with a sharp knife. With great care, I opened my eyes. Jeff Green the Third was still there.

Those teeth again. The smile of a hostile predator. He smoothed down his thick, curly blond hair with the palm of his left hand, displaying a glint of gold on his wrist and on the fourth finger. A bulbous fraternity ring, I shouldn't wonder. It wasn't top Chinese communist cadres alone who had a thing for gold jewellery.

This was the Agency's version of the *Great Gatsby*, but I told myself to stop it. The British could make fun of Americans as much as we liked, of course, as the East Germans, Czechs and Poles loved to sneer at the Soviets behind their backs, but there was no mistaking who called the shots. It wasn't us.

'We've been keeping an eye on you, Mr Fisher.'

Use of my last cover name pissed me off no end. Anybody could have been listening, but at least he didn't call me Brodick. Presumably he'd got the former from the registration book at the Bangkok hostel.

'How kind. We? And who is this *we*?'

'My colleagues and I. Fisher's what you're calling yourself these days, isn't it?'

'What do you want, Mr Green? I assume Langley, Virginia, comes into this somewhere.'

'A chat between friends – and allies. It won't take long. And if it makes you feel better, buddy, it's off the books. It never happened, and we never met. All I ask for is 5 minutes and then you can go back to snoring your head off.'

How reassuring. I had the distinct feeling this wasn't going to end well.

19

Fang stands barefoot on the sand, facing out to sea, her black hair streaming behind her in the warm, onshore breeze. She's dressed in loose white linen – long pants, a wide-sleeved shirt, embroidered at collar and cuffs. Her look – that of a well-off holiday-maker – is complemented by gold hoop earrings and the sandals she carries in her left hand.

The image of serene leisure, of wellbeing, of a privileged life, of urban sophistication, is misleading.

The only sounds are children playing in the shallows, the wind in the palms, their trunks bent away from the shore, and the yapping of a dog from one of the guesthouses. She knows that in another 24 hours she must take the first steps to implementing her plan – if she's still determined to proceed, that is. The question is: *is* she so determined? It won't be easy. It will be dangerous – for her, for her *Guoanbu* comrades, indeed for everyone involved, and that thought brings her around again to Bo Deli.

Fang has argued with herself about him and about the action she's about to launch. She's told herself off, in the tones of a severe school-teacher. There's no reason she should take this on. It is none of her affair. Her professional duty is counter-intelligence, not saving the Party or the country. She's loyal, always has been – until the fateful first meeting with Bo Deli and her devising of their pact. That does not include taking sides in Party disputes, in defying authority, in challenging the existing order.

People don't question. It's not safe.

She has an opinion about Deng Xiaoping, of course she does. Fang has an opinion about the Eight Elders, too, and what they are trying to achieve. She has opinions on many issues, but keeps them to herself, and none of that justifies what could be construed as a treasonous act of rebellion. How could she even think of it?

Failure in this venture means death, and she knows that, too.

So walk away. Be smart. Go back to work. She's saved the life of one foreigner. She's damaged Yao's nascent power grab, snuffed it out. She's supplied vital intelligence to Bo Deli, and he has reciprocated in full. Much of it has been faked or contaminated, but so what? What else is there? The partnership of betrayal has worked over the years and that's because they've both been careful, she and Brodick. They've been professional in their trade craft and they've been careful in selecting material to feed the insatiable appetites of their respective masters. As a result, she's climbed the ranks, and so has he; their pact has borne fruit beyond her greatest hopes and she has no reason to think that her career won't take her on to the very top at a time when her country's intelligence apparatus is growing fast. The Party needs people like her. She's good at what she does. Isn't that enough?

Why risk everything?

And for what, exactly?

It's never bothered her before who runs the Party and the country.

Power-struggles have never interested her. They happen. Personalities don't matter. The leadership is too remote to be an issue. China has suffered long periods of stability and civilised rule only to be broken by unexpected and violent spells of turmoil, struggle, flood, drought, war. Like any Chinese with a strong sense of self-preservation, she's stayed clear of factions and schisms. Like many Chinese, she has sought a way that will provide her with security. Why should this change now? Why invite disaster? So what if a group of corrupt, power-hungry old gangsters of Maoist bent take over by deceit? So what if Deng wants to open up the West, to embrace capitalism 'with special Chinese characteristics'? What does any of it matter? Nothing is permanent in this world except impermanence itself. All she has to do to prosper is keep working – and close her eyes and ears to everything else.

There are several potential hazards. One is Xie Rong's habit of boasting to colleagues about Fang's successes with her UK agent. It doesn't help at all. Fang has heard murmurings from within the Chief Military Commission's office that military intelligence, or PLA2, of which she is a member and holds the rank of full colonel, would like her to run her agent under PLA2 auspices. They ask the right questions, too: what does counter-intelligence have to do with running an agent at the heart of an imperialist power? She knows they are discussing her resigning her leadership of the *Guoanbu*'s 5th Bureau and transferring all her intelligence gathering to PLA2. Military intelligence is aggressive, hungry, somewhat crude in method, but there's talk of further promotion if she goes along with it.

She'd have a major-general's epaulettes and stars on her PLA uniform.

Only Xie stands in the way. What would happen if he falls out of favour once his alleged involvement in the opposition to Deng is exposed? Fang will lose her champion.

It's not without irony.

Fang digs her toes into the sand and, enjoying the physical sensation, watches the lines of waves breaking, pushed by the wind. It's been 10 years or more since she's stood idling on a beach like this.

She's sure that If Bo Deli could hear her jumble of thoughts, her playing devil's advocate with herself, he'd laugh and mock her, telling her that a personal conscience is not something permitted to Party members and that she should know that. It's a bourgeois failing, nothing more. He'd mean it as a joke, but he would be right.

Bo Deli. When she'd trapped the naïve young Westerner, graduated from the Secret Intelligence Service's 6-month-long officers' training course at Fort Monckton back in 1984 and packed off on a futile assignment in Beirut, she'd no real certainty that it would work out quite as well as it did. He could have laughed in her face, dismissed with a shrug her threat to leave him in the hands of the Lebanese military intelligence, the *Deuxième Bureau*, which in turn – so she'd said – would sell him on to the Syrians, the Russians or the Iranians. It hadn't been an idle threat, though she had no intention of carrying it out quite in those terms. As expected, he'd lacked the confidence to defy her, to risk his freedom by challenging her. Yes, she would have left him in the detention centre in the hills above Beirut but they would have released him – after a matter of days or weeks.

But he'd taken the bait. Fang had vowed to help his career, and said that by helping one another, he would be helping hers, too. At the time, it had sounded plausible, nothing more than that, and she hadn't expected it to work. It was what Beijing called a 'win–win' situation. In Party terms 'win–win' meant in reality 'we win, you lose.'

But it had worked.

Richard Brodick had passed to her what every intelligence service would want: highly classified material on military technology, on government policy and on the personalities behind those policies. He'd also betrayed three of Langley's Chinese agents on the mainland and sent them to their deaths, polishing Fang's image as the dedicated counter-intelligence officer, China's premier spy hunter, and displaying on video her ruthlessness by pulling the trigger on the enemy agents herself.

Brodick's aim had been simple; to increase the dependence of both London and Washington on Fang's input, and to remove any competition from Langley.

They showed the video clip of her executing the agents throughout the *Guoanbu*, and Fang had heard rumours that the Party chiefs, including Deng, had all seen it. It was as close to a best-seller as anyone could get, aside of course from *Thought of Mao*.

Fang had done the same for Brodick. She'd provided enough material so that UK Station employed six analysts and translators full-time to process her material, with eight more in the United States, divided between the CIA and National Security Agency. She had provided 4,880 images so far on her Minox camera – a device given to her by Brodick in Beirut back in '84 – along with 130 hours of face-to-face meetings, reduced to 1,500 pages of transcript. Brodick's career has blossomed. He's a star in his own rather small Service.

Never mind that a sizeable proportion of it is fake, contaminated, and that the same goes for his product. Who knows, who can tell?

Human nature is such that we believe what we want to believe, even before we've decided what it is that we need to know.

They've both shot up the ranks, Fang now running the *Guoanbu*'s 5th Bureau, tasked with global counter-intelligence, Brodick heading UK Station in charge of agents recruited from, and operating in, so-called denied territories, such as the Soviet Union, its East European empire, North Korea and the People's Republic of China.

Is she going to risk destroying all this on a single roll of the dice?

Let those old men do their worst. Stay out of it!

Trouble is, she's already up to her neck.

Fang bends, scoops up a shiny black pebble and throws it out as far as she can.

When Fang turns away from the sea, she spots Yang sitting on the seawall behind the beach, a little way from the sand-strewn concrete steps. Yang isn't looking at Fang, but at the few people walking along the seafront and a line of food stalls and cheap guest houses. She watches motorists and motorcyclists. Fang eyes couples holding hands. Yang Bai is doing her job and doing it well – watching Fang's back.

Fang is all too aware of her own way of thinking, and how it can obstruct clarity of mind. What is a 'personality' after all, but a bundle of habits of thought, of feeling and ingrained from the very start, in the womb? To the Buddhist, cutting away habitual ways of living leads to freedom, to an end of grasping, hence of suffering. Buddhist teachings have always intrigued Fang, but she has never dared take it further. She's a Marxist–Leninist, a materialist, and a servant of the CCP. That's it.

Yet she accepts (how could it be otherwise?) that her own background has to be a factor in how she perceives the world. It's not a background she likes to think about, let alone share with others. It's buried in a file somewhere, in Party records, or in the *Guoanbu*'s own registry. She hopes it's been destroyed, but she can't be sure. Fang assumes that every time she is considered for a promotion or a new position, her record is resurrected, the dust shaken off, and its contents perused by the old men, the killers of hope, the so-called experts in looking for faults, for something they can exploit. It's there for those who have the eyes to see.

Bo Deli saw. Very early on, he saw. It shocked her – and she had to improvise.

Did he understand it, though?

Bo Deli had shown her the US Defense Intelligence Agency report on her and she had gone to great pains to insist it was all wrong, that the Americans had mistaken her for someone else, and she'd had to invent – on the hoof – a new set of names instead.

Whether she convinced him and his masters of the truth of her version, she has no way of knowing. But she remembers the US report, almost word for word:

SECRET//UKUS EYES ONLY

Source: US Defense Intelligence Agency

Subject: PRC national CHEN MEILIN work name FANG (see also CHEN AIGUO)

CHEN MEILIN work name FANG believed to be the eldest child of CHEN AIGUO, latter appointed head of ILD in 1982, aged 56. See also International Liaison Department of CCP Central Committee or *Zhongyang Lianluobo* abbr. *Zhongkianbu* (political intel, liaison with foreign political parties).

CHEN AIGUO has taken control of the security committees: the ministries of Justice, State Security (*Guoanbu*) and Public Security (*Gonganbu*) as well as National Minorities. CHEN AIGUO's *guanxi* (relationships) said to be extensive: his primary protector reported to be CHEN YUN, inventor of economic intel, as well as BO YIBU, app. deputy premier 1978, also father-in-law JIA CHUNWANG, rumoured to be in line to take over the *Guoanbu*.

CHEN AIGUO's wife JIA LIHUA (subject's mother) is currently a producer on the BBC's Chinese language service in Hong Kong. Intel role not known.

CHEN AIGUO led missions to Tehran, Algiers, Pyongyang. Visits technical nature, including arms and technology transfers. Proposed setting up paramilitary police force, People's Armed Police (PAP) (*renmin wuzhuang jincha*). Reportedly inspired by Royal Ulster Constabulary (RUC) handling of public disorder in Northern Ireland.

CHEN AIGUO has been associated with arms transfers to Syria, Iran, Iraq, Libya, N. Korea. Regarded as hard-line advocate of active PRC support for *Khmer Rouge*, Afghan resistance to Soviet occupation, counter-insurgency in Tibet, special ops against DALAI LAMA in exile. CHEN AIGUO, of Hakka origin, seen in PRC as bastion of authoritarian old order but supporter of economic reform. His CPC reputation said to be 'firm yet flexible'.

184

CHEN AIGUO is reported to have three children. CHEN MEILIN is the eldest. The second, also a daughter, attends medical school in Baltimore. The youngest, a son, currently a pupil at a private Hong Kong high school, lives with his mother.

LIHUACHEN MEILIN (birthdate unknown but thought to be 1956) attended Tsinghua University and Berkeley UC as postgrad. At the latter believed to have acted as ILD agent targeting overseas mainland Chinese and Taiwanese and reportedly succeeded in persuading an unknown number to join CCP and/or return. Monitored by FBI during this period. She then worked as a correspondent in Hong Kong accredited to Xinhua. Intel activities suspected but unsubstantiated. (See UK/HKG/Local Intelligence Committee)

CHEN MEILIN has carried out short-term, solo missions throughout the Middle East, and is thought to have been a *Guoanbu* cadre since 1983 while maintaining links with ILD and Xinhua as 'honourable correspondent'. Handler(s) not identified. Rumoured to hold PLA2 (military intelligence) rank of colonel.

It was all too accurate.

She had improvised. Chen Meilin, she told Bo Deli, was in reality Zhang Pusheng, and Zhang Pusheng wasn't the eldest daughter of Zhang Chen Xiang after all. Zhang Chen Xiang, Fang's father, was head of the United Front Workers department or UFWD, responsible for persuading Chinese and Taiwanese to join the Party and return to the homeland. Contrary to the US report, Fan Jinn was her mother, and she didn't work for the BBC but was an artist and a cultural adviser at the International Studies Centre or *Zhongguo*

185

Guoji Wenti Yanjiu Zhongxin, established by Den Xiaoping to analyse foreign developments for the Party leadership. An intelligence body as well.

All in all, it was a fair piece of improvisation, with enough truth in it to be plausible.

But she almost made a mess of it. Fang also recalls, with less clarity, further conversations with Bo Deli, sometimes broken off, interrupted, then resumed at a later stage during the early days of their mutual seduction, both professional and personal. How close she came to the truth, to the awfulness that has made her what she is. That phrase in English: pillow talk – she knows all too well with hindsight how dangerous it was, the two of them lying in bed in a Beirut hotel, all hell breaking loose outside, and talking of herself, of her world, before and after making love.

How foolish was that?

The Briton seemed to buy it, but she still can't be sure.

Has he pieced it all together since? She hopes he's forgotten their conversations.

She began her bedtime tale in Canton, in 1924, at the Huangpu Military Academy, established by Sun Yat-sen and the Soviets, to train officers to fight the warlords of northern China. Mikhail Borodin, the Comintern's permanent representative in China, was in charge along with the head of the Soviet military mission.

In October '26, Borodin sent his bodyguard, Gu Shunzhang, to Vladivostok, for training in clandestine, revolutionary methods.

Gu was born in 1902 on the wrong side of the tracks in Shanghai. As a teenager, he got to know the bars, opium dens, the tarts. He had affairs, and he survived by cunning and brute force. Gu was a street fighter. He joined the infamous Green Gang and became a secret member of the CCP. Gu led a double life. With a public persona as Hua Guangqi, he performed as a magician – an illusionist – in top nightclubs and casinos.

Back from the Soviet Union, he and the notorious sadist Fang Sheng formed a special unit to defend communists from the *Kuomintang* or KMT. In 1927, Chiang Kai-shek formed his KMT army and government base in Nanjing. As the CPC was preparing for an insurrection, the nationalists struck – Green Gang thugs slaughtered thousands of communists.

That was in March 1927.

Gu – along with other Party leaders – hid in the French concession. In Hunan, Mao Zedong's insurrection failed, while the Canton Uprising of December 1927 was defeated with 15,000 comrades killed.

Fang remembers telling Bo Deli that even today, this Gu is seen in the PRC as evil – a traitor of the worst kind. A drug fiend, a womaniser, gambler, a liar – every crime and vice is attributed to him in Chinese communist history books.

In 1931, Gu was head of the Shanghai Special Services Section, part of the Party's intelligence apparatus. Despite Gu's talent as an illusionist, a nationalist – an alert KMT agent – spotted Gu in Wuhan as he emerged from a cinema.

Gu had a choice. He could tell his captors what he knew, which was a lot – names and addresses, safe houses, organisational structure, communications and more – or be tortured to death, knowing that his wife and children would also be murdered. Gu agreed to defect, even agreeing to head up a new anti-communist investigations unit and to write a special manual on how to track down communist cadres.

Gu sought a meeting with Generalissimo Chiang Kai-shek, who agreed to meet him. No doubt Gu wanted to appeal for the lives of his family.

There were soon roundups in several cities, many arrests, and Gu was compelled to give them everything he had – rationing it as best he could to ensure he stayed alive long enough to secure his family's safety.

It didn't work. Zhou Enlai ordered the Gu family's execution.

The assassins murdered 10 family members, but they left an infant alive. A girl. Someone may have hidden her, thrown a blanket over the child and the killers didn't see her. The slaughter took place when Gu was actually meeting the Generalissimo, or so it was said. The victims' bodies were buried under a patio and it was only the stink of their decomposing corpses that led to their discovery.

Fang remembers that in telling Brodick this old story, she was almost in tears and had to take control of herself and her runaway feelings.

Bo Deli asked Fang the question she wished he wouldn't ask.

'What happened to the child, the little girl?'

Fang had shrugged, turning away as if distancing herself from the incident, but not wanting to let Brodick see her face at that moment.

'No-one knows,' she'd replied.

It was a lie. Fang knows all too well.

That little girl is her mother.

The story of the traitor Gu is her story, and a bloodstain on her ancestors' secret escutcheon that will never wash away. Mao used to tell visitors that everyone should *chi ku* – taste bitterness.

Fang climbs the steps away from the beach and out of the corner of her eye, she sees Yang move. She's on her feet at once, walking, then drops back, bending down as if tending to a problem with her feet. This allows Fang to draw ahead, while Bai can check what lies both ahead and behind.

They haven't gone more than 300 yards, past some ramshackle stores, ancient bicycles, a white-and-red barber's pole, climbing plants and bunches of low hanging electrical wiring and telephone lines, when they come to a wooden building, over two floors with an iron roof, a wide veranda around it at ground level and the structure – which seems to list to one side – is set upon piles or stilts on the seaward side, part of it protruding out over a rocky shore. It's been painted red, the wooden shutters in white. Out front are some huge water pots containing lotus plants. In big, white letters painted with the curly Thai script, on the wall facing the street, is the name: *Bansabai Guesthouse*. Another sign, outside on the pavement, reads: 'English breakfast 40 baht', and accompanies a faded and torn colour photograph under plastic of what appears to be a plate of baked beans, sausages and egg. In case there's any doubt that this is an English breakfast, there's a useful footnote: *Chang beer special 38 baht*. The price is written in chalk so it can be updated according to the season and time of day.

A backpackers' paradise.

A man sweeping the pavement outside his shop in short, light strokes glances up and away. A woman in an apron sitting on a low stool outside a food stall fans herself with a bamboo fan and ignores them. A shiny blue Suzuki motorcycle with two people in identical helmets cruises past – for the third time. Fang pretends she's noticed none of this.

Sat out on the veranda in the shade, facing the road, is a *farang*, an empty bottle of Chang lager and a pint glass in front of him. He recognises Fang at once and she, in turn, recognises Brodick. He doesn't seem normal; there's no hand raised in greeting, no broad smile. He looks straight through her, then looks away.

She expected him to be happy to see her. But Bo Deli seems indifferent.

He seems better, fitter – it's extraordinary what rest, food and sunshine can do, she thinks, but he's acting like a stranger. He doesn't signal.

Fang keeps going. Yang is right behind, 10 metres back.

Trouble.

The blank face, the beer – the signal is the lack of signal; he's saying they've been made – or might have been.

Shit.

Fang and her shadow turn away but keep moving, heading for the market in the centre. It's only a couple of minutes on foot. They don't hurry. Fang keeps her expression blank. They have agreed a fall-back rendezvous and will try that.

Fang moves from stall to stall, selecting food, or seeming to do so. The stalls are set in long rows; the umbrellas provide a kind of improvised roof, protecting sellers and customers alike from sun and rain. It's hotter than ever without a breeze. It's also darker. Yang Bai is haggling over the first Durian of the season. It's a fruit that stinks like rotting flesh, but is delicious, and its price ranges from the expensive to the cheap and everything in between. Yang loves her Durian, and is haggling with determination, using the chat as an occasion to watch her surroundings. From the next row, Fang buys pork on a stick – grilled pork threaded onto slivers of bamboo, along with a plastic bag of sticky rice. She buys enough for three or four people.

There's a glass-fronted, air-conditioned coffee shop on the corner. It's quite a smart, upmarket place. Yang goes in first, mounting the steps, the door hissing open with a blast of cold air. She's ordering, looking around, pretending to admire the home-made cake and cookies in a display cabinet, and gives the slightest nod to Fang, who follows.

There's upstairs seating, and a way out through the back to the alley beyond.

Cars can't get past. It's pedestrians only or the odd motorcyclist who's prepared to cut his speed right down and walk their machine past the shop and the stalls.

Yang jabs at the ice in her coffee with a straw and then sucks at it and gazes out in contemplation of the dusty street through the window.

Fang is drinking a freezing Diet Coke. The two women are the only customers. The owner, a well-groomed young Thai woman, well-educated by the look of her, wants them to try her homemade banana and chocolate cakes, but they aren't interested. She invites them to take a seat, but they don't respond.

'See anything you like?'

Fang raises her eyebrows in reply. It's a gesture that means 'no'.

The door hisses open again and Brodick walks in.

He turns to the woman behind the counter, who smiles at the *farang*. She's not bothered by him, but by the Chinese customers, who seem so watchful yet indifferent.

In bad Thai, he too orders an iced coffee, and a piece of cake. Fang looks at it. It's very dark, very glutinous, she thinks. Does he want it?

Out they go, Fang leading, Yang behind her, Brodick bringing up the rear, trying to drink his coffee, carry his cake in a little cardboard box and look where he places his feet, so he doesn't trip. City pavements in Thailand are obstacle courses for the unwary.

Fang turns to him on the street corner. Yang swings by, walking in a wide arc, watching their six. She uses the window of a pet shop, with its budgies and fish tanks, to mirror whatever's behind them and across the street on the far side.

'You checked in?'

'At the guesthouse? I have, yes.' They stand looking at each other.

'Walk with us.'

He swings his Bergen from one shoulder to the other, sees Yang Bai look at him and nods a greeting. She sees the gesture, but doesn't respond and immediately looks away.

'Where to?'

'You'll see. It's not far.'

Fang is aware of the owner watching through the glass door of the coffee shop.

They walk at a moderate pace away from the coast and the centre of the town. Yang is sometimes ahead, sometimes behind. Fang and Bo Deli are close enough to each other to be able to talk in brief exchanges.

Fang decides to say as little as possible about the surprise she has in store for Bo Deli, if only because they can't be sure they're in the clear.

'We have a problem?'

He doesn't answer Fang immediately.

She tries again from a different angle. 'How was the train?'

He falls back so they are almost abreast. 'Pretty good. Comfortable. Not at all busy. I got some more sleep. I don't know if you know this already, Fang – you might have had someone else on the train I didn't know about – but an American interrupted my pleasant journey. He sat down opposite me and introduced himself. He said his name was Jeff Green. That's Green with two 'e's. Jeff Green the Third. We can assume it isn't his real name. He's Agency and while he didn't admit as much, he did not deny it. He looked the part. Green was polite but quite pushy. Not the kind to take no for an answer.'

'Was he alone?'

'As far as I could tell.'

'Did he get off the train with you?'

'Earlier. Some place called Bang Bamru. A couple of stops before Hua Hin.'

'He could have come on by road. Do you know him? Do you think he was from the local CIA station in Bangkok, the guy responsible for the watchers at the hostel?'

'I'd never seen him before. It seems to me very likely that he was leading the team in Bangkok. That's why I gave you the "not welcome" signal.'.'

They stop at a broad intersection and wait for the lights to change. Two scruffy vans, a truck carrying wood, a farm tractor and several motorcycles pass by. Fang is not happy. She's thinking hard. Should they call this off? The sensible thing to do would be to defer it for another day. But it's not as if she has the time. The operation can't wait. There's too much to do and too little time.

Yang is watching their rear as well as scrutinising the traffic. They cross over and Fang gestures with her chin to their destination: three identical blocks of condominiums on three sides of a rectangular plot – seven storeys tall, the fourth side open and facing them as they approach. There's an Olympic-size swimming pool running down the centre between the buildings, but no-one's swimming and the sun loungers – new and much smarter than those at the hostel back in Bangkok – are all unoccupied. The rest of the place is given over to a grass lawn and new trees, the branches supported by wooden posts to keep them upright. A worker is pushing a lawn mower around.

Fang stops, touches Brodick's arm and turns to face him. 'So, what did the American want? Did he say?'

'What do you think he wanted? Same thing Langley's been after for years. He wants you, Fang, and your product.'

20

'See, it's like this.' Green put both hands down on the little folding table between us. We both admired his big ring. 'I know you're a senior guy working out of UK Station and that can only mean one thing, right? Executive spooks like us don't run around the world servicing deep cover agents. You've come to meet one of your assets in person. I guess that, like us, you would use a temporary case officer – rotating several TCOs through over a period of months – to service your people for the routine stuff, but you're seeing to whatever it is yourself this time, and that has to mean the asset is right here, in Thailand, and that it's important. You've brought him – or her – out to a third country where it's safer for both of you. No, please say nothing – I'm not asking you to break any of your rules on confidentiality, buddy. Listen.'

The CIA man who called himself Green looked up, took a deep breath and gazed out at the landscape juddering past. He had a lean face, tanned and close shaven. I would have put him down as a tennis coach if I didn't know any better; fit in any case. Smart, too; I'd guessed his alma mater was Stanford – and Oxford. An Anglophile. Did he know I was Scottish? No reason why he should.

'This is pretty damn important, and as I say, it has to be one of your top joes. Your Bangkok Station doesn't know about any of this. Neither does your Beijing Station. It's the way these matters are handled and when it comes to denied territory we are not dissimilar in our methods, right? Now you and I, we're allies, close allies, and we see a lot of the product your agents bring to the table. Wonderful, it is too, some of it. I mean that. You Brits are unbeatable in matters of HUMINT. Congratulations are due, okay? Accept the fucking compliment and don't be an asshole.'

Thanks for the warning. Green made eye contact, and I thought it was because he wanted to see my reaction to his flattery and his insults and to whatever else he was planning on saying.

'If one looks over your product over time, say 6 months, one can draw certain conclusions, make a few inspired guesses.' I waited. 'I'm guessing, okay, but UK Station has nothing in Pyongyang. Fuck all, unless you're keeping something back from your pals at Langley.' The jokey tone changed. 'Are you?' He gave me a slow smile. 'No, say nothing, it's okay.'

So he knew who I was. Did he want me to offer my congratulations? Fuck him. He raised a hand, broke the eye contact and looked out of the train window again. 'I'm thinking to myself you've got one pretty high in Hanoi. Military, top cadre. Trio of sub-agents in Cambodia, all false flag jobs, would be my guess. A single in Laos. This walk-in we're handling jointly in Moscow, one scientific type in Prague, another in Warsaw, a network in the GDR naval yards soon to be redundant, if it isn't already. Oh, I forgot the asset in Odessa, a big fish. How am I doing with your order of battle? Missing anything, am I?'

I said not a word. He was far too close to the truth.

'I know you guys are having a hard time. Your budget's under attack. They want to close half your overseas stations, retire the older folk, the Soviet veterans. Moscow Men and Camel Traders are out of fashion. We know the cuts in personnel are deep – around 25 per cent of what is anyway a small staff of around 2,000 officers. Whitehall is taking chunks out of you. They've brought in auditors from outside. Un-fuckin'-believable!' Green shakes his head. 'The military wants to take you over. It was always thus, right from the start, back in 1909. Those pinkos in the Foreign Office want to charge you rent for the office space you use in embassies abroad. Assholes! We're going through something similar. People don't want to know you. You don't get to all the meetings no more, right? Your 'C' doesn't get to meet your Prime Minister in 18 months. The nineties suck, man, and they've only just begun. Am I right, or am I right?'

He was.

Again, I gazed back at him and forced myself to think of something else. I thought of the sea, thought how warm it was in the Gulf of Thailand, like a tepid bath, with a very high salt content and even the waves came in all soft, without force. Swimming off the beaches here was strange. The air was hot and sticky, and so was the sea. It offered little relief because you went into the water the way you came out: hot and sweaty. During the monsoon, it all changed and became quite dangerous, so much so the authorities would fly red flags along the beaches to keep people out of the water.

I encouraged my mind to wander, if only to keep my pulse normal and stop myself punching the bastard for his impertinence. Someone of my grade wasn't supposed to beat up friendlies on a whim – and certainly not friendlies with all the cards and deep pockets.

Green tried again.

'So, we can help ease the pressure, you know? You've managed to keep hold of some pretty serious people on your payroll on the mainland. Two top agents, the best, and they're fantastic, a fucking industry. Hats off to you for keeping them safe from the wolves prowling the corridors. I mean it, buddy. One in particular. A top cadre working in the Ministry of State Security, or military intelligence, what we refer to as PLA2. So productive – Jesus! We figured that out by reverse engineering. Who knows – you could have one in each. They have brought home the bacon in a big way, while we've had some setbacks of late. You may know about it or not. If you don't, let me give you an update. The bastards shot three of ours. So, my heartiest congratulations. I mean that. Whoever it is has changed the way we view events in the CCP. That's making a real difference in our world, agreed? What I can tell you is we ran your assets' material through our computers and we believe you've got a very senior official indeed inside Chinese foreign intelligence and close to the top. Your people could be grooming your guy for the top job in the *Guoanbu*. That would be a hell of a thing, wouldn't it?' He took on a dreamy look, but I wasn't fooled by any of this. 'It's hard to imagine.'

I waited. There was nothing else I could do but put up with this mauling. He was rubbing my nose in it, and all I could do was smile.

His voice dropped. He was all seriousness now. 'Washington has, as you know, asked London to share with us and the NSA. The dedicated 24/7 satellite comms, the support teams, private aircraft on tap, the safe houses, inter-agency analysis – the whole damn shoot – and we'd foot the bill as well, for a full defector resettlement package if it came to that, including any close family. But London said no. Nothing doing. Feigned ignorance. We tried at station level. Nothing doing there, either, because they haven't been indoctrinated. You know all this, of course you do. Even the White House and Number Ten got involved. Nada. Gossip has it that your man C is a stubborn s.o.b. He killed it stone dead.' He spread his hands wide. He had a slight tic under the left eye and he kept his face turned so I wouldn't see it. Interesting, I thought.

I watched a trio of white storks motionless as statues in the paddy fields.

'So now I'm asking. From one professional to another. I know this is real important to you, Mr Brodick, I know you're going somewhere significant today, doing something special, see, and I want to play too. I want in. I do. And I know how we can make this work, you and I, and everyone comes out of it well. Name your price. You, me, whatever it is you've got hidden away down here. We all win. So let's deal. God knows, you guys could do with the cash. I want you to take it. I want you guys back in top form, right? It's in everyone's interests. That much is obvious. So fuck the politicians.'

He had my real name and wanted me to know it.

'Win–win,' I said, managing a smile, but I don't think he got the joke.

Green looked at me, his head on one side, waggled his blond eyebrows. He wanted my answer.

'I'm taking a couple of days off, Mr Green. That's all there is to it. I'm so sorry for any confusion and of course I take full responsibility if you feel you've been led astray.'

I did my best to sound sincere, but I think he understood what I really meant: go fuck yourself. 'A weekend break, if you like, Jeff. I need the rest. And I like trains and I like to fish.' Those storks hunting frogs and fish in the rice fields had given me that idea. 'This has been an unfortunate misunderstanding and I am sorry.'

It was a terrible lie.

He looked furious and did his best to conceal it.

'*If I like*? Love it. So British. It isn't the weekend, OK? What are you going to do, sit in a bar, get arseholed as you Brits say, pick up a tart with gonorrhoea or worse, take her back to the hotel and do the same all over again the next day? I don't see it. I can't picture you with a fishing pole, either. I can't. I don't believe this for a moment. It's not your style.'

'What about my style?'

'I don't think you're the type.'

'For whoring or fishing?'

'Both.'

'Been checking my record, have you?'

'Wouldn't you, sir? Mr Brodick? That is your name, right? Richard, may I say that If you had a taste for hookers, we'd know it already. I'm being straight with you here, man.'

We had progressed to first names, which was a step forward. Americans were more formal than Brits.

'Thai whores are different, though, aren't they, Jeff? Amateur enthusiasts mostly. Isn't that what you're going to say?'

'So they tell me. I wouldn't know.'

'Had a friend, once, a paratrooper, shacked up with a sweet Russian girl. Gorgeous creature and very affectionate. Paid her rent, looked after her. They lived together in Moscow. It was love. After 6 months, he discovered quite by chance that she was married all along to an impecunious officer in the GRU. How about that?'

He knew I was trying to distract him, play for time.

Green said, 'I hope he turned the bastard.'

'He did. Of course he did. The GRU officer shot himself and she went off with someone else.'

200

He didn't care for my story, which was true. 'You're going to need my help, Mr Brodick, sir.'

So much for cover. I'd insulted his intelligence, but he recovered fast. 'And why's that?'

'Your ChiCom friends have something going on. Sharp increase in diplomatic traffic, for one thing. But what's more interesting to us are the numbers stations. That's picked up, too. Then there's their people on the move. Not the usual by any means. Bodies moving in and out of Shanghai, Hong Kong, Bangkok. Ministry of Public Security people heading into Hong Kong, strange goings on at night, a robbery, shots fired. Then Ministry of State Security operatives mob-handed at a hostel they use in Bangkok, as well as a safe house. That was yesterday. We noted a *farang* there with them. Our people visited both locations, out of curiosity. You wouldn't know anything about that, would you?'

He knew it was me or Peacock, or both. If we allowed the Agency to get anywhere near Fang, they'd have me figured out in no time, and I wasn't having it. It was a matter of my survival.

'Sorry, no.'

'Thought you'd say that. Richard, I'm gonna put one of my cards face up on the table, to show goodwill, which is wearing a little thin right now. Our little inquiry suggests your asset is a female cadre close to the top of the *Guoanbu* and head of the 5th or 9th Bureau. Now that cuts down the number of possibles, doesn't it, given that the ChiComs don't take equal opportunities that seriously. Right? It's a matter of time until we come up with a name, wouldn't you say? Because we will, you can be sure of that.'

A rhetorical question, which I wouldn't answer, but I was feeling the heat. This wasn't good. He knew it was Fang aka DRAGON. Why else would he say all this? He knew, and he was dangling it in my face, and enjoying my discomfort as I would in his shoes. My verbal slap hadn't worked at all – instead, it had earned me a thorough kicking. As long as it stayed metaphorical, I told myself I didn't mind too much.

Green glanced at his watch and looked out of the window, but he wasn't going to let me off the hook, not yet, not until he'd delivered the rest of his message – because that's what this was, a choreographed message from Langley's top man in East Asia to the head of UK Station, no less.

'The first thing they do is make a box. That's what we call it. The outer perimeter has its mobile watchers, *jianshiren*, the inner one a series of static posts, and right inside, they'll have their operations centre, like a giant Faraday cage, shielded against hostile electromagnetic emissions. They've developed this paint – ink, really – to block electromagnetic attacks, and they have these gaskets they use so they can continue their own broadcasts. The ChiComs copied ours, which they stole. They're getting pretty good at this technical stuff. You know what they call it – R, D and T. Research, Development and Theft. Anyway, they run everything from in there until the job is done, then dismantle it all fast and disappear. You get this, of course you do. Thing is, once you're in the box, it's almost impossible to get out again without help. So much of what they do still comes out of the Soviet playbook – with special Chinese characteristics.'

'I appreciate the advice, Mr Green, and the offer.'

'No, you don't. Funny how similar all the services are, isn't it? We're copying procedures from one another, making modifications we envy in our enemy's operational methods, regardless of which side we're on. Hey, this is my stop. Don't say I didn't warn you, buddy. We wouldn't want you to get trapped in their box, now, would we?'

He got up, stretched, looked up and down the carriage. He picked up his jacket, shook it out, put it on, shot his cuffs again. He was wearing brown loafers with tassels. I could never trust a man with tassels on his shoes, or anyone wearing a bow tie, either.

Green didn't seem the least put out that he hadn't achieved his stated aim, the acquisition of Fang along with my co-operation, but I doubted that was what he was after. Or at least, not yet. He'd signalled his intentions and would now sit back and watch.

There was some play in progress that I didn't know about and to which I wasn't invited.

It seemed so quiet as the train slowed, though I saw a couple of passengers dragging their luggage towards the exits. They looked like locals, at least to me; a little shabby, not at all well off judging by the quality of their bags, talking to one another happily in rapid Thai, pleased to be arriving at wherever it was.

'I wish you the very best of luck, Mr Brodick, sir.'

Langley's Gatsby offered me his hand. I shook it. I wasn't his pal, his buddy, his chum or his mate – but we were allies when all was said and done, weren't we? Allies and competitors. Fang had once given me some friendly advice, passed on from her mother. 'If someone asks you a question, say that you have toothache and cannot talk and that you are deaf and cannot hear. That way, you stay out of trouble.'

I didn't say that I was deaf or had a toothache, but I was staying shtum all the same.

There was something Mr Green wasn't telling me. I had the strange feeling it was of immense importance – the proverbial elephant in the room or, in this case, in the train – and that once I found out, it would be too late to do much about it. A senior Agency executive doesn't leap on board a local train headed to some inconsequential fishing village to score points off his British opposite number.

'Thanks, Jeff.'

I spoke to his retreating back. It was lame, but it was all I could think of.

I soon saw signs of the box Green had been waffling on about. First, the guys on the move, the procession of motorcyclists and pedestrians circling around us, all of them Thais as far as I could tell, passing one way, then the other, following and ahead. They weren't at all bad. They covered up, the way Thai manual workers do in the heat, wearing loose, long-sleeved shirts, cloth caps with flaps and face masks attached to them. Then, the second ring of static posts, even guys on the roofs. Construction workers in hard hats. What Thai construction worker – a day labourer – ever wore a safety hat? There was no health and safety here – it was a case of floppy hats and flip-flops on bamboo scaffolding, up 20 floors or more. That's the way it was here.

Women sat in doorways of their shophouses in the shade, chatting, dangling a naked child on one knee, or feeding it something, the men pretending to fix a bicycle, the two old guys playing backgammon, four youngsters in good cheer with a cluster of beer bottles in front of them – but trying hard not to see me. That Thai cop in reflective aviators, I'd bet a tenner on him being one of theirs, staring at nothing, picking his nose. It could be any or all of them. Or none. The give-away was their not looking. Thais stared at *farangs*, if only for something to do – because *farangs* looked so peculiar. These didn't, and that wasn't right.

A guy in a white sun hat was cutting the grass at the condo with a manual lawn mower – hot, sweaty labour. He was from Isaan in the north-east, if I wasn't mistaken; Thailand's poorest region. Of light build but muscled, he had coppery skin and that wasn't suntan. He was making a neat job of it and he wasn't looking at us, either. He was looking down, concentrating hard. His forearms glistened with sweat. Trouble was, the grass didn't need cutting.

But then no-one's perfect.

Fang said the condo was up on the seventh floor, that it was new and owned by an Australian called Pelletier. It came furnished. Pelletier liked to rent it out for the 9 months of the year that he was absent – the rent covered his condo fees and made him a little profit, enough to cover his costs while on holiday in Hua Hin. Of course, he didn't know he'd rented his place to a *Guoanbu* front company. There was no reason he should. As long as the tenants looked after the place, kept it clean and paid the rent on time, he had no reason to question who they were.

Fang said, staring up at the lights showing each floor as we moved up. 'I can guess why your Mr Green paid you a visit on the train. Something happened yesterday and I haven't had time to tell you.'

We were alone in the shiny new lift.

Not only alone, but close. Far too close.

Of course, I wanted to know what it was – that went without saying. But it would have to wait, at least for another minute. I had other matters on my mind. I took her hand, and she turned and smiled. She didn't pull away. Her fingers curled around mine with an inevitable effect on my libido. I sensed her warmth, her softness, her femininity.

I turned to her as she turned to me. We kissed, held each other in ferocious want.

It must have lasted all of 6 or 7 blissful seconds, no more, and then – as the lift stopped – we disentangled ourselves and sprang apart, staring ahead like a couple of naughty school children caught stealing sweets.

We straightened our clothing, and both struggled to get our breathing and heartbeats back to normal.

Anyone seeing us at that moment would have been in no doubt what we'd been up to, but fortunately for us, the corridor was empty.

Wasn't me, sir. Not me, miss.

We moved away from the lift; Fang was about to insert her key into the lock of the flat door.

'So, what happened?'

'Yesterday, in Shanghai. You won't believe this. I didn't. Not at first. Du Fu – remember Du Fu, head of public security in the city, Du Lan's brother and Yao's bother-in-law, the guy who so supplied the shellfish toxin to Du Lan to murder Roger Peacock?' She spoke in a low voice; better than whispering.

How could I forget? I wasn't stupid or suffering from amnesia. I remembered the name.

'He walked into the US consulate in Shanghai yesterday morning. Left his driver and bodyguard and went in alone. Showed his ID and demanded asylum. Told the woman on the reception desk he had important information relating to national security, and would divulge everything he knew if they arranged for him to defect, and once they'd agreed on a resettlement package and he was out of the country. In the conversation that followed, and before he was taken off somewhere more secure, he said he was in danger and would be killed if the Americans turned him down. Hinted that he knew about an imminent change of Party leadership. I have a verbatim report from our people who work at the consulate.'

Talk about a mess.

'We're fucked. He knows far too much.'

Fang pushed in the key, turned it, and shoved the door open. She went in ahead of me.

'What does he know, Fang?'

'Enough, Richard. Enough for it to hurt both of us.'

We went through it together. We needed to share a damage assessment. Du Fu knew about Roger, his role as an SIS agent and his target, Yao Tie. That much was obvious. He had supplied the poison to his sister so she could carry out Peacock's murder, which he presumably believed had taken place. He knew they had detained Du Lan. Peacock was the link to UK Station, and Langley had sent along a senior CIA Clandestine Services officer who called himself Jeff Green the Third to discover what I was up to in Thailand and whether I had been running Peacock and had been in contact with Du Fu.

That much we knew.

There was no reason on Fang's part or mine to assume either Green or Du Fu had made Fang yet in any of her guises, and that was our primary concern. But Green was getting close. Peacock had left the country, was on his way back home, and was no longer operational. Uncovering his identity would cause no great harm to our interests – but Fang's security was something else.

That said, could we assume they had not made her?

We agreed we would have to wait to see what the fallout might be, because there was no action either of us could take to improve matters.

Neither of us was happy about it, but of the two of us, Fang seemed more philosophical and content to bide her time. Neither of us had any inkling how the Americans would react to their latest Chinese walk-in. Would they reject him, or exfiltrate him for a lengthy debrief Stateside?

The two-bed condo was a surprise. Fang's helpers had stripped the living area and lined it with some kind of metallic material. There were tables and office chairs on wheels and three computers and monitors of varying size, along with bundles of wiring and consoles I didn't recognise. Whatever furnishings there had been, the team had taken them out, including curtains. The metallic material lined the ceiling, the windows, and a raised floor. The place was bright with artificial lighting that made it even hotter – two of Mr Pelletier's new air–conditioning units were roaring away, but failed to make much of an impact.

Two technicians in navy overalls – I assumed they were Chinese – stood up when we entered. They showed neither surprise nor interest in the fact that a big-nose was with the boss. They seemed careful not to look at either of us.

Fang spoke in staccato bursts of Mandarin. She was no longer the slender, scented, feminine creature with the soft mouth who'd grabbed my balls in the lift. She was back in her dragon mode. Fierce and very much in command.

The senior of the two engineers, or whatever they were, answered in kind, no words wasted, no unnecessary asides or attempts at humour. Nothing spurious. Strictly business, ChiCom style.

'Are we ready?'

We were.

'Bring up the house on Barker Street in Shanghai.'

An immense and hideous colonial style mansion flickered and settled on the biggest of the screens. There were vans and trucks outside, and people hurried back and forth, carrying stuff up the wide flights of steps to the double doors of the stucco monstrosity.

They carried flowers – huge, ornate displays in urns, pots, glassware.

'This is in real time,' Fang said in English. 'Encrypted satellite link.' She sounded proud of it, happy to show it off. I reflected on the fact that the ChiComs always feel they're less than the Americans and even when they're ahead – which they often are, nowadays – they suspect the United States has pulled a fast one on them and is ahead of the game, even when the numbers show the opposite. They can't quite believe they've beaten the imperialist enemy, even when they have. Could be an inferiority complex, rubbed in by generations of poverty, illiteracy, hunger and colonial misrule.

'Know where this is?'

I didn't have to answer.

Fang answered her own question. 'It's the Tao family home in Shanghai.'

'What are all those people doing?'

'Florists. Flowers flown in from the Netherlands and Israel. Around the back – if you want to see, you can – they're taking in the food and drink.'

'What for?'

'It was the Chinese New Year last week and Comrade Yao Tie likes to throw a masked ball, usually a few days later. He saw one – or it could be it was his wife – in Venice. Or maybe it was a Hollywood movie they watched together in their home cinema. He had one of his own, and now it's Shanghai's big social event of the year. Two hundred people plus in fancy dress. The *nomenklatura*. No expense spared.'

'Including ...'

'The Eight – that's right, including them. If they're fit enough to hobble up those steps with the aid of their nurses. I have the guest list from Du Lan. They're all there, along with many other Party Princes. They come from all over the country. Along with favoured billionaires, air force generals, artists and academics. But top Party cadres mostly.'

'And …'

'We're going to be there too, Richard. Our people. The wine servers, the dish-washers, the guys who park the guests' cars – they're ours.'

'What are you going to do?'

'Tell you what, I'll give you a taste of what's in store.'

21

The woman has her head down, chin on chest, dark hair cascading forward, hiding her face. She's seated before a metal table and behind her is a light blue screen which could be a papered wall or a sheet. She's wearing what appear to be yellow pyjamas or a jump-suit, the kind that prisoners are forced to wear. She raises both hands and places them together on the table, fingers locked, and it's clear that she's handcuffed. The cuffs around her wrists are steel.

She raises her head, shakes her hair aside, stares into the camera lens. She wears no make-up, her uncombed hair hangs limp on either side of her face. No jewellery is visible. She looks tired, stressed out. Fang has put her through four rehearsals to get this right, which means both speaking and acting as schooled. The recording itself has been made in stages, then edited and put together.

Fang is proud of her handiwork. She believes her captive strikes exactly the right note for the intended audience, right down to her expressions and gestures.

'My name is Du Lan.'

Her Mandarin is subdued, hoarse. Her lips tremble as she pauses, but she regains control and continues, more confident now. She knows her script off by heart. In that slightest hesitation, Fang knows, her name will sink in. Du Lan. People will get it. Yao's notorious tai-tai from Shanghai. Everyone who's anyone in the Chinese communist ruling class will know it, will know her or know of her by reputation. Right now, she bears no resemblance at all to the wealthy socialite whose excesses they used to hear about and read about in Hong Kong papers with a mixture of envy, amusement, disapproval and horror.

Where's your pride now, darling? Where's your power, your privilege?

'I want to apologise. I want to apologise to the Party, to my community, to my family and to my friends. I have let you all down and I am sorry. I ask for your forgiveness. I beg the Party's forgiveness. I ask my husband, Yao Tie, to forgive me for my betrayal.'

That word alone should hold their attention. *Betrayal.* High society brought low. That's something every Chinese will enjoy, something Fang believes the Germans call *schadenfreude*, pleasure at another's painful fall from grace. Fang smiles at the woman on the screen. It's a sneer of triumph – not sympathy.

Yao, watching this tomorrow along with his hundreds of friends and associates, will understand that he's a dead man standing, that he has lost everything, including his right to life. His millions, his properties, his mistresses, his insane power grab – they mean nothing. They have all the substance of mist, of smoke. Vaporised in a few words on a video recording. One moment he had everything, the next nothing.

He will never live to enjoy any of it.

Fang feels a slight pang of regret about the son. He might be vain and spoiled, the teenage princeling, but it isn't his fault. It's the way he's being raised. The boy doesn't deserve what's coming to him, just as Fang's mother and her family didn't deserve to

212

die violently, their bodies concealed under paving, their memory smeared as traitors.

Can't be helped. There's always collateral damage. At least he'll live. Probably.

Fang catches Brodick's look. It is one of incredulity, even shock – but he doesn't know the worst of it.

Du Lan is only just getting going with her prepared speech.

Fang hits the forward button and the recording proceeds.

'I confess I was the lover of an English spy, Roger Peacock. He advised my husband and I on financial matters. He was tutor to my teenage son. He helped us export funds abroad with which we bought expensive properties in foreign countries, including Australia, the United States and Britain. He helped us set up bank accounts in overseas tax havens, and showed my husband how to import profits from his property deals as tax-free foreign investments.' She takes a breath, glances up at the camera, then looks away, a furtive glance that seems to combine guilt and shame. 'Peacock and I slept together on several occasions, in foreign hotels.'

Another pause.

Fang imagines she can hear the round snapped into the chamber of the executioner's pistol. There's no defiance, no bravado left in her words or gestures.

She blurts out another sentence. 'This money laundering and the evasion of tax law are, of course, illegal. It's called corruption.'

Du Lan has been told that a full confession in which she implicates her husband and herself might – *might* – save her life and protect that of her son. Fang has said nothing to disabuse her of the notion, though Fang thinks it's delusion. Nothing can save her.

'My brother, Du Fu, head of the Public Security Bureau in Shanghai, discovered during an investigation by his colleagues in the Ministry of Public Security that the foreigner Roger Peacock was an English spy. Peacock had spied on my family. He had too much information about my husband and his business dealings. Du Fu wanted to save his brother-in-law and me. I told him I would deal with it. I decided to kill Peacock. My brother gave me the poison, which I, in turn, gave to Peacock in a Beijing hotel after we spent our last night together. I used a toxin from the sea anemone because I knew it to be quick-acting and fatal. I am truly sorry and regret my actions. I apologise to Mr Peacock's widow.'

She hangs her head again and says nothing for a full minute.

Fang taps her foot with impatience.

Come on!

Du Lan sniffs, tries to use her cuffed hands to wipe the tears off her face, with mixed results. 'I also want you to know that my husband paid millions of US dollars from his illegal activities to senior Party members who, with my husband's backing, plan to force Deng Xiaoping to stand aside. Aside from my husband, there are seven senior comrades, all military and intelligence cadres, who have decided that Deng is taking the Party and the Chinese people down the wrong path, that he has allowed himself to be contaminated by his contacts in the West and that he is not defending our revolution but on the contrary, is scheming with counter-revolutionary foreign elements, including the colonial rulers of Hong Kong and their secret services.'

This is the crux of the so-called confession.

There's a break here in the video, but Fang doesn't think it shows.

'Here are the names of those involved in the conspiracy, all of whom received payments from my husband … Here, I have the list of payments, the account numbers and the banks.'

From papers on the table in front of her, she reads out the name of each alleged plotter, along with the total amount each of the plotters has received. As she moves the sheets of paper, her manacles jingle and catch the light. Her tears fall on the papers.

Du Lan continues to spell out the details, but the screen is now taken up with images of the conspirators. They are shown one by one, full face and close up. Without exception, they are elderly, male. The portraits are of poor quality, comprising enlarged copies of photographs from Party identification cards.

Du Lan is back on camera and she returns to her confession, but Fang can detect changes she missed earlier – it seems that it's some time later; the lighting is a little different and Du Lan is sitting at a different angle – and indeed, the camera has been set up at a different height and seems a little lower. Not that it matters. Most viewers won't notice and considering the whole thing has been edited and put back together over a period of 24 hours, it's pretty good – even if she thinks so herself.

'I am ashamed. I ask the Party's forgiveness for my misdeeds. I was proud and greedy and I recognise my faults. I thought I could do whatever I liked because my husband was so powerful. I beg the Party to be merciful ...'

Du Lan clears her throat. She's on the verge of tears. No, not on the verge. Tears are rolling down her cheeks again, a veritable flood this time. Is it genuine regret – or is it fear? She's a pretty good actress.

Even Fang, director, script writer and producer of this performance, feels uncomfortable and embarrassed watching this woman – any woman – humiliating herself in this way.

Fang notices this in Brodick's appalled reaction and turns down

215

the volume, then switches off the video. 'You've seen enough for now, Richard, haven't you?'

'What will happen to her?'

'To Du Lan?'

'Yes.'

Fang sighs, shrugs. 'Oh, Richard, come on now. Corruption and collaboration with a foreign intelligence agency are both capital crimes in our legal system, as you know.'

'That's it?'

'What do you expect? Realistically, what do you expect?'

'But Du Lan *didn't* kill Peacock, for fuck's sake. She's confessing to something she didn't do, to murder.'

'She knows that, we both know it, but the court will want a perpetrator and it's better than trying to deny it – even though she didn't actually carry out her plan. She intended to kill him and we stopped her. The military court will accept her confession. Not that it makes much difference either way. She wants to save her son and her brother, in that order. She'll do anything. That's why she's co-operating – her regret and expression of guilt are a pretence, a show. She knows it's expected of her. Public penance. A formality. The judges will have their instructions and will carry them out even if Mr Peacock walks into the court before sentencing and declares himself to be a witness for the defence. Not that he would be allowed access. That's how it is. This is a stage play in which everyone has a part to play in the drama, the script having been written beforehand. What you would call a morality play.'

'I thought *I* was cynical.'

'We have to be, Richard. It's our vocation, no?'

'So this self-abasement and confession is for nothing?'

216

'Not nothing. It might save them, the boy in particular.'

'You persuaded her to confess to a murder she didn't commit.'

'It didn't take much. Du Lan knows the score.'

'And you believe you did the right thing, Fang? You approve, even now?'

'Depends on what you mean by "right", Richard.'

Fang looks at him, thinking that the English are such sentimentalists. Considering the suffering they caused in filling their own pockets and creating their great empire at the expense of millions of people, including the Chinese, over a period of some 200 years, it never ceases to surprise her that English people will go out of their way to look after the welfare of animals but step around – or over – the hungry children and homeless folk living rough in their own wealthy cities. A cute kitten seems to have greater emotional impact than some terrified refugee family fleeing a conflict caused by the actions of the so-called Western 'rules-based international order'.

Such hypocrisy!

'Who said anything about approval, Richard? My approval or disapproval is irrelevant. Our opinions don't matter, never did. I am a servant of the Party, you of Her Majesty's Government. I do my duty, you do yours.'

'But we *don't* do our duty, do we? Which is worse, do you think, your Party or my state?'

'You tell me – though I'm biased.'

'Aren't you taking matters into your own hands – and breaking with your own Party in the process?'

'Aren't you? Aren't we both? We're twins in treachery, Richard. I'm carrying out my duties as a Party member to the best of my ability, as you do.'

'As you see it.'

'No. As my Party wishes it and as required of me in my professional capacity – as head of counter-intelligence.'

'No doubts at all?'

'No, none.'

'You're doing this without seeking authorisation?'

'In the field I'm allowed to exercise a degree of personal judgement, okay?'

'I thought you didn't do personal.'

Bo Deli can be a real pain sometimes.

'I meant professional judgement.'

'Oh, right. If you say so, boss.'

'What authorisation do you have, Richard, for what you do?'

They are both rule breakers. They are both traitors. They have formed an alliance in defiance of authority, of the norms of loyalty and trust. They are no better than nihilists.

She punches him lightly on the arm. He's annoying yet somehow loveable, and Fang resists the temptation to hug him. This is neither the time nor place for demonstrations of affection, not while watching a member of the *nomenklatura* condemn herself to death.

He surprises her sometimes.

Brodick changes the subject. 'I'm sorry, I didn't wish you a happy Chinese New Year. We both seem to have forgotten. But here's my New Year gift – better late than never. A little something to remind you of our relationship.'

Bo Deli hands her a paperback book.

'What's this?'

'I thought you'd prefer it to an expensive perfume or a silk scarf. It's the latest security handbook for all new NSA staffers.'

'That's so romantic.' She gives him a peck on the cheek. 'Thank you so much!'

Fang has sent Bo Deli back to his beachfront guesthouse for the night, insisting he ride pillion on the scooter she's arranged for the purpose. It's an 8-minute walk or so as the crow flies, much less on a scooter, but her man has orders to take the *da-bizi* on a circuitous route through the town, past the bars and nightclubs and through the alleys and lanes of the night market, where he'll change to another scooter and two machines – each with two people – will split up, testing the abilities of any team on his tail. Fang wants to know if he's still shadowed – by the Americans, the Thais or anyone else. Not that she'll do anything if he *is* tagged, other than lead his watchers on a dance around Hua-Hin before depositing him back at the Bansabai.

Brodick has his instructions, too. If he detects no surveillance at the guesthouse, he's to leave a towel or shirt tied to the railing of the covered verandah that runs along the side of the ground floor on the beach side, and Fang has told him to place his footwear outside his room door. At any hint of watchers in place, he'll withdraw both signals.

Fang has the condo to herself. It's such a relief! She walks into the bathroom – she's struck by its size, the expensive tiling and costly fittings – throws off her clothes and runs the shower, testing the temperature of the water until it feels right, then steps in and luxuriates in the hot needles pounding head and body. By this time tomorrow, her task will be complete. She should be free to return to Beijing, but being honest with herself, she has no clear idea how the full ramifications of her action will work themselves out. Will Xie Rong still be there behind his immense desk, puffing on those cigarettes of his, his teapot steaming away?

219

More to the point – will she be safe?

Fang knows that arrests have a momentum of their own, with over-zealous law enforcement bodies indiscriminate in scooping up all manner of innocent people who happen to be in the wrong place at the wrong time – and with unforeseen and unpleasant consequences. Simply by being placed under arrest is in itself an act of criminal guilt on the part of the detained.

When Party sharks are unleashed in a feeding frenzy, no-one is immune.

Not even the head of the *Guoanbu* 5th Bureau.

The bigger and higher the target ...

Fang, wrapped in a white bath towel, perches on the edge of the sofa and dries her hair as she tries to weigh the risks.

What's the alternative?

Defection.

For Fang, going over to the other side would amount to not so much betrayal of Party and country but an admission of failure, an admission of failure in her own eyes. Even if she took that route to safety, one offered by Bo Deli, what kind of life would it be in a decaying state, a failing society, to say nothing of terrible weather on a small, overcrowded and self-centred island governed by rightists with no real future except its self-centred dreams of a mythical past? The West generally was dying on its feet – well, according to secret Party assessments, it was. Fragmenting and regressing. Would she be happy working as a Chinese Studies academic in some second-rate, provincial English university and going home to Bo Deli, two children and a dog each evening, cooking them supper and reading the kids a bedtime story as they did in sentimental Western movies? She can't take that idea seriously. It's an absurd fantasy.

And anyway, she's a lousy cook.

Fang puts off the lights, walks barefoot into the master bedroom, drops the towel on a chair and slides naked between the sheets.

She has so much still to live for in the People's Republic of China, provided she survives this crisis. For one thing, there's Xie Rong's job as chief of the *Guoanbu*. She'd be so much better at it. He's a Party hack – she, on the other hand, is a professional.

She'd be the first woman in the role and the first incumbent under the age of 50.

If she does capture the post, she'll begin by launching a whole-sale reform from top to bottom and turn the *Guoanbu* into a lean machine on a war footing rather than the many-layered and comfortable bureaucracy it has become under Xie's lazy oversight.

Maybe she and Bo Deli can maintain their partnership, taking their intelligence collaboration to new levels in both quality and quantity. He would rise, too, of course, in his quaint little organisation, the Secret Intelligence Service, but there'd still be masses of material he could harvest from his country's intelligence allies in the form of the Five Eyes partnership of the United States, Canada, Australia, New Zealand, the United Kingdom and – if reports are correct – a new addition waiting in the wings, Germany. For the *Guoanbu*, Germany is the number two intelligence target after the United States, along with Japan. The United Kingdom is small beer – its only value lies in being a window through which the *Guoanbu* can penetrate more important targets.

The risk of operating at such levels will be greater for them both, of course, and will have to be factored into her plans.

No, she decides, it won't work. Once she's secured Xie Rong's position, the link to Bo Deli will turn out to be too risky to maintain – and also superfluous, if only because she can no longer perform as an agent runner. It wouldn't be tenable in her new, elevated role. Oh, well. She turns over in the bed, stretches out her legs. It's wonderfully comfortable. Sleep laps at the edge of her mind. Her final thoughts before succumbing to exhaustion are that in her capacity as future head of the *Guoanbu*, she can't expect to continue to run Bo Deli as an agent, but it'll be a big loss. There can be no question of handing him over to another case officer. It's unrealistic. Discovery would follow and it would prove fatal for them both.

She'll have to draw a line under the operation.

That will mean choosing between loving her funny British spy, heading off with him into a romantic sunset in British suburbia, or disposing of him – and the latter would have to be final. A clean break. There can be no resurrection, as in Peacock's case.

It's going to be one or the other. You or me, Bo Deli. There's no middle way.

Fang knows she has to make the choice soon, in a matter of hours or days.

Sorry, Richard, my love. So sorry.

22

I enjoyed the ride around town; the streets deserted well before midnight – in contrast to Bangkok, which never seemed to sleep. Between mounts, I paused long enough to buy some chicken and rice to take back with me. Like everything else, even cola, it was handed to me in a plastic bag, fastened with a rubber band with a flick of the shopkeeper's wrist. Once I was back, I watched the scooter speed away, his colleague following on the second machine. I checked the wedges I'd left in my door, then the rickety wardrobe with its three bent wire hangers and bedside drawer. They were still in place. The place was clear as far as I could tell. I bolted my door, having left out the signals according to Fang's wishes – or rather, instructions – both towel and shoes. I unpacked my gear, located the satellite, received the green, blinking signal, and looked for any signals waiting for me. There were two.

One was unexpected.

010484–54–658UK

TOP SECRET. UK EYES ONLY. FLASH.

1. YOU WILL IMMEDIATELY ORDER DRAGON TO STAND DOWN.

2. SUBJECT MUST REPEAT MUST AVOID JEOPARDISING ROLE BY ACTIVELY ATTEMPTING TO PREVENT OR DISRUPT ALLEGED CCP PLOT.

3. STRESS DRAGON'S ROLE OF VITAL IMPORTANCE TO SERVICE AND MUST BE PROTECTED.

4. INTERVENTION RUNS HIGH RISK OF EXPOSURE. SUBJECT'S PRIORITY MUST BE INTEL COLLECTION NOT REPEAT NOT FREELANCE POLITICAL OPERATIONS.

5. YOU WILL INSIST DRAGON COMPLY.

6. ACKNOWLEDGE.

I wouldn't insist on anything. All right, all right. London – or at least the TCI committee – had got its collective knickers in a twist over Fang. Century House seemed to have hardened its stance on not doing anything to prevent a putsch by hard-liners. As if Century House had a better sense than the case officer in the field of what was – and what was not – deemed too risky. It wouldn't be the first time or the last that a committee panicked and started sending out orders to field operatives to rein in their agents. It was office politics, of course, but I would play the dutiful case officer and go through the motions of tugging my forelock. OK, so London wouldn't authorise any action on my part, or DRAGON's, to forestall the move – the alleged move – against Deng.

224

Or maybe it was the ChiCom conspiracy itself that had everyone confused and they didn't want to get involved for fear of exposure – or because they weren't yet sure where our national interests lay and how the Firm should react, if at all.

Could be we were waiting for Washington to tell us.

There was little I could do. Fang had the proverbial bit between her lovely white teeth; the race had begun and there was no stopping her. I was a bystander in this high-stakes drama, not a participant. I was prohibited from travelling to the mainland. Century House had made that clear. I had no skin in the conspiracy either way. Should I care? Not really. Fang wouldn't 'stand down' – she wasn't going to take orders from London. Why would she? It was ridiculous to think she would – but then Century House didn't know the whole story of our relationship, and I hoped they never would.

I would witness the event she was planning. I would hold her hand if she needed it, but I didn't think she would. She'd never needed a case officer to hold her hand in the past – it was usually the other way around, with Fang grabbing me by some more sensitive part of my anatomy and dragging me along. Fang had her team here in Thailand and she seemed to know what she was doing and doubtless had thought it all through. There was no role for me. I was a supernumerary. In fact, I might as well go home and take part in GLUTTON's debrief and, after it was all over, buy him a few drinks. We'd get plastered together and I'd sympathise with him over the loss of his marriage, his business, his access to the PRC. If he'd let me, that is. By now perhaps Peacock saw me as the main instrument of his destruction and hated my guts. If so, he wasn't wrong.

I acknowledged the signal.

The second message was straightforward.

010484–54–658UK

SECRET. UK EYES ONLY. IMMEDIATE.

1. GLUTTON RETURNED SAFELY AND IN GOOD SPIRITS.

2. SUBJECT IN PROTECTIVE CUSTODY PENDING DEBRIEF.

3. DEBRIEF TO COMMENCE IMMINENTLY.

4. WILL CONSULT/KEEP YOU ADVISED OF PROGRESS.

5. GTFL ADVISE ESTIMATED TIME OF RETURN.

6. ACKNOWLEDGE.

As instructed, I acknowledged this signal, packed away my gear, put the wedges back in place and went outside, locking the room door behind me and pocketing the key. After slipping on my deck shoes, I stood still for half a minute, counting up to 30, waiting for my eyes to get used to the dark so I could identify the unfamiliar shapes – chairs and tables, a bird cage suspended from the eaves, shophouses with their shutters down, cars, pickups and motorcycles parked on both sides of the road, telegraph poles at peculiar angles, topped by huge bundles of chaotic electrical wiring like storks' nests. A dog barked in the distance, a cat on heat yowled in the alley. The air was warm, the sea breeze welcome if only because it carried off the stink of drains. I padded around the building, trying to make as little noise as possible on floorboards that creaked at every other step. I found a wooden chair, picking it up and setting it down again so I could rest my feet up on the railing.

Out beyond the sand and rocks, white lines of foam marked the waves, rising, lengthening and vanishing again in their serried ranks, driven by the onshore breeze. The continuous sound of sea water swarming up and down the beach was especially calming.

I had thought hard about Fang, about what made her the way she was. I puzzled over her as her case officer, as her kidnap victim, as her agent, as her occasional lover and as someone who found her desirable and not a little scary. Well, fear had something to do with the desire. Fear and danger. They were aphrodisiacs. They were to me. I was no psychologist; I had no special insight into her character, but ambition counted for a lot of what made her the way she was, the way she approached her work and the world generally. Professional success mattered to Fang. Like many Chinese who'd survived the Cultural Revolution and the Great Leap Forward, she'd known extreme hunger, poverty and brutality. It was no wonder she was that way. I knew that much. She wanted to survive and prosper. Didn't we all?

I also knew her past was something she wanted not to bury but obliterate under the weight of her accomplishments. She couldn't do so, of course, but it didn't stop her from trying to rub it out and in that sense, a successful and all-powerful *Guoanbu* officer played a vital part in that longed-for internment of the family history. She too revelled in pseudonyms, in changing identities. It wasn't a coincidence that she was working for a Party that had wiped out so much of the past, not only hers but an entire country's, razing the truth and destroying millions of lives with the tools of Marxist–Leninist–Maoist ideology, marking history as forbidden territory, as a minefield, even to the extent of 'modernising' Mandarin so that new generations could not access their ancestors' real lives in their libraries.

Fang wanted security, safety, stability – but she had no clue how to go about it.

So much for trying to understand Fang – what of me?

Sitting out there in the darkness, with only the dark sea, the coming and going of phosphorescent waves and a few stars above – the sky being veiled in a thin mist – I had exhausted and over-thought tomorrow's plans. All I could do was match what little I knew of Fang with the little I knew – or imagined – of my own origins.

I took off my shirt and tied it to the railing as instructed.

We lived – my mother, father and I – in a tiny, two-bedroom, rented cottage in the Cape Town southern suburb of Kenilworth, whites only, of course, middle class, with its suburban train station and quiet residential streets, its neat gardens and clipped hedges, its brown-skinned servants and its polished cars in the driveways. I'd hear my parents shout at each other after I was sent to bed; I could hardly do otherwise – the thin walls and limited space made sure of it. The shouts and shrieks ended in blows, dull thumps, my mother's crying, then silence. I buried my head under the bedclothes; what made things seem better was the line I whispered to myself.

It doesn't get worse than this.

But it did, of course. It had to, but I didn't know that at the age of five, so the idea that it *didn't* get worse gave rise to another thought: in that case, it had to get better. I was an optimist. There was no self-pity. When I was taken to hospital and examined for possible broken ribs, I recited it again through clenched teeth.

It doesn't get worse than this.

I remembered little of the incident – my surprise more than anything else at being hurled out of my high chair across a restaurant dining room, sprawling on the floor, tears and cries of shock more than pain was all it was, along with the sheer surprise. I had done nothing I knew of, said nothing to trigger the sudden rage.

When my lips were split open from a swinging slap still later, I still recited it as the doctor sewed my mouth back together again, weeping with the pain of forcing my lips to move to say the words in a whisper.

As so often in these cases, I blamed myself for the outbursts and violence. I must be a wicked child to have caused so much anger.

There was nothing unusual about my having recurring nightmares, bed-wetting and sleep-walking. Several of my pals at boarding school had suffered much the same.

This was my mantra then: *things will get better*. But for them to do so, I must escape to something better. I would achieve nothing by waiting. All I wanted was to escape from my parents, from what passed for a home, from boarding school, from the military, from the country, from the first wife, from myself. I wanted fresh places, new identities, new loves and hates, new adventures, new cuisines, new wines, new ways of talking, new girlfriends, new sexual experiences, new styles of clothing. I could not stay still and wait for a better world. I had to be the doer. I had to make it better myself. I learned to be a chameleon, always changing colour, changing names, changing jobs, changing accents, changing relationships. There was never a time when I didn't want to be someone else, so much so I practised different voices, ways of moving, of acting, of behaving. People I admired, I imitated – their ways of speaking, of movement, their gestures and habits.

People watching and imitating was my favourite pastime. I was a professional foreigner even at home, wherever that was.

Yet I was always wary of anyone getting too close; I was on the run from others and myself, and I made sure I bit every hand that fed me, without exception.

In my teenage years, drugs helped, especially low doses of LSD – enough to put an edge on objects, to bring the mundane alive, from the sap of a tree trunk to the writhing innards of a loaf of bread. For some people, it was drink that gave them the edge they sought. I too wanted to make the world blaze from the inside out, because it helped me laugh at the absurdity of living. Acid helped me laugh; later on speed in the form of a fast bike would replace the drugs, then sex – lots of it.

If necessary, and in short bursts, I could charm. I could impress, entertain, even amuse. I was good at telling jokes. I could seem interested, concerned, even kind. I'd open doors, pull out chairs for females and help the elderly across the street. I'd befriend dogs if anyone was watching and give them a good kick if they weren't. Like a tart, I knew how to get what I wanted. I could give pleasure – and inflict pain. I could hate and smile at the same time.

I was almost ideal spy material, in fact, a shapeshifter, a mobile and adaptable lump of ectoplasm, an amoral survivor under the blanket, someone who could mould himself to any shape of conduct required of me.

It doesn't get worse than this.

Sorry to disappoint, old son, but it can and will.

I wish someone had told me that at the outset.

I had the feeling I was being watched. Odd, given I heard nothing

230

but the sea. I was sitting back in my chair, feet up on the wooden railing. I turned my head this way and that, listened hard. I was imagining things.

A scrape of a foot on the floor, followed by a familiar male voice.

'How's the fishing, Mr Fisher? Catch anything today?'

Fuck.

'It's going splendidly, thanks.'

I pulled my shirt off the railing.

'Great. I bring news.'

'How long have you been standing there?'

'Oh, a couple of minutes. Making sure you're alone.'

'You don't give up, do you, Mr Green?'

'As I said, I'm the bearer of news.'

He came closer, back against the wall so I had to turn around to see him. Gone was the well-cut linen suit, the loafers, the bow tie and in their place was a Grateful Dead tee, baggy shorts with lots of pockets, flip-flops, a dark baseball cap. Mr Green looked like 100,000 other foreign tourists, which was doubtless the objective.

I waited

'I'll take this from the top. It's official: the emperor's on holiday. Of course he's not.'

It wasn't in the papers.

'Before he announced his family holiday – and we're talking 17 family members going along for the ride – he did, of course, pass the baton to his anointed successor.'

This conversation reminded me of Bamber Gascoigne and *University Challenge*, a series I'd enjoyed. I could play this game, too.

'Jiang Zemin.'

'Right first time. And why? First, Deng believes that unless his reforms are expanded and driven forward, the PRC will face a similar fate to that of Eastern Europe and the Soviet Union. He believes it's a matter of the CCP's survival. He could be right. Washington thinks so. Deng is relying on Jiang to do just that. Hell, the old man is 87 or thereabouts. He knows he's not got much time. His sight and hearing are failing. He gets tired. He's a tough old bird, but even he can't escape the ageing process. Right?'

'Right.' Where was all this leading?

'OK – so now the Party's preparing for the 14th Party Congress sometime later this year. It will mark the changeover, the succession, the enthronement of the new guy. So Deng has made it known to Jiang that if he supports Deng's faster reforms, the old boy will support Jiang for the top job – if not, Deng will back some other candidate. Jiang understands this, and has thrown his weight behind a more rapid opening up of China.'

'You'd make a great political science lecturer, Mr Green.'

'I'll take that as a compliment, Mr Fisher, and not as the insult it's intended to be.'

'No offence intended.'

The man who called himself Green was fiddling with his pockets. He pulled out a crumpled pack of Lucky Strike.

'Want one?'

'No thanks.' I did, but I didn't want to admit it, and in fact I knew that if I smoked after such a long period of abstinence, it would make me nauseous and I'd only make a fool of myself in front of Langley's man by vomiting over his flip-flops.

Green's lighter flared. He sucked at the cigarette so that it glowed in the dark and the pungent smell filled the air before being whisked away by the sea breeze.

'I don't have to tell you that there's a lot of resistance in the Party. Now, there's at least a dozen old men who don't much care for Deng's ideas. Chen Yun is one Party veteran digging in his heels, or so we hear. One of Deng's old comrades, but unlike Deng, born into poverty, self-taught, joined the Party in the twenties and fought the Japanese ...'

'Yes, I know the name. Shanghai underground with Deng under Zhou Enlai in the 1930s. Differences emerged in the eighties.'

'Right again, chief. Then there's this fellow called Li ...'

I was getting bored and tried to hurry things along. 'Premier Li Peng. Front man for the old school of hard-line Maoists.'

'That's the one. It was Li Peng who criticised several anonymous articles – a series – in Shanghai's *Liberation Daily*. This was last April. You saw them?'

He was asking for it and I couldn't resist the bait.

'But they weren't anonymous, were they, Mr Green? They appeared under the title *Huangfu Ping* or Shanghai Commentary. The clue was in the name. *Huang* refers to the Huangpu River that runs through the city while *fu ping* can be taken to mean *fuzhou* Deng Xiaoping or 'to help Deng Xiaoping'. The Central Propaganda Department tried to put Deng back in his box by refuting the articles in the *People's Daily* and *Guangming Daily* and again when Premier Li opened Shanghai's Nanpu Bridge a couple of months ago ...'

'November,' Mr Green added.

'Thank you. November, as you say. On behalf of the old guard, Li attacked the articles, saying they'd mislead people into thinking the Party's political direction had changed, knowing full well, of course, that the author was Deng himself. Deng fought back, pushing for one of his own supporters, vice premier Zhu Rongji, to direct the economy, but Li blocked the move.'

Green flicked the glowing stub of cigarette into the night. 'We agree then that this struggle is going on behind the scenes, so Washington and London and everyone else have to rely on intel to know what the hell is happening – and we don't know enough, but I'm sure your deep cover agents could help us.'

I remembered McGregor's parting questions – who was up? Who was down? What the fuck was going on over there?

Green hadn't finished his lecture. 'It seems Deng has decided not to get bogged down in arguments, but to act, to take the lead himself.'

'Meaning?'

'This one's free, buddy. On the house. He's about to embark with those 17 members of his family on a family holiday. That's the Party line. Of course, there are rumours, some of which might be closer to the truth. Some say he's ill and is in hospital. Or that he's in forced retirement, if you get my meaning – that is, he's under house arrest in the government complex in Beijing. Others say he's turned to drink and gets plastered every evening on that evil *Maotai*. It's foul stuff. It's a distillation of fermented sorghum and goes way back to the Qing dynasty.'

'I read about it in last week's *Economist*.'

'Very fuckin' funny, Mr Fisher.'

'And?' I didn't trust Mr Green the Third at all.

'A related matter. At least, I believe it's related. A certain Du Fu – I guess you've heard the name – who heads the all-powerful Shanghai Public Security Bureau happened to stroll into our consulate there a couple of days ago. Day before yesterday. Did you know? He wants to defect and requested political asylum.'

'Will he get it?'

'It's under consideration. We're of a mind to throw him out, on

234

the grounds that it's likely a provocation, coming as it does at a sensitive time in US–China relations. He has some interesting things to say, though.'

'I can imagine, but beware Greeks bearing gifts, Mr Green.'

'He talks about a brother-in-law named Yao Tie. One powerful *hombre*. Shanghai Party Secretary, wealthy, allegedly the money bags behind the conservative faction opposed to Deng. They're planning a showdown – I reckon before the Party congress.'

'So a coup – is that what you're saying?'

'Something of the kind, yeah. My people think so.'

'A coup, which your people want to kill stone dead?'

'Hell, why would we? For once, we, the Pentagon and even State are on the same page. Think about it. I mean, if Deng fails, and we're betting that he *will* fail, then China falls apart. In terms of the economy, it stagnates or goes backwards. Bye-bye to all that foreign investment, job creation, lifting hundreds of thousands, if not millions, of very pissed-off peasants out of poverty. The CCP collapses, like their commie brethren in Moscow, Prague, Warsaw and Berlin. OK, so the equity and currency markets will take a fall, but that's temporary. Now you have to agree that's an attractive proposition – attractive to us, anyhow. And if that doesn't happen, and a gang of inward-looking Maoists takes over, hey, it'll usher in a period of little or no economic growth and a prolonged period – decades – of political and diplomatic isolation. I say, and a lot of folk inside the Beltway agree, that we should leave well alone.'

'And the bloodshed, the hunger and poverty, the chaos that will follow – even another civil war?'

'Not our concern, buddy. Not yours, not mine. It sure as hell isn't our job to save the ChiComs from themselves. Aren't they always accusing us of interfering in their internal affairs? If the hardliners win, it weakens China, puts it on the back foot – and for us in the West, that has to be good. Good for human rights, for world peace, for Taiwan. Right?'

He was right, of course he was – except for Taiwan. I'd been slow on the uptake. Neither Washington nor London wanted China as a direct competitor in manufacturing, in services, in seeking raw materials and stealing advanced technology, in extending its influence throughout Asia, Africa and the Middle East. Washington didn't want a new Asia Pacific superpower challenging the established American hegemon. It was going to be Athens and Sparta all over. The established, status quo power – Sparta – was scared stiff of the new kid on the block – Athens. US taxpayers expected a peace dividend now the Cold War was over – not yet another struggle for global dominance. America was running scared of Beijing's red barons.

'And this Du Fu?'

'Oh, yeah. Almost forgot. Sorry. Du Fu mentioned someone named, uh, let's see – yeah, Roger Peacock, that's it – Du Fu claimed this Peacock was an English spy who was a financial consultant and adviser to Yao and was at the same time banging Yao's wife, Du Lan, who happens to be Du Fu's sister. He was pretty sore about it, too. Does this ring any bells, Mr Fisher? Du Fu said his sister murdered Peacock in his sleep with a shellfish poison that Du Fu had given her.'

'Why would he do that?'

'Give his sister Du Lan the poison to kill the Brit, you mean? Well, according to Du Fu, Peacock had details of Yao's illegal financial dealings as well as payments made by Yao to military and intelligence people involved in organising the anti-Deng movement. You know as well as I do that contact with a foreign intelligence organisation is a death sentence. Du Fu might be a big man at the Ministry of Public Security in Shanghai, but he's justified in fearing for his life, don't you reckon? Peacock was a threat not only to Yao but to his extended family, including the wife and Du Fu himself. Does this make any sense to you? We'd love your take on this, especially as this Peacock must have been one of your UK Station assets, right?'

I didn't respond, and the darkness hid whatever my facial expression might have shown. I pulled my shirt back on but left it unbuttoned. At least being this close to the sea meant fewer mosquitoes.

Green flip-flopped over to the railing and looked out to where the dark waters drew back to prepare another assault on the shoreline. 'My condolences, by the way, if you did lose your agent. Sounds like he was a good 'un while he lasted.

'This Du Fu character of yours is some fantasist, Mr Green. Maybe he is a provocateur. Best put that particular fish back in the sea. For what it's worth, that's my take on it.'

Mr Green got in the last punch.

'Yeah, guess you're right. Thanks for the advice. But it is odd, don't you think, Mr Fisher, that someone named Roger Peacock travelling on a valid UK passport from the mainland should check into an international youth hostel in Bangkok 2 nights ago – and then catch a British Airways flight to Heathrow? Has to be the same feller – can't be coincidence, right? People who saw him say he was no stiff, but very much alive at the time. You wouldn't know anything about that, either, would you?'

Of course I didn't. Not a damn thing.

23

Fang rolls off him and sits up in the bed.

They're both naked and slippery with sweat. 'That was wonderful, the best,' she says, but I've been in better beds.'

'The best?' Bo Deli is surprised.

'We could take our time. Compared to the first. It wasn't such a crazy wrestling match as before.'

'If I remember, that room in Beirut – we were under fire. It was …' Brodick hesitates – 'distracting.'

'Speak for yourself. I wasn't distracted. I found it exciting.'

'You would. You're addicted to danger.'

'What's that supposed to mean? That's so unfair. Anyway, we weren't under fire. The hotel was. The western sector of Beirut was. It wasn't personal.'

'It felt bloody personal. It became personal.'

'That was afterwards. You were unlucky. Wrong place, wrong time. Isn't that what you say?'

'Have it your way. Why've you cut your hair?'

Fang touches it with her fingers. 'You don't like it? It's a bob, if you know what that is. More practical and formal – and I like it. It's smart. It goes with my work clothes.'

'I prefer it long.'

'Too bad. You'll have to wait a few months. I'll grow it out by winter.'

'I don't have months and I won't be there in winter. Did you get any sleep?'

'Enough. You?'

'Not enough, but you're right, it was great. You were great. You had someone watch this place until the American left?'

'He's left Thailand.'

'Finally. Your people were following Green?'

'Not following. Monitoring.'

Fang looks around, changes the subject. She has an urge to talk about ordinary stuff, simple things, the mundanities she imagines ordinary, decent people like to talk about after making love. 'I like your room. It's big, old-fashioned, and I like all the wood. I love the ceiling fan, especially the whirring sound it makes, though it's not effective. It's like being in an old movie. I adored *Casablanca*, by the way. I saw it in Manila a few years ago. I loved that beautiful actress, Ingrid Bergman, and the American actor. What was his name? An old time Hollywood star.' Now she remembers. 'Bogart. Humphrey Bogart. It was so romantic.' She sees he's not interested. 'OK, what did the CIA spy want?'

'Green. He calls himself Green, remember? He wanted to talk about Du Fu. According to Green, they're considering his request for asylum. Green seems to think it might be a provocation. Du is talking already, though. He's mentioned Peacock, his wife's murder of the English spy, his supply of the poison and Yao's payments to hard-liners.'

'Anything else?'

'Green knows that Peacock's alive. He knows he flew to Thailand from the mainland, stayed at the hostel and has since left for the UK on a scheduled flight.'

'I've something to add to that, Richard. When I get back, I've orders to see Du in person at the US consulate in Shanghai. I'm to persuade him to withdraw his request for asylum and escort him off the premises. The Americans asked our *Guoanbu* liaison people for the meeting. Maybe I'll see this Mr Green. The Americans don't want Du. They've already decided to ditch him. The Americans think we're professional and not as corrupt as some departments I could mention, and they want the *Guoanbu* to handle it, not Du's *Gonganbu*. They also want to smooth things over with Beijing and not let this make matters worse. It's progress, I guess.'

'They're right, but how are you going to manage it? They might want you involved, so they get a good look at you. They may have worked out that you're my agent.'

'American consular officials insist on being present at the meeting. But we won't agree to meet at the US consulate. We want a neutral site. We might ask the Swedes or the Swiss, or our Lao friends to host the talks. I will make a solemn promise to Du that he won't be executed, that he'll be detained for a short while we question him. No rough stuff. I'll say we have an agreement with the Americans and will keep our bargain. We'll throw in his sister, too, as a humanitarian gesture, but that will be a harder sell after today.'

'He won't believe any of it.'

''Course he won't. He's *Gonganbu*, and senior enough to know how this plays out. He'll be suspicious. Du won't like us being involved. But he'll want to stay alive. He'll entertain false hopes of survival. Most people do, I guess, and he of all people knows we

240

can reach him wherever he goes, even with a new life somewhere. Australia, Canada – wherever. We'll track him down if we put a mind to it. He's no option but to go along with our proposals, especially after the Americans have denied him refuge. He won't know about today's little presentation, though – not until it's too late. Anyway, you know the Americans. They love the word "humanitarian". They'll love my presentation, too, because I'll say all the right fluffy stuff.'

'So he walks out of the consulate into your embrace.'

'I wouldn't call it an embrace, no. More like a neck-lock.'

'Thinking of neck-locks … we've caused a lot of casualties, Fang, you and I.'

'You think? A lot? Not by Chinese or Russian standards. Ask Stalin or Mao about numbers. Not by imperialist standards, either. They brought it on themselves. Why? Are you developing a guilty conscience? It's a bit late for that. We both knew what we were getting into, didn't we? We've got to live with the consequences – and right now, I'm loving the consequences.'

'You said a moment ago you were going back later today.'

'Tonight or early tomorrow. I must.'

'They could be waiting for you, too, telling you a pack of lies to get you to return. It could be an ambush, a trap. You don't know you're safe.'

'That's true, I don't. No-one ever does. The Party isn't a safe place; didn't I tell you before?'

'So don't go, Fang. Finish it. Come with me. I'll arrange everything. The Firm will be sorry to lose an agent, and so will I. But at least you'll be in one piece and can start a new life. They'll set you up with a home somewhere and a job that pays well. They'll employ

241

you as a China analyst. Imagine that – a staff job with SIS or one of our other agencies, such as the Defence Intelligence Staff. You know how this works. We can be together.'

'Is this a marriage proposal, Richard? How sweet. Aww. Do you have the ring? Is it a genuine diamond? You're meant to get down on your knees and ask me. Isn't that how it's done? That's how it's done in Hollywood movies. Go on – on your knees. I'm waiting.'

'Hilarious. I'm serious.'

'I know you are. So am I. Where I come from, you'd have to play a lot of mahjong with your mother-in-law and you would have to make sure you lost every time. That's the first hurdle.'

'For God's sake, be sensible. Stop playing the cynical, tough spy for once. Come over to us. As soon as you've completed whatever it is you're doing today. We could leave tonight. Together. I mean it. I don't want to lose you.'

'The time now?'

Brodick looks at his watch. 'It's 0450 hours local.'

Fang turns onto her side, facing Brodick. 'That's 0550 in Shanghai and Beijing.'

'It is, yes.'

'We ought to make the most of the time, Richard. This may be our last fuck. We have a few hours. Are you ready?'

'Ready? Ready for what?'

She's laughing to herself, but doesn't show it. She takes hold of him, squeezes. 'Is there life in the old man? Can you get it up again – or must I wait? You need some ginseng tea. It might help, though I don't know if it works on counter-revolutionary English spies and their floppy dicks.'

* * *

242

'I want you to see this.'

Fang checks her watch yet again.

The screen flickers, an image appears, goes away, returns in a burst of static, then stabilises.

'Now watch.' Fang fiddles with the dials, trying to get a better focus.

'This is in real time?'

'Live streaming – that's what you call it, isn't it?'

They're back in the condo on the top floor, in the darkened living room with its monitors, blinking boxes, masses of wiring, the peculiar lining on the walls and ceiling. An engineer, one of Fang's people, kneels on the floor under a table, wielding various tools and mumbling to himself. Brodick is on his feet, leaning forward, hands spread on the table in front of him, peering at the screen. Fang is so close to him that her shoulder brushes his arm and she feels a static charge, but it isn't electricity. It's the aftermath of their love-making, the embers still hot. She wants to keep it that way. Miraculously – and it does seem like a miracle to Fang – they've spent the morning in bed, followed by fresh fruit and iced coffee and a stroll through the town, back to the condo. She has experienced nothing like it. She had to resist the temptation to disregard the rules and common sense. How wonderful to walk with her lover hand in hand, arm in arm – like any other young couple, unashamed, unembarrassed. To enjoy the luxury of it, even if it is a pretence, make-believe. So much of what they do is play-acting, after all. In their case, they're on the verge of middle age. The thought of having Brodick to herself for the rest of the day excites her.

It's not going to happen, though.

243

They've waited 2 hours, Fang excited, Brodick impatient, not knowing what this 'surprise' is all about. The lovemaking has also made Fang hungry.

'What is this place? What are we looking at?'

'Wuchang rail station. That's in Wuhan if you didn't know. Today, the 18th January' Right now.'

'What's going on?'

'Somehow, people have got wind of his arrival. Look at that crowd – that's unexpected. I hope they can cope. The police, I mean.'

'Whose arrival? Who is it?'

'Can't you see? There. It's Deng.'

'Deng Xiaoping?'

It is, too. A small, elderly man with a broad grin, surrounded by family, police and well-wishers, pushes his way through the throng on the platform. Even Brodick can't mistake that face and smile. Fang feels emotional. This surge of feeling brings tears to her eyes, and she turns so Bo Deli doesn't see her reaction.

She doesn't know why she feels this way. It's the same with the national anthem and the flag. It's social conditioning since childhood. Nothing more than the science of social control. She tells herself a lab rat could be trained to respond the way a billion Chinese have been drilled to respond.

'So this isn't television, then ...'

'No. This is the PLA police feed. They've organised the visit in the strictest secrecy. Not even the Politburo knows. No-one in Beijing does. Officially, he's on a family holiday. That's why you're hearing all the rumours – that he's hitting the *Maotai*, that he's finished, that he's dead, that he's under house arrest. So now you know. He's taken things into his own hands. He's pushing his reforms forward and leading by example. But if those crowds are any sign, word is out.'

'Military police, you said?'

'Right. And you're watching their PLA security video. Did you forget I'm an officer in military intelligence and *Guoanbu*?'

'Christ. I should report this to London.'

'What difference will a few hours make? What are they going to do? Send a gunboat? Or those funny soldiers in bearskin hats? You can send your report later. Your bosses are sound asleep in their London mansions, dreaming of the empire they no longer have, or their share options. Let them sleep. Now watch. You're seeing history made, Richard.'

She can't help making fun of Bo Deli and his ridiculous English government. Punching above their weight, that's what the British call their foreign policy. It's absurd. They want a place at the Americans' table so they can pretend they have a role. They're like children crying for attention – why don't they stick to their toys and leave the adults alone? Why bother? What on earth for? It's a dream of the British upper classes, but Fang can't see why they still want to strut the world stage. How can it be in their interest, now that they're a middling European power? Why don't they live within their means and be content to lead quiet lives?'

She lets her fingers touch his, but he pulls away, irritated.

Fang tells herself they'll have time later, before the main act.

Wuhan is a major railway junction in central China where the 1911 revolution started, but Fang doesn't think she needs to explain that to Bo Deli.

'That man there – that's Hubei's Party Secretary. Guan Guangfu. And that's the governor, Guo Shuyan. See? Now Deng's speaking – it's a speech. He looks annoyed, d'you see? He's lecturing them! That's his daughter – she's shouting in his ear everything that's said, so that he doesn't miss anything.'

'I don't care what they say. What's he saying?'

Fang tried to translate. '… There are too many meetings … the reports are too long … the speeches are too long, the content is too repetitious … You should do more, talk less … Whoever is against reform should leave office …'

Fang and Brodick look at each other. So there it is. Deng has thrown down his challenge to his opponents and critics. Get with the programme or fuck off.

'Listen.' Fang turns up the volume.

'What are the people shouting?'

'They are greeting him. They're friendly.'

'Such as?'

'*Shushu hao*. That means Uncle Deng.'

'What else?'

'Listen to that – those younger people are calling him *yeye hao* or Grandpa Deng.'

The screen goes blank.

'Now you understand why I have to try to stop the Eight. Deng needs our help, Richard. So do the Chinese people. You can see that, can't you? No-one has the right to deny us our moment of fulfilment. No-one, not even in the Party, and especially no-one abroad.'

Fang sees the hesitation in his eyes, the doubt in his expression. She's not surprised. Why should a *waibin* throw himself into this struggle? Bo Deli isn't a Party member, he's not even Chinese. He's not only a foreigner, but an imperialist spy, in bed and out. How could he ever understand?

It's not his fight.

Lunch in Hua Hin.

Fang can't wait. She likes spicy Thai food, and she chooses a classic *ton yam goong*. It's a hot and sour soup with prawns, cooked with lemongrass, lime juice, fish sauce, galangal and red chilli peppers strong enough to take the roof off anyone's mouth.

With some care, and after asking the woman behind the counter in his bad Thai, a cautious Brodick picks out another popular dish, the *massaman* curry. It's mild. It comprises chicken, shallots, garlic, coriander, bay leaves, cloves, cardamom, cinnamon and cumin.

They drink cold bottled water from the restaurant fridge because the stuff that comes out of the taps isn't potable.

They sit on white plastic chairs at a Formica-topped table. They talk little. One reason is the place is busy, all manner of people around them. Students, office workers, holidaymakers. There's a plastic roof, a cement floor, several servers hurrying this way and that and a number of flea-bitten stray dogs lying in the shade, an eye on the diners in the hope of a scrap. Fang knows Thais like to give food to birds, fish, dogs and cats because they believe it will bring them 'merit' in their next rebirth. She's watched people buy birds in cages – usually at stalls set up outside the temples – and then free them, or live fish (supplied in the inevitable plastic bags) and then drop them into the city's many *klongs* or canals. She wonders if the fish survive in such a filthy environment. Generosity is important to Thai Buddhists. Everyone wants a good rebirth. The ideal is to return as a human, not a lower animal. It's all part of the accumulative effect of good thoughts and deeds – or bad thoughts and deeds, known as *karma*.

Fang finds all this both amusing and puzzling.

Brodick looks at her. 'You don't mind us being seen out together?'

'Should I? The American has left. I mean your Mr Green, along with his local helpers. Yang Bai says there's no-one else now.'

'He's not "my" Mr Green.'

Fang laughs. 'I do apologise.'

It's boiling in the pavement restaurant, but one of the waiters, seeing the *farang* looking hot and uncomfortable, brings a large floor fan closer to them and puts it on maximum. The blast of air ruffles their clothing and hair and threatens to blow away their paper napkins. Brodick thanks him with a smile and a nod.

'I like this,' Fang says.

'What?'

'I enjoy being here with you. It's calming and pleasant being together, don't you think?'

'I do.'

'We don't get a chance to do this often. It feels special.'

He smiles back at her.

'When did you first go to school, Richard?'

'It was play school. Kindergarten, it was called. I suppose I was around three.'

'Did you enjoy it?'

'Pretty much. It was OK. Why?'

'Just curious.'

'They expelled me at the age of five. The head called my mother and said her son was getting a bit big for the place and should move on.' Brodick smiled at the memory.

'Why? What happened?' Fang finds this odd. For a Chinese family, it would be shocking, an embarrassment, to be told to take a child out of school for misbehaviour.

'First, I tried to burn down a big gum tree that stood in the playground. I rolled up some scrap paper, climbed up and put it in the branches and lit it with a match. It didn't burn, though, to my great disappointment.'

'You were a child arsonist!'

'It gets better. The school itself was a prefabricated wooden building set up on cement blocks because of the voracious ants and other insects. There were around 12 to 18 inches of clearance between the ground and the wooden flooring. So a friend called Derek and I collected used gunpowder from all the discarded bits and pieces of fireworks left over from Guy Fawkes night. You know what that is?'

'Yes. I know. Some ancient schism between Christians in England. Some radicals called Catesby and Fawkes – there was a third, but I forget – had a religious grievance and they tried to blow up your Houses of Parliament. The King's spy discovered the plot. I've done my homework about you English. Go on.'

'I'm Scots, by the way. Not English. We gathered all the gunpowder remnants that hadn't burned and packed them into a box and pushed it under the school, laid a trail of gunpowder across the playground and set it alight at a safe distance.'

'You young scoundrels!'

'It fizzed and fizzled and there was a lot of blue smoke and at the start it was impressive, but it made very slow progress and one of the young female teachers spotted it. She ran out with a pan and brush, and stamped on the live bit of it until it died and then she swept it all up. She gave us a very long, hard look. I remember feeling disappointed and not at all guilty.'

'What about the people in the building? The children and their teachers?'

'I don't think that at that age I'd quite grasped the link between cause and effect.'

'Do you think you understand it now?'

'I hope so.'

'I wonder if you do. You were a little terrorist back then and I don't think you've changed at all.'

Brodick seems to have had enough curry. 'Do you want anything else, Fang?'

She's still hungry. 'Ice cream for me.'

'I'll have an iced coffee, but with less sugar this time.'

They give their orders to a waitress who appears to be the daughter or niece of the owner. Fang is sure there's a strong family likeness.

'When does the show begin?'

'Guests are invited at 1830. Most won't turn up until later, though. I want to be there in time to see who's there and who isn't. I've got the guest list and I want to check off as many as I can. It won't be so easy if they're wearing fancy dress and masks.'

'So we do have time for a decent nap.'

'A *nap*? Richard, who said anything about sleeping?'

But he does sleep, later. Fang watches him. She thinks he's beautiful naked and stretched out beside her, all the tension gone . Their love-making was wonderful once again – despite her teasing – and she thinks it's because he knows something about female anatomy, and is careful to make sure she's satisfied. Well, she's never satisfied, so it's relative. It's not so much the pleasure – of course it *is* pleasurable – but it's something else, something more basic, and she struggles to find the words in her language and his.

It's the closeness, she decides. The human closeness. He's brought her face to face with what she realises she's always needed and not had: closeness to another person. People buy pets for companionship, for the proximity of another living being to talk to, to hug. She's thought of doing so, but her Beijing apartment is too small, and Fang is away too often and for too long – at short notice, also – so no animal would survive alone without her, and she has no close neighbours whom she trusts to look after whatever she might decide to get: a puppy, a kitten, a goldfish.

Fang knows it's not going to happen.

This rare feeling is more special than embracing a pet animal, though.

Intimacy. That's it.

Intimacy, closeness, belonging.

Three words that mean so much. This is what people must mean when they talk of heaven. It's not up in the sky, or in a bank vault. It's right here in this crappy old room for rent with its noisy fan, lumpy mattress and threadbare sheets. In the midst of this, of the recognition of her own needs, there's a stab of memory, of guilt. Those three Chinese she shot – traitors working for the CIA, giving away China's secrets to the main enemy – they were people. They had mothers, wives, girlfriends, siblings, even children. Yes, she remembers, one had two small children. That would have been the engineer. What would those children do now for the closeness they need? How will they cope without loving and being loved, without a father's love?

To her dismay, tears spring into her eyes, roll down her cheeks. She wipes them away, angry at her inability to control her emotional responses. She tells herself she despises sentimentality. All this love-making is responsible for her fragility, that's all it is. She's tired.

They weren't the only ones. Including those three spies, she's executed a total of 11 enemies of the state. She remembers them all, and she cups both hands over her mouth and nose, stifling a sob. This colonel in the PLA, this head of the 5th Bureau, so ruthless, pitiless, ambitious, patriotic, weeps in silence.

Bo Deli sleeps through her pain and guilt, oblivious.

Calmer now, she looks at him again. He lies on his front, head turned away from her, right arm trailing off the bed, the fingers almost touching the floor.

It will be time to go soon, to begin the show. She should wake him now, so they both have time to shower, dress, and prepare themselves.

Fang enjoys watching him sleep. She leans over him, whispers something. The words are so faint, so slight, she might have imagined them. She thinks he might hear them in his sleep and when he wakes imagine that he's dreamed them. She'll never say them aloud, in a normal voice, and to his face. She can't. They're too embarrassing, too cloying. Fang still sees such sentiment as weakness and she can't admit to it. Never.

'You complete me, Richard.'

252

24

This time, one of the Chinese technicians acknowledged my presence. He grinned at me as I followed Fang into the living room of the condo and he followed it with a thumbs-up. The place had been tidied and reorganised. Two black, executive-style chairs faced the biggest screen. Fang and I sat side by side. The two technicians sat over to one side, their boxes of blinking lights and bundles of wiring all around them.

'We're on,' said Fang.

In the gloom the screens came on, big rectangles of bright, hard light. The images were clear. They were also in colour. I could see why the engineer was in a cheerful mood.

The Yao family's Shanghai mansion loomed before us, a carbuncle of architectural ugliness. The word 'grandiose' didn't do it justice. It was as big and as useless as a beached aircraft carrier. Who the hell would want to live in that? It seemed the Yao family did, or at least the patriarchal Party Secretary Yao Tie did.

Two gardeners worked out front. I knew that's what they were because of their overalls, wheelbarrows and rakes. There was more movement. Figures in black moved in pairs across the screen, right at the bottom, close to what must have been the edge of the property.

'Security.'

'Your people?'

She shook her head.

'So whose are they?'

Fang didn't answer. They wore black suits, and it was impossible to tell if they were carrying, but I assumed they must have been.

The two technicians went out and stood in the corridor, speaking Mandarin in low voices, arguing about some technical matter. One had what looked like a fuse in his hands, but I couldn't tell if he was explaining something or criticising his colleague. The Mandarin sounded, to my Western ears, abrasive, aggressive.

Fang leaned towards me and spoke while watching the screen. 'You have this rule, don't you, in your country? Your security service – what you sometimes call MI5 – operates at home, on your territory, right? As well as your colonies? And your SIS operates abroad because it is restricted to collecting foreign intelligence. Right?'

'More or less. Sometimes there are joint operations and there are arguments over which agency has jurisdiction. Battles over turf.'

'We have a similar system now, ever since the reorganisation in the eighties. The *Gonganbu* – the Ministry of Public Security – takes care of domestic matters. The *Guoanbu*, to which I belong, comes under the MSS – the Ministry of State Security – and we work overseas in embassies, trade missions… like your people. And yes, there are grey areas – such as Hong Kong and Tibet. Though, of course, they aren't really grey. They're part of China.'

'Does that mean you don't have people on the ground?' I gestured at the scene we were watching via satellite link.

'A few. Catering staff.'

'So who are these guys, then – the ones in black walking around in pairs outside?

'Yao's private security. Ex-cops, ex-military.'

'And Du Fu's people? The Shanghai Public Security Bureau?'

Fang gave a slight shake of her head. 'They won't show. They've heard rumours about their boss and his wife. They'll keep a very low profile and wait to see how things pan out. They won't want to come anywhere near this place. They'll make their excuses and not turn up. You have a saying – about not wanting to be tarred with the same brush.'

We sat close together, so much so I could smell her scent. After our lunch, lovemaking and a deep sleep, I felt super relaxed – I wanted to rest my head on her shoulder. If it hadn't been Fang, I would have. When she leaned her head closer to mine, I had an even stronger urge to take her by the shoulders and kiss her again. It was hard not to. Despite this peculiar room crowded with all the electronic gear, the shuttered windows, the hum of air conditioners and the excitement, I wanted a hug. Did she? I was supposed to feel excitement watching Yao's property for what was billed as the social event of the year, yet it seemed to count for nothing compared to how I felt about Fang.

Yes, Fang was also ruthless, a killer, a risk-taker. A traitor to her Party, her country.

I was certain she had no clue how I felt, either, or how much she meant to me.

She leaned right over, her eyes on the door in case the technicians came back in. I breathed in the scent of her hair, her skin, felt the warmth of her. We were so close I almost fell into her lap. Mellow? I was about to melt right there.

'Have you heard of the Central Commission for Discipline Inspection, the CCDI?'

Fang was all work.

'I have, but I heard they'd been shelved some years ago, their powers reduced and their numbers dwindling to almost nothing.'

'Now they're back. Deng has given them new powers and more resources.'

That was news to me. 'To do what?'

'Their primary task is protecting the leadership.'

'To protect Deng himself?'

'Sure. Along with the rest of the *politburo*. Their second task is to root out corruption in the Party.'

'They've got one hell of a massive job, in that case. And they're in Shanghai right now, at Yao's place?'

'I sent them copies of everything on the discs, as well as a video cassette of Du Lan's confession. They've launched a full investigation. They do have a team deployed at the house, yes.'

'You did so anonymously, I hope.'

She didn't answer, but moved away from me and sat upright. The technicians had returned, slipping back into their chairs as the first guests started to arrive at the Yao palace.

I couldn't get enough of Fang. That was my trouble, always had been.

'Do you see what I see?'

I almost choked, trying to stifle my laughter.

'It's Julius Caesar. At least that's who I think it's supposed to be.'

Fang, too, gaped at the screen. Welcoming guests in person was Yao Tie himself, standing at the top of the steps outside the giant double front doors. He wore a white toga and on his thinning hair sat a gilded crown of olive leaves. He was too short, too plump, for either the costume or the role – but the message was clear; the part of Dictator was what he – or rather his wife – sought in real life. The problem was that Du Lan, who no doubt would have played the role of a svelte Cleopatra at this expensive shindig, was nowhere to be seen – not yet, anyway.

The guests' cars were bumper to bumper in a long traffic jam up the drive. And what cars! This was no ordinary procession. The first to arrive was a silver Humvee, followed by an immense white Rolls-Royce, a red Ferrari, a Bentley, and twin black Range Rovers that sounded their horns with self-important impatience.

When the twin SUVs finally reached the front of the queue, body-guards sprang from them, rushing to open the rear doors and stood back, hands inside their jackets as the VIPs disembarked – an old man in a dark suit from the first vehicle and, in a concession to the event, he held a red mask to his face with one hand, leaning with the other on a Zimmer frame. From the second vehicle came his very thin, very tall but much younger wife, resplendent as – no, I couldn't believe my eyes. It was too surreal.

'Jesus Christ.!

'Who's she supposed to be?' Fang said.

The bodyguards helped the octogenarian up the steps. They seemed to carry him up by the elbows, his legs left dangling while another thug picked up the Zimmer frame and carried it up behind the old man.

'Marie Antoinette,' I said, 'the last Queen of France before the Revolution. Interesting choice for the wife of a leading figure in the Chinese Communist Party. Or do you think she's sending a message of her own to this august gathering?'

'You know who he is?'

257

'No.' In response to my ignorance, Fang prodded me hard in the ribs with her elbow.

She hissed the name at me. 'Wu Xian. One of the Eight.'

'How can you tell? He's wearing a mask – at least he's holding it up to his face.'

'I know the *tai*. I know *of* her. She's 44 years his junior. She's a singer.'

'Nice work if you can get it, I suppose. No wonder he looks tired.'

Someone switched on the fountains in the grounds, geysers of water rising 40 feet and falling, drenching some of the guests downwind. And although it wasn't quite dark yet, all the lights went on, thousands of them. The facade of the mansion was also lit up, but it didn't make the pile any prettier.

The welcoming procedure worked smoothly, staff in dark suits on the steps checking invitations and faces. There was no intrusive security that I could see, no physical patting down or electronic scanning. Hell, why should they? They were CCP loyalists to a man – and woman.

The guests went up, most in pairs, waiting their turn to show their tickets. Julius Caesar greeted them in person. They wore dazzling outfits, silver and gold, lots of sequins and stars with a variety of masks, some beaked, some with plumes of feathers, others meant to represent a historical figure, while most held glittering masks on short sticks – useful if you wanted to chatter, eat or drink. The women were in gowns, some of them low cut or backless, the men in sombre black tie or the most ridiculous outfits.

I caught sight of a couple of red-nosed clowns, a donkey, a giant chicken, two popes and a huge duck.

'Who's that?'

A man and a woman clambered out of a huge black BMW.

Fang ticked a name on her list.

'That's Napoleon Bonaparte,' I told her.

'He's another one. Ling Qiwei.'

I thought it odd how the plotters, despite their professed loyalty to the CCP, dressed up as emperors. I almost forgot – it was the party of princes, and princes needed an emperor, didn't they?

Running up the steps, taking them two at a time despite his advanced years, was a big, burly man. A woman followed, tripping after him in heels and dressed as a Tyrolean barmaid – at least, that's what she resembled, in a wide skirt, tight waistcoat that emphasised her bust, rouged cheeks, blonde braids.

Fang identified him at once. 'That's General Zhou Lijun.'

Another plotter. He dressed not in a PLA general's uniform but one from the past: brown jackboots, khaki riding breeches, Sam Browne belt, pistol holster and what appeared to be an Italian military cap with a tassel hanging from it. His mask was a fetching shiny black, perfect for a fascist.

'Mussolini,' I said.

'Who?'

I was always happy to show off my profound knowledge of twentieth-century history. 'Benito Mussolini – Italian fascist dictator in World War Two. Nasty piece of work. Hitler's ally. He also saw himself as an emperor after he sent troops to invade and conquer Ethiopia in 1935. They called him *Il Duce*, the leader.'

Now I really thought I'd seen everything.

Hang on. There was more history on the way. Waiting to be welcomed by Caesar, two guests faced each other on the top step, both with identical moustaches, in identical masks and wearing the boots, tunics, red tabs, stars and epaulettes of Soviet Red Army marshals. Grinning and laughing, they stamped their feet and punched each other on the chest. Standing behind them, enveloped in the scarlet and yellow outfits of Spanish flamenco dancers, were two women I assumed were their wives, both the very opposite of tall and slender.

The punches and slaps exchanged by the two marshals didn't seem especially friendly.

They were none other than twin Josef Stalins.

None of this was especially Venetian. There were no gondolas or gondoliers in evidence, or none that I had seen. At least no-one had been foolish or suicidal enough to attend the party dressed as Japan's wartime leader, Emperor Shōwa, better known in the West by his own name, Hirohito. Or as the anti-communist commander-in-chief of the National Army in China's savage civil war, Generalissimo Chiang Kai-shek.

Led by their imperial host, the guests in all their outlandish finery flowed like glittering lava through the front doors into the mansion.

'We'll follow them,' Fang said.

And we did.

Fang's people had tapped into the internal security cameras fixed high on the walls in the public rooms and, given that the view sometimes changed and seemed to come from monitors lower down, from under furniture or affixed to works of art. We watched the same scene, but shifting from one place to another in rapid succession, a process Fang seemed to control with a keyboard in front of her. That would mean Fang's *Guoanbu* operatives had put spy cameras in place.

We watched as guests were herded along by black-clad security staff and waiters and waitresses, the latter all wearing red bow ties and bearing fixed smiles and trays of champagne flutes and canapés. On they went through the immense hall, past some immense Chinese ceramic pots, and down a wide flight of stairs. There's nothing like the allure of food and drink to get people headed in the right direction. Even via the satellite link, I could sense their anticipation and curiosity as they chatted and laughed, giggling at each other's masks and outfits, clutching at the bannisters in an effort not to topple down the steps in their outlandish costumes.

'The canapés were flown in from Milan,' Fang said. 'And the champagne is Krug or Bollinger – it's nothing but the very best for Yao's high society guests.'

At last, the *pièce de résistance*, and I didn't mean the food. I meant the huge gold statue of the Great Leader himself, a young Emperor-to-be with a benign smile on his face looking out over the heads of the crowd, many of whom stared up, mouths agape, at this extraordinary rendition of Mao as revolutionary leader.

He wore his Sun Yat-sen suit and a worker's cap – in solid gold.

A vast screen on the wall of the basement cavern, which I hadn't noticed before, sprang to life, showing an image of the hall, emptied of Yao's car collection and dominated by the statue. Now the guests could see themselves partying, and some waved at one another or jumped up and down – those young enough to do so, anyway – in their delight. The oldies – the ancient men with their canes and Zimmer frames who mostly had decided not to dress up, gathered around their host at the foot of the golden Mao. These were the senior Party people, or so it seemed to me, distinguishable by their extreme age, their frailty, their drab attire.

They all seemed to watch themselves on the screen.

'Now,' said Fang, and she hit a button. The images on the screen changed.

A loud, commanding voice boomed from hidden speakers.

'Ladies and gentlemen, your attention please.'

First in Mandarin, then Cantonese.

'Please watch and listen to this announcement. Thank you.'

It was none other than an enlarged image of Du Lan in her bright prison jumpsuit, the blue screen behind her, her chin on her chest, hair flopping forward and covering her face.

Her recorded confession began.

No-one moved. The guests had been immobilised, struck dumb. They gazed up, spellbound. They must have known who it was they were seeing.

The mood changed abruptly when Du Lan got to the payments from Yao to the alleged conspirators.

'Here are the names of those involved in the conspiracy, all of whom received payments from my husband ... Here, I have the list of payments, the account numbers and the banks.'

There was a commotion, centred on the old men and their host. The private security people were pushing their way through the crowd of guests, making a passage for Caesar himself, the Party's oldsters hobbling along as best they could in his wake. He shouted, waved his arms about – but he couldn't make himself heard above Du Lan's confession, broadcast so loudly that it drowned out everything else.

In fury, he tore off his olive crown and tossed it aside.

Du Lan was reading out the names. The faces of the Eight appeared one by one on the screen. Including Yao's.

She read out the last name.

A loud pop. Another, followed by screams.

Our own screens turned black.

The audio was still on, at least for a key short time, 15 or 20 seconds. There were more popping sounds. I thought it might be the start of a fireworks display outside, but no, this was gunfire. Single shots, more shouts and screams, then what I was sure was the sound of double tapping, the way a trained shooter puts two rounds into each of his targets, the way they had taught me at Fort Monckton as a trainee intelligence officer.

I could only imagine what it must have been like, with hundreds of people trying to escape in panic, fighting to break out of the garden doors or fight their way back upstairs.

A rippling sound followed. Automatic fire. A single burst of three or four rounds – whoever was firing the automatic weapon was disciplined, doing it the way he or she had been trained.

More pops, only much louder. They were definitely gunshots.

Then the sound went, too.

We sat in silence in the dark operations room.

It was night outside.

The technician turned to Fang and said something in a low, tense tone.

Fang turned to me, upset and shocked. 'We've lost the satellite link.'

Her fingers raced across the keyboard, tapping in a frenzy.

'Everything's down. I can't receive or send.'

263

25

Fang takes immediate control. Up on her feet, she issues her orders. First things first: the technicians are to take everything down and pack up, starting now.

Yang hands Fang a telephone receiver at the end of a long cable. It's still live, and she's got an encrypted call through to the duty officer *Guoanbu*'s Bangkok Station. There is a short, staccato exchange in Mandarin and, after a brief wait, another brief exchange with someone more senior, the station commander himself who's been dragged from his bed to take the call, much to his disgust. Apparently satisfied with the result, Fang hands back the phone to one of the engineers. It, too, is disconnected, packed in a large metal trunk.

She explains nothing to Bo Deli because she doesn't have the time. She tells him in a brusque tone to return to the guesthouse, buy something to eat on the way, and get some rest. He's no use in the flat; he's taking up space and getting in the way. She'll follow, she says.

He tries to argue, to delay, but Fang has already turned away from him and he's led to the door by Yang, who passes him to another member of the team. He accompanies Brodick down in the lift to the ground floor, walks him over to the street to a comrade waiting on a motorcycle. The helmeted rider carries him to the night market, waits while Brodick buys an omelette and rice, then drops him off at the guesthouse and leaves him there.

In the condo, everyone works quickly. The team members exchange few words; they've worked together before and each knows what he or she must do. The technicians pack the electronics into the trunks, take them down in the service lift and stack them in the back of a pickup. The team dismantles the Faraday cage; the wall, window, ceiling linings and the false floor are taken apart – the material is hinged, and they fold up the sections. They bag, bundle, roll up the equipment, fastening it all in place with tape.

Yang tells Fang she should go too, get some rest while she can, that the team can do the rest – but Fang won't do so until she's satisfied with their work. She insists on being the last to leave and on making sure the place is left in the state in which it was found – pristine, with no visible sign of a *Guoanbu* presence and fit for the owner's return, whenever that is. She helps by taking the screens down from the windows, then uses a broom to sweep the floor throughout the condo and wipes down the kitchen tops and sink, then the bathroom. Fang also scrubs the lavatory. These are the jobs no-one else wants. But this is the Chinese Communist Party and everyone is a worker! The rapid pace of activity helps her deal with the monsters circling in her head. She's going home – but to what?

The pickup with the electronic gear and dismantled Faraday cage is finally ready to leave for the capital. Someone has lashed down a tarpaulin over the cargo in the back.

The technicians jump on board and they're off.

Fang, Yang and her *dui* hurry to complete the housework.

It's already first light, a grey glimmering to the east. Fang is last out of the door after switching off the air-conditioners and the lights – and having made a final walk-through inspection.

As the sun rises, the team sits down to a meal together in a simple eatery in central Hua Hin. Everyone looks weary; their shoulders slump, their eyes are puffy. They're too hyped for sleep now, Fang especially. Too tired to talk, to joke. They eat in silence, companionable silence, but silence nonetheless.

Fang is sure that if she went back to the guesthouse, she wouldn't be able to rest. Brodick would be awake too, and he'd want to talk, to interrogate her. He'd ask all manner of awkward questions, such as what was next, what about this, what about that – and whatever she said in response, it would provoke a deluge of objections, complaints and queries. She can't face that now.

With a metal spoon, Fang eats boiling rice porridge with chilli and pork, along with two sizeable pieces of deep-fried dough, not unlike doughnuts, though they aren't sweet.

In China, people call this breakfast you *mizhou*, or 'congee with rice'. People use the expression when they receive something unexpected and positive, such as a cash windfall. In contrast, *wu mi zhou* refers to 'congee with no rice' – which is little more than hot water and refers to wasteful government projects or work that fails to earn money.

Have all their efforts turned out to be *wu mi zhou*?

She has no idea what happened at the Yao mansion. Whatever it was, it wasn't part of the plan.

Fang likens their situation to suspended animation. What's happened to her *Guoanbu* colleagues who were undercover, playing the role of catering staff? What's happened to Yao? To the undercover CCDI squad meant to carry out the arrests? Who was responsible for the shooting? Were there casualties? And the Eight Obstacles – what has happened to them? The Bangkok Station would have known nothing when she called late last night, and she has no secure link to call or contact them again to find out.

There's a television above the cash register in the outdoor restaurant and it's showing Thai national and international news, but as far as she can tell, there's nothing from the mainland. Some criminal incident in Shanghai wouldn't make headlines abroad. Why should it? The Party censors would make sure of it.

Wait. There is something from China, after all. It's Deng, of course. He's viewing the vast construction sites from the top of Shenzhen's 53-storey World Trade Centre. It's an amazing view. When he descends, there's a big crowd clapping and cheering. But Fang knows this friendly, casual Deng is very different from the Deng his Party colleagues will see and hear in private, behind closed doors, and on the back seat of his official limo.

The newsreader is saying that Shenzhen had an average annual per capita income of 600 yuan in 1984, and that it has risen to reach 2,000 now, in 1992.

That's something to cheer about. On the bus returning to the guest house, the cameras catch Deng repeating his basic points. Fang can make out some remarks. Planning is not the same as socialism. Markets are not the same as capitalism. There are markets under socialism. Socialism is not poverty.

The news switches to the weather forecast for Thailand. Hot. Humid. Sunny.

There's only one thing Fang knows she can do, should do.

267

In a low voice, she gives her last instructions to her colleagues.

What awaits her she has no idea.

There is no alternative, though, not a realistic one.

Fang has to go home.

26

The morning sun burned off the low mist among the palms. It became warmer by the minute as the white-hot disc rose in the eastern sky. No-one said anything because there wasn't anything to say. The plane was late, 2 hours late, and there was nothing that Fang, Yang Bai, the remnants of her *dui* or I could do about it.

They were all tired, hot, irritable, anxious – and it showed on their sullen faces. I was lucky – I had managed a few hours' kip.

A motorcyclist had picked me up from the guesthouse, brought me to Hua Hin airport and sped away again. No-one said as much as good morning, so I didn't say anything, either. I stood there, a few yards from the 35-metre-wide single runway, and observed the others. Fang looked furious. She had one large, wheeled suitcase and a bulky shoulder bag, which lay at her feet. Yang stood well to one side and back, behind her boss. There were two young men – the rest of the team – who stood well apart and faced the terminal – a low, ramshackle building on the far side of the runway.

The place appeared deserted. I didn't see anyone else around and there were no aircraft standing on the apron. Crickets provided a sonorous soundtrack. There was little wind; the palms barely moved at all. Sweat ran cold down my back.

Something about Yang and her two male companions – it was the way they stood and carried themselves – told me they were armed, though I saw no real evidence to support my opinion, no tell-tale lumps or bulges under their shirts. The guys sometimes patted their stomachs or reached behind their backs – checking their hardware, no doubt. That was the giveaway.

Fang wore a dark trouser suit, a white blouse – her work clothes.

Then I heard it, a distant whine.

We all did, but there was nothing to see quite yet.

We all looked, swivelling about, necks craning to search the sky.

It was upon us all at once, making me flinch, for the white plane swept in low, below tree height, a sudden roar out of nowhere from its turboprop engines. It flashed low overhead like the shadow of some immense bird, carried on up the runway, rose, turned, straightened out, and came back in, descending in a straight line.

The *dui* members had all, except for Fang and myself, thrown themselves flat on the ground. One of the men dropped his pistol.

The pilot seemed to be having fun, and I imagined him laughing at the sight.

I recognised the plane as a twin-engine Harbin Y-12 (11) transporter, powered by Pratt & Whitney (Canada) engines. It usually carried two crew and seated up to 17 passengers. As it turned around in front of us and the engines died, the Chinese flag was visible on the tail, and the wing and star emblem of the People's Liberation Army Air Force on the fuselage.

The door opened, the steps unfolded, and dropped down. Two crew in uniform trotted over to us and, without a word, picked up Fang's bags and took them on board.

270

Fang spoke to Yang and her colleagues, thanking them, then turned to me and switched to English.

'Richard, they'll drive you to Bangkok right away. They'll drop you wherever you want. That's up to you. Let Yang Bai know. Please book your own flight back to the UK, all right?' There was just a hint of a smile, a softening of her expression.

'Fang.' I walked up to her. I spoke quietly because I didn't want the others to hear me. 'Don't do this. Don't go.'

All at once she took a step forward, and I felt her cheek against mine, the brush of her hair.

'You could be walking into a trap.'

'I must,' she whispered in my ear. 'I've no choice.'

'There's always a choice.'

She stepped back and turned away. What had I expected her to say? Fang had made up her mind and it would be useless to argue. She walked to the plane, mounted the steps. She did not wave or look back at any of us. The door shut behind her; the engines rose in pitch and the aircraft started to roll forward.

It was just another day in the life of a senior *Guoanbu* officer.

I stood there like a fool, not knowing what to do.

It was over.

Yang Bai drove me to Bangkok, along with her two comrades. They dropped me off at a five-star hotel on the banks of the Chaophraya river. It was modern and extremely grand, and I would, of course, charge it to expenses. Many years before, an old hand in Beirut – a newspaperman – had advised me on how to make up my expenses claim; I should always claim for something called porterage. It was for all those little expenditures for which there were

271

no receipts, such as tips and bribes. They added up to a few hundred quid, usually. No-one in accounts would want to look foolish by querying 'porterage', and that meant I always had a little cash left over for myself with which to buy a jacket or a decent bottle of malt whiskey in the duty free.

I spent most of my time until my UK flight the next day by either sleeping or lazing at a table outside on the river bank, eating and drinking and watching the long-tailed boats and other river traffic, the golden Buddhist temples shining on the far bank.

It wasn't until the next morning, when I came out of the shower, that I saw something on CNN Asia news that made me turn up the volume on the television in my room and pay attention.

'… Thai aviation officials say the Chinese transport aircraft disappeared off radar screens yesterday at 1130 local time in the vicinity of northern Laos. The mountainous and remote area shares borders with Myanmar, China, Vietnam and Thailand. An unconfirmed account from a local reporter in the town of Luang Prabang suggests that at least one witness in a village on the border saw an aircraft on fire, and that there was an explosion. It is not yet known how many people were on board the plane …'

By the time I boarded my flight to London, there were more details. The type of aircraft was known. And yes, it was a Harbin Y-12 (11). Wreckage had been spotted from the air and was scattered over a wide area. It was believed that all four people on the flight, including the pilot and two cabin crew, had died. All were PRC nationals.

I felt numb.

27

MacGregor had a well-equipped room to himself in the Lister Hospital on the King's Road in South Kensington. The building was Victorian, unattractive in red brick and stone, but inside it was contemporary and welcoming – as one would expect of a private establishment. MacGregor paid – as we all did – into the Firm's medical insurance policy, and now he was reaping the benefit after all his years of service. He sat up in bed in faded blue pyjamas, a pile of pillows supporting head and back, a sheet over his knees and the pages of *Le Monde* spread out in front of him.

If I hadn't known better, I would have said he was having a lie-in at home on a Sunday.

No-one challenged me or asked who I was, and why I wasn't sticking to the visiting hours. The Lister was relaxed and seemed to operate an open door policy. I followed the sign to the oncology section, walking along cream carpeted corridors and peering through the glass windows set in the doors of blond wood until I found him.

He was alone. There was some kind of apparatus over the bed, like one of those complicated machines found in fitness centres – it had a bar he could grab hold of to pull himself up, to change his position or exercise his upper body. The bed itself he could adjust by tweaking a control panel. MacGregor had a telephone, a carafe of water, a pile of books and magazines, and flowers all over the place. There was an emergency button, and another he could use to pump painkiller into himself.

'I ask them to take the flowers out each day, but people keep bringing in more.'

'Well, I didn't bring any. I didn't bring anything.'

C motioned me to a chair of chrome and brown leather.

I took off my coat first, shook off the rain, and propped my dripping brolly up in a corner.

'I'm sorry,' he said. 'I keep dissociating.' The pages of *Le Monde* slid off the bed, fell to the floor, and I bent to pick them up.

I wasn't sure what he meant, other than the drugs. I didn't know if he was in pain and didn't like to ask. I couldn't imagine being ill, confined to a hospital bed and suffering constant pain, only to be asked by visitors who'd strolled in off the street how I felt and whether it hurt. What would I say? Of course it's fucking hurting, numbnuts – fuck off out of here!

They must be giving him serious pain killers by now. Maybe morphine sulphate was being added to the saline drip. It was effective; it would suppress pain, but it would also – once the dosage was increased – send a patient into a state of semi-sleep and continual dreams.

Not an unpleasant way to go.

MacGregor had kept working, though he'd had cancer for more than a year. He kept it quiet from most of us. 'Therapy,' they called it – using some kind of cocktail of poisons to kill the poison. The only people who knew, other than his family, were the suits in what we used to know as the Personnel Department, which had been renamed Human Resources recently, to appear corporate and modern. Finally, when getting to the office and trying to work proved too much, he'd taken indefinite medical leave and stayed home, but after a while he needed full-time care, and this was it.

His white hair was gone.

We didn't talk about work. We didn't talk about anything very much. I never found MacGregor's preference for silence disconcerting, unlike some of our colleagues. So we sat, and said little.

After a while, I got to my feet, grabbed my coat, went over to him and shook his hand with both of mine, holding it for a little longer than normal.

'Leave the door open,' he said.

We didn't talk about DRAGON or GLUTTON. No-one was going to trouble him with work-related issues now.

It turned out I was the last member of the Firm to see him alive. In another week, he'd gone.

I was late for my next appointment that morning, partly because I spent too long not talking to my boss on his deathbed, and partly because I confused the address of the meeting. It was supposed to be Carlton House Terrace in Westminster, and not Carlton Gardens around the corner. The former had been the home of royals, prime ministers and spooks. Number three had for a time housed our very own Section Y. The unsavoury Nazi ambassador to London, Joachim von Ribbentrop, lived in numbers eight to nine before World War Two, during which it suffered severe bomb damage from Herr Ribbentrop's pals in the *Luftwaffe*.

By the time I rectified my error and found the right number in the long Corinthian facade, I was 15 minutes overdue. In Whitehall terms, this qualified as a shooting or hanging offence. Although I tried to be as quiet as possible, everyone at the long conference table, which was covered in green felt, noticed my flustered arrival, and pretended not to do so, which only made it worse.

What was this?

My hanging jury?

An inquisition?

I'd only been back in London a couple of days and I was still not quite adjusted to the city and its ways. No-one had briefed me about the purpose of this meeting, and I didn't know what to expect.

I recognised Sir Martin Scope, a doleful and wealthy aristocrat who headed Foreign Office Liaison, the pugnacious and burly Eric Frobisher who sucked on a pen and who headed Requirements, Edwina Evans was there in her twinset and pearls in her role as chief of Production, and several deputy directors who served SIS as regional controllers, all of the last being male. Baroness Mildred Askew, MacGregor's number two, the seldom-seen Assistant Director-General, wearing Chanel and a bright smile, was in the chair. She was both charming and far too intelligent for Whitehall's liking. She was someone who even dared to come up with the odd original idea.

Conversation died away.

'Thank you for coming,' someone said. Heads turned. They were all looking in my direction. My presence was thereby acknowledged.

Sir Donald Kramer, chairman of the Joint Intelligence Committee, spoke.

'Richard, may I welcome you back home and say on behalf of us all here today that you have done a remarkable job as head of UK Station and we owe you our thanks and congratulations for outstanding service and some extraordinary successes.' There was a subdued clapping, heads nodded and there were a few restrained 'hear hears'.

My stomach churned. Whatever decision they'd taken, I had not been consulted.

'Changes are afoot in the Service, as I'm sure you're aware. We've been discussing them prior to your appearance here today. For once, I'm not referring to budget cuts, redundancies or closures of stations abroad. Thank heaven. Let me come to the point as I'm sure everyone would like to escape. It is Friday, after all, and the weather forecast for the south-east looks promising. Richard, we have reached a consensus and I know the Foreign Secretary supports our decision. We would like to offer you the position of Controller Asia–Pacific Region. With that, of course, comes the rank of deputy director. As you know, there are seven and you will be one of those. It's a significant promotion, and well-deserved. We can't think of anyone better qualified than yourself. How do you plead?'

Smiles from my fellow Controllers, more nodding heads bald and grey.

'If you want some time to think about it ...'

What I was supposed to do? Burst into tears and run screaming out onto the street? It's what any sane person might have done, and with good reason.

Let's face it, I wasn't sane.

'Thank you,' I said. 'I accept – with gratitude.'

I knew they loved it when people said they were grateful.

It seemed that crime did pay, especially treason.

No-one at that meeting, or on any other occasion, mentioned Fang. I wrote up a final report on her death. No-one knew if the plane had been shot down or bombed out of the sky, and guerrilla forces operated in the area where the wreckage was found. No-one mentioned Yao Tie, Susan Ho Ping, Du Lan or Du Fu, Major Ma, Xie Rong, Yang Bai or the Tanka boat crew – not even Roger Peacock. No-one mentioned the Eight Elders – or Eight Obstacles, as Fang called them.

The Hong Kong papers had picked up on the Shanghai incident and splashed it on their front pages and I saw some coverage on my way back to the UK. Here was one example on a tabloid's front page: *PARTY BOSS DIES IN SHANGHAI SHOOTOUT*.

They were referring to Yao Tie, hit at close range by two rounds, one to the chest and the other in the abdomen. He was pronounced dead on arrival at a Shanghai hospital. There were arrests, but it wasn't clear what had happened at the fancy dress ball. Had the coup failed? Who had shot Yao, and why?

Here was another: *TYCOON GUNNED DOWN AS RED MILLIONAIRES PARTY*.

And so on. The British tabloids weren't far behind, but Shanghai was a long way away and the actors in the drama had been all Chinese. Tabloids didn't think foreigners mattered, so the story of the violent end of a Chinese communist billionaire dressed up as Julius Caesar wasn't considered worthy of more than an inch or two of 9-point Bodoni, hidden on an inside page.

The following week, brief items appeared in the broadsheets, in particular the *South China Mining Post*, the *Guardian*, the *Independent* and the *Washington Post*, citing unnamed diplomatic and security sources reporting a spate of arrests of senior CCP members, as many as a dozen Party cadres of senior rank, in Beijing and Shanghai but also other, unspecified cities. There were also reports of a 'purge' at the top of China's security and intelligence establishment, though it wasn't clear – according to these unnamed sources – whether the personnel changes in the *Gonganbu* and *Guoanbu* were in any way linked to the reported arrests.

Of Deng Xiaoping, there was plenty of coverage. He was even on the nine o'clock evening news. No-one could remember when he last went shopping – in fact, it was more than a decade before – but now he appeared at Shanghai's No. 1 Department Store, inspecting the brisk trade in consumer goods. His daughter, Deng Long, helped him buy pens as gifts for his grandchildren. Staff at the *Shenzhen Daily* were so confident that Deng's economic offensive had been a success that they published a series of eight articles on his southern tour. Jiang Zemin declared his support for more reforms. Party bosses in Shanghai and Guangdong fell into line because they too wanted faster moves towards open markets.

The crusade was deemed successful, even if conservatives could still be heard muttering in Beijing about the dangers of a market economy.

A month on, and more snippets appeared in Asian publications. Citing unnamed diplomats, they reported that 11 senior CCP officials had been tried, found guilty and sentenced to death for espionage and corruption. No names, no dates, no locations identified.

On 23 February, a single intelligence report from the CIA, redacted for consumption by Washington's Five Eyes partners, circulated among the appropriate departments at SIS, GCHQ and the Foreign Office. It crossed my desk, also. According to this, the heads of both *Gonganbu* and *Guoanbu* had been asked to retire to make way for the next genera- tion. It said the ministers of both MPS and MSS had been replaced.

On 11 March, the day after a *Politburo* meeting and almost 2 months after Deng began his southern tour, the New China News Agency, *Xinhua*, finally broke the news to the public about Deng's journey and called, in an editorial, for people to be more daring in reform and in opening up the country.

The coup attempt had failed.

Of Fang there was no word.

Not yet, anyway.

Some images – imaging intelligence or IMINT – came my way, thanks to our Australian sister service, ASIS. Big, glossy prints showed the wreckage of the Chinese plane scattered across a jungle-clad peak, close to the Chinese border in northern Laos. Close-ups revealed punctures in the metal skin and burned pieces of wreckage.

It was grief, or something like it. It was as if I'd had a limb amputated. It itched and it ached and I tried scratching it. I couldn't grapple with the notion that she wasn't coming back, that I wouldn't see her again. I kept imagining that she'd stroll in through my front door and say, 'Hey, I'm here! Sorry, I was held up, but I'm back now,' and we'd hug and laugh, open a bottle, tear our clothes off and tumble into bed.

But she wasn't coming back.

My head told me I had to forget her, but my irrational heart wouldn't let her go, much as I tried. I dreamed of her, awake and asleep. I kept seeing versions of her on London's streets, in taxis and buses, and was tempted to call out and wave.

I didn't envy my successor at UK Station, who would have to face a falling off of intelligence from the ChiCom mainland, along with complaints of customers in Whitehall and across the pond who'd come to rely on DRAGON's contribution, false though much of it was.

28

It was mid-May, and after a damp start we seemed to have a dry summer on our hands – long, bright, hot days. No rain in sight. London was insufferable in the heat, especially on the crowded, outdated and slow public transport. There was even a hosepipe ban in place across some parts of the Home Counties, in a bid to conserve water. It would get worse in June and July, the Met Office said. I was settling into my new role, trying to get used to the combative style of leadership on the part of Frobisher, our blunt new C. Like several of his predecessors, he was ex-Royal Navy and sweary, and didn't mind rocking any number of Whitehall boats. I had the impression he would have liked to see them torpedoed, too. It was just as well; he was one of ours and not some suave Whitehall outsider imposed on us with new-fangled ideas on modern management algorithms.

Poppy Marsh – who had left SIS for a career in the City of London, in disgust over the cuts – was proved right, after all. I had indeed moved up to the top floor with a spacious office of my own, and I was about to be awarded a CBE for public service.

Public service?

I returned from a 10-day swing through the SIS stations in my new bailiwick – the few Asian stations that had survived the swingeing cuts – to find, on my doormat, a handwritten note on expensive paper from someone I'd almost forgotten. Roger Peacock.

Would I care to come down for the Bank holiday weekend if I hadn't anything better planned? If I took the train on Friday from Fenchurch Street station, I would be collected by car from Basildon. He was alone, and he had much to discuss. He added a postscript: he had a pool, and it was warm enough to swim. I should bring a swimsuit.

I replied at once. I would be delighted to accept. I checked the timetable and advised him of my arrival.

The reason was simple: curiosity.

What should I take with me, if the host didn't drink? He must have weekend guests from time to time, like myself, so I thought he'd welcome a decent Bordeaux from England's oldest wine merchant. The latter would appeal to his vanity. I paid for a dozen bottles and asked that they be delivered to his Essex address.

On the Friday, after a short train journey, a driver named Peter drove the Peacock Bentley through the backlands of an Essex I didn't know existed until I arrived at a traditional, thatched farmhouse with exposed beams, a refurbished barn across a field, a stable yard, several acres of woodland, a paddock and a pool.

Peacock emerged, beaming in red shorts and blue shirt, sunglasses propped up on his now tanned and almost hairless skull. He'd put on more weight and seemed more glossy and self-satisfied than ever.

A white-clad server – I realised it was the same Peter in a different uniform – carried out an ice bucket with champagne as we sank into two identical sofas with huge off-white cushions. Peter popped the cork, and poured two flutes to the brim, then handed them to us.

'What a frabjous day,' I said. I liked to show off new words I'd discovered.

He took his flute: 'Nothing but the best for my friend Richard!'

I had expected resentment, accusation, blame, anger.

'I thought you didn't touch the stuff,' I said.

'Decent champagne doesn't count, old man. Anyhow, that was the tropics, and I had to keep a cool head with Johnny Foreigner around.' He was joking and trying to sound like a Tory backbencher. Could be that was what he was destined to become.

'It feels petty tropical in southern England and it's only May.'

We raised our glasses and my host proposed a toast. 'To spies everywhere, whoever they may be, wherever they are!'

We drank like Germans, looking each other in the eye over our flutes.

'What a wonderful place,' I said, gazing around. 'It's so peaceful, too.'

It wasn't a very original compliment.

I waited. We finished the bottle. Peacock asked if I wanted to clean up before supper, which would be served out on the terrace. I took the hint and was shown by the butler, or wherever role Peter was now playing, to my en suite guest room. There, I was left alone to shower, shave and change.

During the delicious if simple meal of salad, trout and ice cream, washed down with a fine Chablis, Peacock thanked me for the wine I'd sent over. I said something about it being marvellous seeing him again after all this time, and congratulated him on his imminent OBE while avoiding any reference to my award, which would not be gazetted for obvious reasons. He asked me how I was enjoying being back in London and working at Century House again, and he said that he'd heard a rumour to the effect that they'd promoted me to stratospheric levels. Polite, inconsequential talk. The clichés flowed along with the drink and we circled each other like boxers, dancing on our toes and reluctant to throw real punches.

Still I waited.

It was only when we were on the post-prandial coffee and brandy, listening to owls hunting in woods and fields and watching bats dart over our heads in the darkness, that Peacock spoke of serious matters.

'I have a confession to make. So let me start with an apology.'

'What on earth for?'

He held up a hand. 'I want to tell this my own way, Richard, if you don't mind.'

'Sure.'

'There was no coup, no conspiracy. It didn't exist. It was an invention. Fang's invention. I misled you. We both did. That's why I must apologise.'

He paused, emptied his glass, reached for the bottle.

'Those guys, the Eight Elders, they were real. Of course they were. They weren't figments of the imagination but flesh and blood and, yes, they were also conservatives and opposed to reforms, to opening up the country. So were a lot of other people. People in even higher positions. As for the payments, they were real, too, and the funds were drawn on Yao's accounts.'

'So?'

'Fang narrowed her targets down to these eight because they weren't the usual paid hacks, the Party ideologues, the smarmy media types, all of whom she despised. She went after those with hard power, people who could cause real trouble for Deng. She followed the money, as they say, and that meant Yao.'

'So Yao was the prime target?'

He waved his hand at me as if swatting a mosquito, so I shut up.

'Yao knew nothing about the payments, but I'll ask you to keep this between ourselves.'

'What?'

'Fang ordered those payments, Richard, but I made them. Do you see now? She wanted Yao. She wanted irrefutable evidence against him. I had access to his accounts, and I supervised the transactions and signed off on them. Here in the UK we'd call it power of attorney. I was secretary of several of Yao's offshore shell companies. My accountancy firm did his books – all three sets, by the way. I moved a lot of money around for Yao. Millions in dollar terms. He had no idea of the extent of it or the details. He was too busy pinching bottoms and showing off. Pathetic bastard. Fang gave me the co-ordinates of the Elders' accounts and she told me how much and when. I did the rest.'

'You were working for Fang and Yao was set up.'

'Isn't that what you wanted – that I should work for Fang?'

He had a point.

'But this started ...'

'I worked for her from the beginning, Richard. I'm sorry, but I had no choice. Before you recruited me for queen and country. Fang blackmailed me, you see. Of course she knew about me and Du Lan, and used that knowledge to good effect. She made the usual threats, and I believed her. Fang had me by the short and curlies. I still believe that if I'd refused, I'd be rotting in some *Guoanbu* labour camp by now. So I accepted her offer. I could become rich, she said, retire back here on the proceeds and never have to do a day's work again – as long as I did as I was told. She promised they would leave me alone in the UK. She'd shown me the stick and that was her carrot – but

285

she kept her word, as you see. She encouraged me to work for your lot, too. Suggested it, in fact.'

I thought about Beirut, where Fang had turned me, too, with threats and promises.

'What's happened to Susan?'

'We divorced on the grounds of my infidelity, agreed a deal, divided up the money and investments. She's started a new life in Australia and has found someone else. I don't begrudge her. I treated her abominably.'

'Why are you telling me all this?'

'I wanted you to know. I owe it to you. There's more – about you and Fang.'

'Go on.'

'I assume you know what happened at that party Yao held in Shanghai.'

'No, not in detail.' Which was true, pretty much, though I'd seen the build-up live, thanks to Fang and her PLA2 buddies.

'An intelligence operative shot and killed Yao, not one of Fang's, but an official from an organisation called the Central Commission for Discipline Inspection. The CCDI had infiltrated Yao's home, posing as domestic staff. Fang had tipped them off, fed them the fake evidence. It happened when Yao tried to stop the arrests of his friends. The others – the seven still alive – were detained after scuffles, warning shots fired in the air, and so on. It must have been very dramatic. They were charged with corruption and contact with foreign intelligence services. But there was no real conspiracy.'

'And?'

'They were kicked out of the Party, lost their posts and were given light sentences of imprisonment on account of their age and because they still had some influence in Beijing. Fang cleaned the stables,

Richard. With our help. An amazing accomplishment, I think you'll agree, even if it was fiction.'

'And Du Lan?'

'I'm sorry about her. She got 10 years, but she may be out sooner. They confiscated everything she had, too, even her precious car.'

'You had something to say about Fang and myself.'

Peacock rose to his feet. 'Do you want a swim before we turn in?'

'I want to hear it all first, if you don't mind.'

He sank back into the cushions.

'I was sorry to hear about the plane,' he said.

'We still don't know who or what caused it. Maybe the Chinese know by now.'

'You remember that raid on Susan's flat in Hong Kong?'

'I do.'

'It was Fang who tipped off Du Fu. She wanted him to have evidence of Yao's corruption and the payments to the Eight so it would look as if Du had suppressed it. Creating the right Party narrative, she called it. She managed to trigger Du's panic and his failed attempt to defect.'

I had nothing to say. She'd outfoxed us again and again.

'And the cop who was wounded?'

'Self-inflicted, a negligent discharge.'

'That didn't get into the media.'

'He was just a kid, fumbling with his sidearm.'

Peacock picked up the brandy bottle, eyebrows raised, but I didn't want more.

'Fang was very ambivalent in your case, Richard.'

'Meaning?'

'On the one hand, she needed to have some hold over you. On the other, I know she worried that if things didn't work out for you

287

in SIS, that you wouldn't go empty-handed. She wanted you taken care of. She felt she owed you. She also had a sense of irony.'

'What do you mean by that?'

'She instructed me to open a deposit account for you. Payments started at 1,000 USD a month, then Fang upped it to 10,000. At first, it was to blackmail you if you needed to be coerced. She didn't tell you. She left that to me. Do you know the name of the oldest bank in the world, founded as capitalism was getting underway in Spain and Portugal, with sugar and slaves as the prime engine of economic growth?'

I didn't.

'She thought that as an imperialist agent, you'd want to bank your communist money there. It amused her. It's the *Banca Monte Dei Paschi di Siena* – which, as the name suggests, is in Siena and it's been around since the mid-15th century. You'll have to go there yourself if you want your cash. You'll need two forms of photo identification. And they'll need your signature. That's it. They'll provide a bank cheque for the total amount, if you ask. I'll give you the account number, sort code and so on before you leave.'

'You arranged this?'

'Of course. Yao paid you your generous stipend, though he didn't know it, out of one of his accounts in the British Virgin Islands. That tickled Fang no end.'

'How much is there?'

Peacock rubbed his chin. 'Oh, at current prices and taking interest into account, enough to buy this place twice over, I should think.'

'It's under my name?'

'It is, squire.'

'Is this some bloody booby-trap left behind by Fang to fuck us up?'

'Not at all. It's genuine. Of course, if SIS ever found out, you'd have hard questions to answer, though. Don't worry. Mum's the word.'

'And your debrief – didn't they ask about Fang, about Du Lan?'

'Why would they? They had no reason to connect us. It was a stroll in the park. They put me up in a country hotel and we went on long walks and chatted about this and that. It was all very amicable. I was well looked after. The food was great. They told me my OBE was in the post, so to speak.'

'I don't know what to say, Roger.'

'Take the cash. You earned it.'

'It's Yao's dirty money.'

'So what? They tell me tenners and twenties are all tainted with cocaine these days, and that the City of London is the world's money-laundering capital. Cartel money. Mafia money. Gulf money. Russian money. Now Chinese money. Government ministers are awash in the stuff. Don't say anything, old man, just enjoy it. She loved you in her own way, Richard, she really did. Will we have that swim now?'

29

In November 1994, Singapore hosted a security co-operation conference. Senior officers from Asian and Western intelligence services were
invited. In all, 16 governments had accepted. It was the intention of the
so-called Western powers and their Asian allies – not yet made public –
to raise the issue of the South China Sea and Beijing's claims to it.

Frobisher fronted the UK team, and I would, as SIS Asia–Pacific
Controller, be doing most of the work in my role as his deputy. The
third member represented GCHQ. Our local high commission had
sent a diplomat along to assist, whatever that meant. I thought he
was likely tasked with trying to suppress Frobisher's habit of calling
everyone he met by a four-letter obscenity. Perhaps the Foreign Office
would pick up the cost of this junket. I certainly hoped so. Frobisher
was due to retire at the end of the year and I was tipped to take his
place as director-general. It was known throughout the global intelligence world who Frobisher was by now, and what I did, too. It was
inevitable. Our pictures had even appeared in the broadsheets. We
were modern spy chiefs, open and accountable. (If you believed that,
you'd believe anything). It went with the job in the 1990s. It was all
about showmanship, even as our budget and workforce were slashed.

Langley's number two would join us, as well as representatives from the NSA and FBI. Officials from Japan, Australia, New Zealand, Vietnam, the Philippines, India, Malaysia, Indonesia, would attend. The PRC, of course. Taiwan, after a lot of the usual bullying by Beijing, accepted observer status for the island under the name of 'Chinese Taiwan'.

It was no surprise that the Chinese communists were bringing the biggest delegation – 36 officials, including translators and secretaries. The UK had sent three, including me, plus the embassy staffer.

I enjoyed a coffee in the delegates' lounge on the opening morning, turning the pages of a magazine on southern French properties. I was tempted by a *maison de maître* for sale just outside Sarlat that would be perfect for my retirement – while watching a televised screening of the arriving delegations. The Chinese were the last. It was deliberate, timed for maximum impact, the message being that they did as they pleased, made their own rules, and we would have to wait until they were ready to start. They would not follow any imperialist agenda. The CCP wanted respect and deference, it demanded both as a world power equal to the United States in every way. Not that I could blame them, given what China had been through and what it had achieved.

The Chinese delegation trooped down the aircraft steps to be greeted by Singapore's deputy foreign minister and the chief of the country's Security and Intelligence Division, or SID. There were half-bows, fake smiles, handshakes. A dozen children in red waved PRC flags. A bouquet was handed to the visiting delegation chief. The formalities were well-oiled and brief.

A Chinese woman led the team. She handed the flowers to a flunkey, waved to the children and strode along the red carpet to the VIP entrance to the terminal building.

She was tall, slim, immaculate in a black suit with a CCP lapel badge.

That unsmiling, iron mask caught my attention.

I jumped, choked on my coffee, spilling half of it down my brand new Yves Saint Laurent silk tie.

I wasn't mistaken, not this time.

It was none other than a resurrected Fang, aka Chen Meilin, aka Zhang Pusheng, formerly DRAGON and newly-appointed head of communist China's foreign intelligence service, the *Guoanbu*.

Select Bibliography

Aldrich, Richard J., GCHQ, *The Uncensored Story of Britain's Most Secret Intelligence Agency*, Harper Press, London, 2010;

Allison, Graham, *Destined for War, Can America and China Escape Thucydides's Trap?*, Scribe, London and Melbourne, 2017;

Andrew, Christopher, *The Secret World, A History of Intelligence*, Allen Lane, 2018;

Brown, Kerry, *The World According to XI*, L.B. Tauris, London, 2018;

Brown, Kerry, and Tzu-hui, Kalley, *The Trouble With Taiwan, History, the United States and a Rising China*, Zed Books, London, 2019;

Corera, Gordon, *MI6: Life and Death in the British Secret Service*, Weidenfeld & Nicolson, London, 2011;

Davies, Philip H.J., *MI6 and the Machinery of Spying*, Frank Cass, London, 2005;

Clissold, Tim, *Mr China*, Constable, London, 2004.

Faligot, Roger, *Chinese Spies from Chairman Mao to Xi Jinping*, Scribe, Victoria, 2019;

Hoffman, David E., *The Billion Dollar Spy, A True Story of Cold War Espionage and Betrayal*, Icon Books, London, 2018;

Li, Dr. Zhisui, *The Private Life of Chairman Mao*, Random House, New York, 1994;

Mattis, Peter & Brazil, Matthew, *Chinese Communist Espionage: An Intelligence Primer*, Naval Institute Press, Annapolis, 2019;

Piper, Fred & Murphy, Sean, *Cryptography, A Very Short Introduction*, OUP, New York, 2002;

Vogel, Ezra F., *Deng Xiaoping and the Transformation of China*, Harvard University Press, 2013;

West, Nigel, *Spycraft Secrets: An Espionage A–Z*, The History Press, Gloucestershire, 2017;

Yang Jisheng, Tombstone, *The Untold Story of Mao's Great Famine*, Allen Lane, London, 2012.

Acknowledgements

My thanks to the team at Lume Books for their enthusiasm and professionalism in publishing *Spy Trap*, the final novel in the Brodick espionage trilogy.

A friend has gone out of his way to help, given his personal knowledge of China and his fluency in Mandarin and Cantonese. He has provided much insight, without which this novel would be a great deal poorer. Because he lives in the shadow of the 'relevant department', he does not wish to be identified. My thanks, too, to Ned Thacker and Sallie Tilson for reading the first draft and providing frank and detailed comments.

I would also like to thank the authors and publishers of the books that have helped to plug innumerable gaps in my knowledge. Many of the titles turned out to be far more intriguing than my efforts to entertain with fiction. That said, any errors of fact are entirely mine.

CPSIA information can be obtained
at www.ICGtesting.com
Printed in the USA
LVHW090449130422
715999LV00006B/806